THEY WILL DIE

A DCI PHILIP RADFORD MYSTERY BOOK 1

MARK YARWOOD

This novel is entirely a work of fiction. The names, characters and incidents portrayed in it are the work of the author's imagination. Any resemblance to actual persons, living or dead, events or localities is entirely coincidental.

BiscuitBooksPublishers © Mark Yarwood 2025

The author asserts the moral right to be identified as the author of this work Published by Amazon Kindle All rights reserved. No part of this publication may be reproduced, stored, or transmitted in any form or by means, electronic, mechanical, photocopying, recording or otherwise, without the prior permission of the publishers.

For my other Auntie Marie,
never forgotten

PROLOGUE

'There but for the grace of the Devil,' he whispered to himself, then shivered a little as he swept his eyes over the dark and bleak shore. The oily black water glistened under the moonlight and the roar of the waves filled his ears as it merged with the raucous music the wind was conducting. He tasted a mixture of saltwater and rain on his lips as his gaze returned to the figure lying on the stony beach, grey and still under the shadow of the cliff. He took out his phone, turned on the torchlight and shone it over the figure. There was that tell-tale rise of the chest, that shallow breath rattling into the night air, soon swallowed up by the wind and the rain.

He looked towards the sea and the dull grey outlines of the rocks and the sand. In a few hours —very few indeed—the sand would be covered in tourists, having come to soak up the sun that had come earlier in the spring but had now deserted the shore and was replaced by a tumultuous set of grey and stormy days. Still, the tourists would drag their kids down to the shore from the holiday park, set a few hundred yards back from the dunes. Buckets and spades in their pale, freckled hands, ready to dig and swim the whole day long despite the horrendous weather. Such a mediocre life, such banality and he somehow admired them for it.

He shook himself from his thoughts, his dreams, and looked at the body, still and grey beneath the night sky. He lifted his gloved hands and examined them for a moment, the wind howling and scraping at his ears. He stepped across the sand and onto the shingles, barely hearing it crunch beneath his boots. He crouched down over the figure, removed one glove and reached for the neck. Beneath his palm, he felt a weak pulse. He put the glove back on, gripped the neck in both hands and squeezed. He lifted his eyes towards the black and rain-soaked sky as he tensed his hands, feeling the body tighten, trying to return to consciousness. It was no good. He only squeezed tighter and tighter until the body finally relaxed.

For a moment he thought he heard thunder, and he looked up into the night but the sky remained dark and noisy only with the wind. Then the sound came again, a deep rumbling echoing all around, even from underneath him as it seemed to come from beneath his boots. He pushed to his feet, confused, and scared that some beast roared somewhere in the dark. Then he saw it, the cliff moving above him, an oily serpent glistening as the rumbling once again filled his ears.

No, it wasn't some creature but the rocks, falling and tumbling towards him. He stumbled backwards, his boots sinking into the wet sand, the cold waves washing over the back of his trousers. He pushed back through the water, moving quickly as the landslide came rushing, spitting smaller stones out towards him.

Then the movement and the sound ceased. Only the rush of the waves filled his ears and he felt brave enough to go back to where the body lay. But he could no longer see it, instead all that remained was the cold, hard black rock that glistened with the rain. And there it was— the lack of anything. The absence of what he had done, what he had striven for over the months and weeks. He could have cried as he fell to his knees, looking up at the sky in pleading, almost as if he believed someone was looking down on him, on everything and judging it all. But he didn't believe that. How could he?

Then it caught his eye, a little colour among the darkness of sand and stone. The pale hue of flesh. He clambered forward, diving for it, grabbing for the smaller stones and rocks and hurling them aside. He breathed hard and looked up into the rain again. When he lowered his eyes, there it was, a foot, a pale, bloodied and twisted foot.

As he got to his feet, he began to laugh—laughing still as he stumbled along the beach and headed home.

CHAPTER ONE

Sunday morning arrived and the storm had lessened, the sky less grey and miserable, although Philip Radford was perturbed to see the distant match-like figures of tourists walking along the Cobb while waves reached up, seemingly desperate to pull them into the cold and grey lap of the sea. He was happy to be warm and dry inside the beach shack he had hired while he recovered from his injuries.

It wouldn't have been long ago that no one would have found him living anywhere near such perilous waters, but here he was, against his better judgement. Being by the sea was good for one's health, someone had told him. It was one of those old Victorian sayings, and off the poor wretched souls would travel by train or omnibus towards the sea and its hunger for the idiots that dared dip their toes into its wild waters. On so many occasions he had read of another poor child or careless adult that had been swept away by a sudden freak wave. Not he. The sea was only a couple hundred yards away, just beyond the row of static homes that seemed far too close to the pebbly beach and wild and angry sea. At least, he told himself, the shack he was renting was up a steep hill and a little more out of reach. He looked back at the Cobb to see the fools had not moved, even though the sea was once more attempting to wash them away.

'They must be insane,' he said aloud and picked up the strong black coffee he had made a little while ago.

'Who must be?' she said behind him, and he turned to see her, former Detective Constable Michelle Carr, sitting on the well-worn sofa that was also a very uncomfortable pull-out bed.

'Those idiots on the Cobb,' he said and pointed a thumb at the window.

She smiled the old smile, her dark eyes glistening at him. Her deep caramel skin seemed paler, the skin drawn tighter over her skull. Her smile grew brighter, followed by a quick laugh.

A smile quivered at the corner of his lips, and so he lifted his coffee cup and took a sip, feeling the deep and earthy burn of it at the back of his throat.

'Why won't you let yourself be happy?' she asked and tilted her head.

'Who said I won't?' He put down the cup and turned and looked out the window and watched the silhouettes of people dancing along the sand, daring the rolling waves to rise up and get them, while the seagulls came in from the mist, gliding on the thermals. They had the right idea, he thought, coming in from the sea when it got angry. 'I'm here, aren't I? Away from it all.'

'Away from it all?' she asked. 'Or away from everyone? From people?'

He ignored her questions as he tried to decide how windy it was out there as the waves came crashing against the Cobb wall and spitting a great plume of foam into the air. It was windy enough. Too windy for him.

'It's time,' she said.

He nodded. 'It is. Perhaps today…'

'It's time, DCI Philip Radford.'

'That's not me any more.' He finished his coffee. 'I'm just Philip Radford. Man of leisure.'

'Yeah, right. You don't know the first thing about leisure. Anyway, you're on gardening leave. You never resigned.'

'True.' He put down his cup by the kitchen sink, then slipped on his waterproof jacket and faced the door. His hand reached out, a slight tremble travelling down to his fingers.

'You can do it.'

He took a breath, clasped the handle, pulled it down in one swift motion and jerked the door open. He found himself in the tiny front garden, the roar of the waves pounding at his ears while seagulls complained angrily about the bad weather or perhaps a lack of discarded chips or pasties. He trembled but he moved on, not even bothering to say goodbye to Carr. She knew he'd be back, sitting beside her on the sofa for the evening news. Goodbyes were pointless. There were so many he had never had the chance to say goodbye to.

He moved on, pulling up his hood as he fought against the violent wind and the drops of rain that spat into his face now and again. He promised to take a walk every day, to be among people and out in the real world and not cooped up in the shack. It wasn't good for his mental health, he was told. They didn't know what was good for his mind—only he did. Problems were the key to getting his brain working again. But there was nothing here but sand and food and the occasional break in the wild and torrid weather.

He turned his head when he caught the sound of a police siren. Or was it an ambulance? He carried on along the promenade, passing the now-closed fish and chip huts, the tourist shops and the pubs and restaurants.

As he approached the Cobb, he could see the waves pounding against the long, snake-like shape of it, while silhouetted fools still dawdled on the beast's back. He toyed with going further this time and trying to find Mary Anning's statue which he knew was perhaps a few hundred yards away from the museum that stood on the spot where her house had once been.

A police response car raced past. There was no siren this time, just the necessary speed to get it where it was going. Where was it going? It was not his concern any more, he told himself and carried on in the direction of Charmouth.

It was when he was within a hundred yards of Anning's statue that he stopped dead. A horde of people, a few with umbrellas held over their heads, stood close to the steps to the stony beach below, where he knew many went in search of fossils. His eyes jumped from the damp crowd to the police tape that had been tied across from one handrail to the other, preventing anyone from taking the steps down. His curiosity yawned and stretched as he carried on walking, planning on passing it by and perhaps stealing only a glimpse.

'I'm sorry, sir, you aren't allowed beyond the cordon,' a woman's voice said and Radford drew his eyes away from the crime scene and up to a female uniform, wrapped up in her police issue waterproofs. She had a round, slightly freckly face, her dark brown hair drawn back in a ponytail. He examined her uniform and saw she was an inspector.

'I was merely going for a walk,' he said, looking at the crime scene tape speckled by raindrops.

'Well, I'm afraid you'll have to head in the other direction.' She smiled, but only politely.

'Has traffic been kept to a minimum?' he asked, his eyes jumping to the uniforms on the beach who were making plenty of prints in the sand.

She narrowed her eyes at him. 'You mean the town traffic?'

Radford pointed to the beach. 'I was referring to the traffic down there. They are trampling through the crime scene.'

'We don't think there's been a crime committed,' a man said as his head appeared over the steps. 'There's been a rockfall. The last one happened nearly ten years ago...'

'That was the last time someone died,' the inspector said. 'They happen all the time along here, especially after a lot of rainfall.'

The young-ish plain-clothed officer pulled his red, wavy hair from his brow and nodded, then looked keenly at Radford. 'I'm sorry, but you sounded like a police officer just then.'

Radford sighed. 'I am... I mean, I used to be. I was a detective chief inspector.'

'Impressive,' the red-headed detective put out his hand to shake. 'Detective Sergeant Finley Scott. Nice to meet you.'

Radford looked down at the hand and decided to ignore it as he walked over to the railing and looked down at where the rockfall had covered the yellow sand. 'No one perished?'

'Actually, there's been a fatality,' Scott said. 'A witness saw a foot poking out...'

Radford turned to him. 'A foot was poking out?'

'Yes, it's funny but some of the rocks seemed to have been moved by the looks of it. The foot is all black and…'

'You're dealing with a crime. Possibly a murder.'

Both DS Scott and the inspector flinched and looked at him as if he was pulling their collective legs, but it was the young detective who said, 'You're joking? How can you possibly think a rockfall is a murder? Unless the so-called killer arranged for…'

'Who removed the rocks from the victim's foot?'

Scott shrugged. 'I don't know, perhaps…'

'Who discovered the body? A dog walker?'

'How did you know?'

'It's always a dog walker,' the inspector said and lifted the tape so she could slip under the cordon. She stepped closer to Radford, resting her hands on her stab vest. 'You've worked a lot of murder investigations, then?'

'I've had my fair share.' Radford looked at Scott. 'Did the dog walker remove the rocks?'

'No. He said he saw the foot poking out when his dog started sniffing about… So, what are you thinking?'

Radford stepped over to the rail again, then leaned over, his eyes avoiding the grey-looking sea that was creeping ever closer. He focused on the rocks and the many footprints dotting the sand. 'Was he lying down? Foot protruding towards the sea?'

'That's right. Why?'

'Why would he be lying down on the beach? Especially in this weather? I take it the rockfall happened late last night, during the storm?'

'We think so.' Scott exchanged glances with the inspector. 'So, you think someone drugged him and laid him out and waited for the cliff to give way and the rocks to fall on him?'

'No, he was probably dead before the rockfall. Of course, he wouldn't know there was going to be a rockfall. How could he?'

'Exactly.'

Radford looked between them. 'That's why he uncovered the foot.'

'Why?' the inspector asked.

'Because he wanted the victim to be found. This was meant to be a statement.'

DS Scott looked at the inspector for a moment, then back at Radford as he took a step closer to him. 'What would you feel about taking a closer look, Detective Chief Inspector…?'

'Mr Philip Radford,' he replied. 'I'm not a police officer any more.'

'But you're on gardening leave. You haven't left the force?'

Radford shook his head, then looked down at the beach and the sea that was coming ever closer, filling in the rock pools. He could smell it too, the stale scent of stagnant water that almost choked him. 'You want me to go down there?'

'Is it a problem?'

'It might be,' the inspector said. 'If he's not officially...'

Scott faced her. 'Don't worry, Inspector Morris. I'll make sure it's all right.'

'I'm sorry, but I'm the inspector here,' Morris said, 'and technically this is my crime scene, and I'm in charge. You're only a DS.'

'She's quite correct,' Radford said, nodding. 'So I had better not.'

'I didn't say that,' Morris said. 'If you're quick, then you can give us your expert opinion, as a kind of... consultant.'

Radford closed his eyes and pinched his nose. He took a deep breath, then opened his eyes again to see that DS Scott had untied the police tape and was waiting for him to descend the steps.

Radford placed a foot on the top step. 'When does the tide come in?'

'Not for an hour or so,' Scott said. 'Is there a problem?'

Radford shook his head, then put his foot on the next step, getting closer to the rolling waves that kept creeping closer and closer, the roar of the sea growing in intensity until it was all he could hear.

He found himself back in the darkness, his legs moving, propelling him on as his heart swelled in his chest. His fists were pumping as he screamed out, shouting at the figure in the distance that grew and grew until he could see DC Carr's face, her eyes widening. Then he felt it, long before the force of the blast grabbed him and hurled him towards her and he seemed to be falling forever.

'Quick, grab him!' the inspector shouted and the young detective grabbed him under his arms as he fell head first towards the beach.

Emma Ash walked from the back room of the cafe and out into the compact seating area. There were only a couple of tables taken up, some tourists coming out for an early morning coffee away from the lousy weather. But it was good for business, she told herself as she opened the door and looked out, noting the heavy grey clouds that were hanging over the town. Most of the tourists were wrapped up in waterproofs and stood under shop awnings, sheltering from the rain. She went back inside, back into the warmth and saw Jane putting more cheese and onion pasties out on the display.

'Those pasties cooked long enough?' Emma called over.

Jane, who was barely in her twenties and liked nothing better than to chinwag most of the day rather than serve customers, froze and looked at her guiltily. 'Don said they were.'

'Let's have a look.' Emma crouched down

and stared at the pasties, inspecting them, making sure they had the nice golden shine she liked to see. 'Not bad.'

'Look at it out there,' Jane said, nodding to the windows where the rain had started to come down a little harder.

'Well, maybe that's good for us. People like to come in out of the rain and hopefully buy drinks and food.'

'No wonder there's been another rockfall.' Jane continued putting out the pasties.

'A rockfall?' Emma stared at her. 'Really? When was the last one?'

'A couple of months ago, but no one was hurt. Remember when that young lad got… you know.'

Emma grimaced, joined her behind the counter and started tidying up. 'Let's not dwell.'

'No, best not. I heard someone got hurt…'

Emma straightened up, her heart beating a little faster. 'Who got hurt? Not a tourist? That's not good for…'

'I don't know. Happened last night. God knows what they were doing down there at that time.'

'Taking a late-night swim?'

'It's too bloody cold for that.'

Emma laughed. 'True. The only place you'll get me swimming is the Mediterranean.'

'You going away this year? Where's it you usually go? Cornwall, or…'

'No, I'm not.' Emma turned away and looked out at the bad weather again, and saw two tourists looking at their window menu. 'I might stay here for a change...'

'I have to go abroad, it's...' Jane stopped when the door of the shop opened.

Ralph from the bookshop came in, dragging his little furry and quite damp dog with him.

'You're all right with Bella coming in, aren't you?' Ralph asked and pulled her in anyway as he took down his hood. 'It's bucketing out there.'

Bella gave a shake, spraying the air and wetting the floor.

'It's fine, Ralph,' Emma said with a sigh. 'Takeaway coffee?'

'I couldn't sit for a minute, could I?' Ralph was already pulling up a chair on a nearby table when he asked. 'It's cause I've had a bit of a shock this morning.'

'You know what, Ralph,' Jane said. 'I thought you looked quite pale when you came in. You need one of those sunbeds...'

'What happened?' Emma asked, rolling her eyes.

Ralph took a breath and shook his head. 'You heard about the rockfall?'

'I heard someone got hurt.'

'They're dead,' Ralph said a little too loudly, making the other customers stare at him. He said sorry, then looked at Emma again. 'Yeah, someone got... killed, Emma. Thing is, it's me who found him...'

Emma felt her whole body tighten. 'He?'

'You poor thing, Ralph, I'll get you a sugary tea,' Jane said.

'Jane, stop,' Emma said, then focused on Ralph. 'Who's dead?'

Ralph leaned in. 'You know the fella who owned the butchers over the road. I think he's gone back to fishing now... or had, I should say.'

'Ben?' Jane asked. 'Ben Gardener?'

'That's it. Ben Gardener. Life's so bloody short.'

Emma looked out to the street, her mind running in every direction. 'Ben Gardener? How do you know?'

'I saw his foot,' Ralph said as Jane put a cup of tea in front of him. 'Thank you, dear.'

'His foot?' Emma repeated.

'Yep. There it was, poking out.'

'How do you know it was Ben Gardener's foot?' Jane asked.

'The tattoo,' Ralph said as if they were stupid. 'He has that little mermaid tattoo on his ankle. He got it when he was drunk years ago. Anyway, God rest his soul.'

Emma shuddered and stared off towards the door again. Ben Gardener, she thought and shook her head. No, it couldn't be him.

'Are you OK, Emma?' Jane asked, staring at her with concern. 'You've gone very pale.'

'Yes, I'm fine.' She gripped her hands to stop

them from trembling.

'Oh my God!' Jane slipped through the counter and stared towards the rainy street. 'I think I saw him again.'

'Who?' Ralph asked, bending down to feed his dog a treat.

'That same weirdo again,' Jane said and looked at Emma. 'You remember that man who I kept seeing outside just staring in here?'

'What did you say he looked like?'

She shrugged. 'I don't know. That's the weird thing, he had his hood up, sunglasses on and a face mask with like a big painted creepy smile on it. Makes me shiver thinking about it.'

'He was there again?' Emma asked, staring out the window. 'You're sure?'

'Yeah, why? Do you know him, do you think? Have you got a stalker?'

Emma ignored her, walked to the door and opened it, the wind roaring in, playing with her hair as she stepped down onto the pavement. She looked up and down but only saw the tourists battling with umbrellas and running for shop doors. She shuddered again, a terrible feeling coming over her, as dark and threatening as the clouds hanging over the town.

CHAPTER TWO

The first thing Radford saw as he came to, his eyes fluttering open, was grey clouds rushing past. He blinked, then craned his neck and saw the cottages flickering by and the occasional wooded area. He sat up with a grunt and looked round to see the backs of two heads in the front seats. The inspector drove them along the narrow road, while DS Scott turned in his seat to take a look at him.

'How're you feeling now?' Scott asked, looking him over with a sympathetic smile.

'I'm fine. What happened?' Radford fastened his seatbelt.

'You fainted,' the inspector said over her shoulder. 'Good job we were there to grab you. You muttered something about a bomb, and then you just dropped like a brick.'

Scott narrowed his eyes at him. 'Do you have a problem with the sea?'

Radford looked over at the scenery. 'No. It has a problem with me.'

'Does it?'

'Yes, the sea wants to drown me. In fact, it wants to drown us all.'

Scott laughed until Radford stared at him.

'All right,' Scott said, nodding. 'Fine. You weren't there to see the foot. Inspector Morris here recognised the tattoo on the dead man's foot.'

'You are Morris?' Radford asked.

'Inspector Eva Morris. Nice to meet you again.' The inspector smiled at him in the rear-view mirror. 'I think you're right about this being a murder.'

'I am right, but thank you.'

'You're welcome.'

'Why do you agree with me?'

'Well, that foot belongs to Ben Gardener. I recognised the tattoo from one night when he had one too many beers and decided to strip off in the middle of town... anyway, there's no way he would just be hanging around the rocks like that, even if he was drunk.'

'Why not?' Radford asked, sitting forward, his curiosity flickering to life.

Morris looked at him in the mirror. 'He was always going on about the cliffs. How dangerous they were and how crazy the tourists were to go there and dig for fossils. So, there's no way he would just lie down there or... whatever he was meant to be doing.'

'Someone took him there.'

'Bloody hell,' Scott said. 'We've actually got a murder? Is this really happening? I mean, it's usually just drugs, theft... anti-social behaviour. I don't know when there last was a murder here. I'm going to have to call Chief Superintendent Parsons. I'll have to tell her what's going on. She won't like this.'

'It's a murder,' Radford said. 'Nobody likes a murder. Where are we going?'

'To see his widow and inform her of the death of her husband. Molly's going to be distraught.'

'Perhaps she can fill in some holes in the timeline, for example, where he was last night,' Radford said and sat back, trying to clear his mind.

'We're here,' Morris said, indicating as they came to a small white cottage that was sitting a little back from the tree-lined road. She turned the car towards the house and parked up.

'So, who's going to do this?' DS Scott asked. 'I mean, I don't really know her. And I don't think DCI Radford...'

'Mr Radford,' Radford said, then climbed out and stretched, still feeling a little dizzy.

Morris got out of the car, looked at them both and sighed. 'Well, it should be me really, as I know her. It'll be best coming from me.'

'Thank you, Inspector Morris,' Radford said,

then turned towards the cottage as he heard a door opening. Out of the gloom of the house came a short, stubby woman with greying blonde bobbed hair. She looked to be in her late fifties, her wrinkled face set in a worried expression.

'Eva?' the woman said. 'I was about to call you. Ben didn't come home last night. You haven't seen him on your travels, have you?'

Radford saw Scott and Morris exchange awkward glances before the inspector headed towards Molly Gardener.

'Let's go inside and have a cup of tea,' Morris said, taking Molly's arm and directing her back to the cottage.

'Is everything all right?' Molly asked as they approached the front door. 'Do you know where Ben is? He's not been arrested, has he? You know he never does any harm.'

'I think it's best if we talk inside.'

Radford had started to follow them inside, with DS Scott right on his heels, when Molly stopped walking and turned around. Her eyes had become wet, her skin paler as she stared at the inspector.

'You've got to tell me,' Molly said, her voice trembling. 'Has something happened to him? Has something happened to my Ben?'

The inspector drew in a breath. 'I'm sorry, Molly...'

It was the only words Inspector Morris

managed to get out before the bereaved woman grasped her face and tears began to pour. 'No… no, no, no.'

Radford found himself staring helplessly as Morris put a supportive arm around Mrs Gardener and practically carried her into the living room.

'This is the worst part of the job,' a voice said beside Radford, making him flinch. He had forgotten that DS Scott was even in the house.

'Then we are very lucky the inspector is here,' Radford said as he headed for the open doorway of the living room. 'Make a cup of sugary tea.'

Scott pointed to himself. 'Me? But shouldn't I be asking her questions?'

'Leave that to me.' Radford went into a cramped, cluttered and flowery living room that was filled with a cumbersome battered and cigarette burnt sofa, armchair and TV. Mrs Gardener was now on the sofa. 'No, no, no,' she kept repeating, her voice cracking, while Morris rubbed her back and tried to say comforting things.

Radford stepped closer, watching it all unfold, remembering the countless times he had delivered bad news to grieving spouses. Only a few months ago, it had come close to him being the one whose life was extinguished, the difference being that there would be no one for his colleagues to break the news to.

'Is someone making tea?' Morris asked, looking up at Radford.

'DS Scott,' Radford said, then stepped closer, noticing that Mrs Gardener had ceased her outburst. 'Mrs Gardener, can you think of any reason your husband would be on the beach, below the cliffs last night?'

Mrs Gardener looked up, blinking away her tears, staring at him with confusion in her eyes. 'The beach? I don't understand...'

'Ben was found on the beach,' Morris said. 'I'm afraid there had been a rockfall...'

The wailing began again and Radford stepped back as the tea arrived. DS Scott looked a little red in the cheeks as he held out the mug of tea to Mrs Gardener.

'Not right now,' Morris said, rubbing Mrs Gardener's back again.

'Mrs Gardener, are you aware of anyone who might want to harm your husband?' Radford asked and flinched when Inspector Morris' angry eyes jumped up to him.

'Harm him?' Molly Gardener stuttered, wiping away her tears. 'I'm so confused. What's going on? You said he...'

'I know, I know,' Morris said. 'It's a lot to take in. But there is the possibility that we're looking into... well, that...'

'I was told he didn't like to be anywhere near the cliffs, Mrs Gardener,' Radford interrupted.

She nodded. 'That's true. He didn't. He

didn't think anyone should be down there… because of the danger of… why would he be there? He wouldn't be there. No, it can't be him. He wouldn't…'

'Ben has a mermaid tattoo on his ankle, doesn't he?' Morris asked.

Mrs Gardener nodded, then her eyes widened and the tears came again. 'Oh God. Oh God.'

'Where did he go last night?' Scott asked, still holding the mug of tea.

'The pub,' Mrs Gardener said, staring down at the carpet. 'He goes most nights. More since… well, he closed the butchers. He didn't want to go back to fishing, but there you go… It's not right, is it?'

'I'm sorry?' Morris said.

'You said… he was down by the cliffs. Why would he be? It doesn't make sense.'

Morris looked up at Radford, a strange look in her eyes he didn't quite understand, and took it to mean she had come to realise he was right, Ben Gardener had been murdered.

'We are going to find out what happened, Molly, I promise you that,' Morris said, then took the tea from DS Scott and gave it to Mrs Gardener.

The office of the Lyme Gazette appeared almost empty when Emma Ash looked into the narrow building's glass door. The newspaper office was merely a converted shop and had sold shoes at one time, many years ago when she was just a girl. She remembered pestering her mother for a pair of pink jellybean shoes one day and was so proud when she wore them to school the next day. That was until Martin Linnell stole one and pulled it apart.

She shielded her face and stared closer into the darkened interior. There was a light on near the back of the offices, the glow of a lamp or perhaps a computer screen. She tapped on the glass of the door and saw a shape move somewhere in the gloom. Then the silhouette grew in size and soon she realised it was a man coming towards the door.

It was Nathan Sharpe who opened the door. He was a tall and lean man, probably in his forties. He smiled a little, his eyes looking round the street behind her.

'Hello, Emma,' he said. 'What can I do for you?'

'Peter isn't here, is he?' she asked.

'Peter? No, he's not here. He's gone to oversee this charity event thing in Bournemouth. Is it anything urgent?'

'Oh, no. I just wanted to catch up with him.' She was about to turn away, then she thought about what had happened that morning. Sharpe was in charge of the newspaper these days and if anyone would know something about what had happened last night, it would be him.

'Did you hear about the rockfall last night?'

she asked.

He nodded. 'That's what I was just writing up. People need to know, especially the tourists, how dangerous those cliffs are.'

'It's Mrs Gardener I feel sorry for.'

'Yes, it's awful. Poor Ben, and his poor wife. Does she know yet?'

Emma could only shrug, as no one else in town, along with herself, seemed to know what was happening. 'I'm not sure. I'm sure the police will let her know. If it is Ben Gardener they found. Do you know for sure if it's him?'

'My sources tell me it's definitely him, I'm afraid.'

'Your sources? The police? Do they know what happened? Was it an accident?'

He looked at her strangely then and suddenly she feared she had said too much.

'Was it an accident?' he repeated. 'It was a rockfall, wasn't it? What else could it be?'

She shrugged, her face reddening. It was time to go. 'I don't know. It's just... well, he wasn't one for hanging out at the beach, and he was always going on about how those cliffs were dangerous.'

'That's true. But, well, he did like a drink, didn't he? Probably had a few too many and somehow found himself there. Anyway, I'm sure the police will tell everyone what happened when there's an inquest. Did you want me to tell Pete you called by?'

She nodded. 'Yes, thanks. Ask him to call me.'

'I will. I'd better get back to my write-up.'

She smiled. 'Thanks.'

As Nathan sank back into the gloom of the shop, she retreated to the damp and windy street, moving out of the way of the raincoated tourists and then headed towards the promenade. It was where she did most of her thinking, where she felt a little peace. She took down her hood and stared out across the grey water that foamed and roared over the sand, while figures ran and frolicked, trying to avoid getting wet.

Ben Gardener was dead. That was the fact of the matter. Ben Gardener was dead. That was the fact of the matter. What else could it be but an accident? That's what Nathan Sharpe had said. What else? But her mind returned to the fact that Ben had been found in a place he hated to go. She shivered and prayed to God that what was happening wasn't what she feared it was.

Lyme Regis Police Station, situated on Hill Road, a few minutes' drive away from Mrs Gardener's cottage, seemed more like a motorway services station to Radford. Inspector Morris parked in a space in the massive car park, which was packed with a mixture of marked and unmarked cars. The building was a wide white painted box with a grey dome over the top. As they had left Mrs

Gardener's house, DS Scott had received a quick phone call from Chief Superintendent Parsons. From DS Scott's expression, Radford gathered that his boss was not happy.

'What did she actually say?' Morris asked as they all climbed out and headed towards the main reception desk.

'She just told me to get back here,' Scott said, letting out a harsh breath. 'She didn't sound happy.'

'When does she ever?' Morris said.

Radford stopped as they approached the tall glass doors of the entrance, unsure of his part in all this. 'I suppose I'd better wait out here.'

DS Scott turned and looked at him in surprise. 'Oh, no, she wants to see you too.'

'Me? She doesn't know who I am.'

Scott shrugged. 'Well, she said to bring the tall, skinny bird man with us. I'm taking it that she meant you.'

Radford straightened his tie and followed them inside, signing in at the front desk and slipping a visitor's pass around his neck. He followed them up and into an expanse of neat office space that still had that new furniture and equipment smell. The major incident area was at the far end, with a few sectioned-off cubicles filling the rest of the space. As they arrived, a far door to a large office opened and a thick-set woman in uniform in her mid-fifties, with a hard-looking face, came striding out. This was

Chief Superintendent Parsons, Radford decided and took a deep breath, ready for some kind of rebuke.

Parsons stood in front of them all, her hands behind her back as she stared intently at each in turn.

'In my office now,' she said, her voice sharp in a well-educated tone that comes from years at the best schools. 'If you would all be so kind.'

They followed her in as she went round her large modern desk that looked like it belonged in an IKEA catalogue, and sat down in a black leather chair, watching them carefully as they all took seats, apart from Radford.

'And who exactly are you?' Parsons said to him, her cheeks red, her skin tight.

'This is DCI Philip Radford,' Scott said, quietly.

She glared at him. 'I was talking to him, not you, DS Scott. I'll deal with you in a moment. Can you speak for yourself, Mr Philip Radford?'

'It's Mr Philip Radford,' he said. 'I'm on gardening leave, but I don't plan to return to work.'

'You don't?' She gave a short, empty laugh. 'I feel there are some superior officers who are breathing a sigh of relief somewhere. So, Mister Radford, why have you been ordering my people around?'

'I haven't. I merely observed that the dead man was likely a victim of murder.'

Parsons sighed. 'There has been no murder, Mr Radford. Let's get that straight. I've talked to a doctor, a very trusted doctor, who has examined the scene and the body, and he has happily concluded that this was an unfortunate accident. The dead man, Ben Gardener, was known for his drinking…'

'There will be a Home Office pathologist called in, ma'am?' Inspector Morris asked.

'Of course there will,' Parsons said, as if the inspector was daft. 'And he or she will undoubtedly report to the coroner that this was merely death by misadventure. Nothing more. We don't want our locals or, more importantly, our tourists to think some murderer is going around. It's not good for the community. So, you, Inspector Morris, and you, DS Scott will refrain from investigating this matter further and return to your other duties. Mr Radford, I suggest you go back to your gardening leave and then return to your home town. I take it you don't reside here?'

'No, I certainly don't.'

'Good. A relief for us all.'

Then Inspector Morris cleared her throat. 'Ma'am, can I say something?'

Parsons' sigh was heavy and thick with annoyance. 'Yes, very well.'

It's just that DCI—sorry, Mr. Radford—has a point…Ben Gardener had a fear of those cliffs and kept well away from them. His wife even found it extremely odd that he was there…'

Parsons sighed again. 'Let me stop you there. All due respect to Mrs Gardener, but her husband was seen heading towards a taxi, being directed by someone, as he was very unsteady on his feet. But he never got in that taxi home and probably ended up stumbling down to the beach. He was probably disoriented and then passed out. Misadventure, you see?'

'Yes, ma'am,' Morris said.

'What do you say, DS Scott?' Parsons stared at him.

'Misadventure,' Scott muttered. Radford let out a short, dry laugh.

'Is something amusing, Mr Radford?' Parsons looked up at him.

'No. But I realise now my work is done here. I'll be leaving now.' He turned on the spot and headed through the door and back along the corridor. By the time he had reached the stairwell, he heard quick steps behind him and turned to see Morris approaching. She slowed and looked apologetically at him.

'I'm sorry about that,' she said.

'Why are you sorry, Inspector?' he asked. 'It's not your fault that your commanding officer is stupid.'

She laughed. 'I know. But she's not stupid, just trying to avoid a fuss and losing tourists and their money. Her husband is a big deal around here and owns a hotel and a few shops and a restaurant.'

He nodded. 'Now it all makes sense. Well, I will say goodbye.'

'Wait. What about the murder?'

'There is no murder.'

'But we both know there was a murder. What do we do?'

'Nothing. There is nothing we can do. Goodbye.'

'That's it?' Morris called out as he hurried down the steps.

Emma decided to drive out to the little market town where she knew Peter Roberts had gone, hoping to write about the new school that was hopefully going to be built. She knew where the site was and that already machinery and workmen had begun to prepare the fenced-off site for building the foundations. She pulled up at the security gate and the young, almost teenage-looking security guard came over to her window.

'Can I help you?' he asked, scratching at his acne-covered face.

'I'm looking for a reporter,' she said. 'Peter Roberts. He should've been here today.'

'Oh, yeah, he was, but he left about an hour ago.'

She sighed, thanked him and then started to pull away. She braked as a lorry suddenly sped past, then moved off when the coast was clear.

The road ahead was pretty much clear and there were only a few cars coming along. She saw a gap and pulled out and headed back towards Lyme Regis. Where the hell was Peter? She needed to talk to him, he was the only one who would understand. She put her foot down, keeping an eye out for speed cameras. She looked in the rear-view mirror and saw a van behind her a little way back. Then she noticed it was speeding up, getting closer to her bumper all the time. What the bloody hell was the idiot doing? She tried to make out the driver, wanting to ensure they saw her hand gestures, so they knew she was pissed off.

Her eyes widened as the driver came into view. She stared. The person behind the wheel wore a baseball cap and sunglasses. There was the face mask too, and the evil smile painted onto it. Her car was shoved forward, the sound of metal hitting metal. She put her foot down, panic overriding her, trying to think straight. It was him, the person outside the shop who had been staring at them, watching her. What the hell? Then she realised, or at least, the suspicion crept into her mind. No, it couldn't be. She thought of Ben Gardener. Dead. Now this.

She looked up to see the van drifting back, slowing down as they got closer to town. She took the turn to the car park and quickly pulled up. She sat there for a moment, watching the entrance, fearful that the van might appear.

Nothing. She kept staring and only saw people passing as rain started to hit the windscreen. Soon the sky opened up, dark clouds coming over, and the windscreen was awash with rain. She took her seatbelt off, reached for her waterproof coat, put it on and zipped it up. She'd better wait for the rain to ease off, she thought, but after a couple of minutes, she realised it wasn't going to happen, at least not for a while.

She pushed her door open against the wind and rain, pulling up her hood. Her eyes darted around, searching for the man in the mask. Who the hell was he? What did he want? But she knew, deep inside, she felt it, the terrible dread that this was all to do with what happened. She hurried towards the main road. In a couple of minutes she would be back at the shop, safe and sound. She needed to get hold of Peter, and he could tell her what they needed to do.

She went through the back way, heading towards the narrow alleyway that would lead her to the crossing opposite the cafe. She was safe now.

Jane gave the change back to the elderly gentleman who had just bought two cheese and onion pasties, then watched him go off with his wife, before she looked to the street, wondering where her boss had got to. Then she smiled, seeing her coming out of the alleyway over the other side of the street. The rain was hammering down and Jane thought she'd better make Emma a hot chocolate to warm her up. She looked over at Emma and her eyes widened, her mouth opening. Behind her boss was a figure, a man looming up with a mask on, and that creepy smile. His gloved hand clamped over Emma's mouth and he started dragging her backward.

A bus rumbled slowly past, cutting off her view for a moment. She broke out of her frozen state, rushed to the door and hurried out into the rain. The bus went by.

Jane stared at the alleyway, but it was empty.

CHAPTER THREE

Radford pushed the now tepid deep-fried cod around his plate, sitting at the small dining table in the shack. It had been tucked under the small kitchen unit and folded out easily enough. It was a compact place, with only a sofa bed and a small room with bunk beds to cater for small children. There was a small bathroom with a shower. A compact TV sat on a shelf in the living room, but he hadn't even turned it on yet. He was studying the small building and its contents, its brochures and one shelf of paperback books, because it helped him not ponder on the disaster area his life had become lately.

'Are you not going to eat your fish and chips?'

Michelle Carr was sitting at the other side of the table, her smooth, pretty face resting on her knuckles as she stared at him, her eyebrows raised.

'I'm not hungry.' He put down his knife and fork and sat back.

'You're still obsessing over this rockfall business, aren't you?'

'You mean the murder?'

She smiled. 'But is it murder, or are you inventing a mystery to keep your mind off other things?'

He let out a tired breath. 'One might think that, but that's not the case. This man, Ben Gardener, a former butcher...'

'An alcoholic, wasn't he?' She raised her eyebrows even higher.

'Apparently, he liked to drink, but that doesn't necessarily make him an alcoholic. Anyway, as I was saying, Mr Gardener had made no secret of his dislike of the cliffs. He feared them like...'

'You fear the water?'

He ignored her and took a sip of his drink. 'He would not have gone there. That is the point. Especially not during the storm last night. It just doesn't make sense.'

'He'd been drinking. Perhaps he saw someone on the beach and went down to warn them. Then he passed out. Isn't that possible?'

Radford stood up, picked up his plate and put it by the kitchen sink. 'It's possible I suppose. Perhaps you're right, maybe I'm making more of this than it is. It doesn't matter anyway...'

'And why is that?'

'Because we'll be gone by the end of the week.'

'Speak for yourself. I might stay.'

He smiled for a moment, then lost it when he felt his jaw muscles ache from the effort. 'Well, whatever happens, this is none of my business as I'm not a policeman any more.'

'Technically you are. You haven't handed in your notice yet.'

'No, but I will.' Radford stared over at his phone that was sitting on the table, now lit up, vibrating. Before he had left Lyme Regis police station, Inspector Morris had given him her number, and now she was calling.

He answered and said, 'DCI... Mr Philip Radford.'

'Old habits, eh? You're still in town, I take it?' Morris said.

'Yes, I'll be gone by Saturday.'

'Well, I don't know if you're interested, but there's been another murder.'

'Where?'

'The high street. Come and find me.'

The main road was in chaos by the time Radford walked along the promenade and up and into the main strip of the town. There was police tape across the bottom of the road, along with an incident response car parked diagonally across it, while a few uniforms stood guard. He couldn't see much of what was going on, so joined the gang of tourists and locals trying to gawp up the street. The rain had eased, but the wind pushed and prodded everyone, and the police, bundled in their waterproofs, looked miserable.

'Excuse me, but is Inspector Morris about?' Radford asked a male uniform.

'Somewhere around,' he said in a West Country accent. 'Can I help you, sir?'

'I'm expected. I'm Radford.'

'Phil Radford?' the uniform narrowed his eyes and started lifting the police tape.

'I prefer Philip.' Radford slipped under the cordon as the officer sighed, then pointed up the street. 'You'll find the inspector in the Cobb Cafe, halfway up.'

Radford nodded, then hurried up the street, careful to keep a low profile when he passed the centre of the activity, which seemed to be an alleyway. A tent had been erected over the area, and SOCOs were already at work while uniforms were guarding. He kept going and reached the cafe, where a female uniform greeted him.

'Sorry, sir, you'll have to go,' she started to say, so Radford said, 'I'm Philip Radford. I'm expected.'

'Go in,' she said and opened the cafe's glass door for him.

He saw the inspector sitting at one of the tables in the corner, a tearful young woman opposite her. Radford stepped over but kept quiet and listened.

'I can't believe it,' the young woman shook her head and sniffed. 'I just looked out there. She was... she was just over the street... then... he came from nowhere.'

The inspector looked over her shoulder at Radford, nodded and then looked at the young woman again. 'So, you basically saw the whole thing, Jane?'

Jane nodded, balling the tissue in her hand. 'I saw... I saw him grab her. Then he was pulling her backwards, dragging her into the alleyway.'

'What then?'

'I don't know, I didn't see. A bus passed by. When it was gone, so was she. I couldn't bring myself to go over, so I called the police.'

'I see. Did you get a good look at the person who attacked Emma?'

'No. They were wearing a baseball cap, sunglasses and a face mask with a weird, creepy smile printed on it.'

'OK.' The inspector wrote it down. 'That must have been scary.'

'Well, that's the other thing that scared me. I've seen him before.'

'You've seen her attacker before?'

'Yeah, I've seen him a couple of times. Stood over the road, wearing the same clothes and mask, just staring at the shop. Oh God, he must have been waiting...'

The inspector stood up and put away her notebook. 'Thank you, Jane. I'll get someone to sit with you, I just need to have a word with my colleague.'

When Morris had directed Radford over towards the counter, out of earshot, he said, 'Your colleague?'

She shrugged. 'Well, you kind of are. Listen, this is murder number two. Looks like you were right…'

'Of course I was.'

She raised her eyebrows. 'Right, well, the problem is, they're treating this as a separate incident.'

'Excuse me?'

'You heard me. My bosses believe this is a terrorist incident. In recent times we've been warned that terrorists and extremists might try and sneak over as illegal immigrants. So, this is what this is being put down as.'

'I know the kind of terrorist attacks they are referring to. They tend to be more violent. And they usually kill more than one person. She said she had seen them before, watching the shop.'

'A stalker?' the inspector asked.

'It's a possibility. But this has to be linked to the murder of Ben Gardener. I think he murdered him on the beach, in a place he would never be caught dead. The rockfall must have been just bad timing. That's why he removed the stones and left his leg visible. He wanted him found. Same with your second victim left in an alleyway. How was she killed?'

'Her throat was…' The inspector let out a harsh breath. 'Her throat was cut, and deep. It's as if he tried to cut her head off. Who does that?'

'Someone with a point to make. It's a statement.'

'So, there's a motive.'

'Of course. There'll be some kind of link between the victims.'

'It's a small town. They knew each other. I wonder where the latest victim lived.'

The inspector went over to Jane. 'Jane, I'm sorry but where did Emma live?'

'Oh, in a cottage at the end of town, past the park. It's called The Thatch Cottage. I never knew why. It's not got a thatch. I can't believe it, I just… What do I do about this place?'

'I don't know,' Morris said, 'I'm sorry. Did she have family, anyone we should contact?'

Jane sighed, staring off towards the window. 'I think she mentioned a brother in Canada, but she hadn't seen him in years. Oh, God, I'd better tell Peter…'

'Peter?' Radford asked. 'Is that her husband?'

'She wasn't married,' Jane said. 'Peter's her best friend. Peter Mayfield. He works for the paper as a reporter. This is like a bad dream.'

Morris looked up at Radford. 'Let's go talk to Peter Mayfield.'

'After we examine her home.'

As Inspector Eva Morris drove herself and the mysterious and unusual Philip Radford towards Emma Ash's home, she looked him over, wondering about him, wanting to find out more about his past. He was obviously ill at ease with people, and not very friendly, but somehow she found herself warming to his strange ways.

'Do you want to ask something, Inspector?' Radford said, looking out the window.

'I was just wondering what your story is.'

'My story. I don't have a story. I have a series of events starting with the moment I was brought screaming into this dark world we live in.'

Morris managed to keep in her laugh. 'OK, so why are you on gardening leave?'

'I made some mistakes and now some of my colleagues are dead.'

'Oh God, I'm so sorry. Was it a terrorist attack?'

Radford looked at her, his eyes glazed over. 'I suppose you could call it that. But it's more complicated. Anyway, I took my eye off the ball, and here I am.'

She nodded, wondering what to say next, trying to decide if she should say something comforting.

'Did Ben Gardener and Emma Ash know each other very well?' Radford said, and she was glad he changed the subject.

'I don't think so. I mean he was a fisherman, a butcher before that, and he spent most of his time either on a boat or in the pub. Emma on the other hand, didn't drink and was kind of the… bookish type. It's a small town so they probably ran into each other, but other than that I can't think of a connection.'

Radford pinched the bridge of his nose. 'Well, there has to be some kind of connection between them, something we're not privy to.'

She looked at him, a laugh tumbling from her mouth before she could stop it. He stared at her. 'I'm sorry, it's just I like the way you speak.'

'The way I speak?'

She smiled. 'Yes, you talk as if you belong in the Victorian era or something.'

'Do I indeed? I hadn't realised.'

Just at the right moment, Morris saw the turning for Emma Ash's house and indicated, keeping an eye on the diverted traffic that was now avoiding the town centre and congesting the arteries of the rest of Lyme Regis. She pulled up out the front of a small, whitewashed cottage that sat close to the road. There were hanging baskets filled with bright flowers all about the front of the building. It was the kind of picturesque house that she had always seen herself living in, instead of the ramshackle, crooked flat she rented over the pet shop on the high street.

Radford climbed out and joined her as she

looked over the building, her mind filled with questions both about the murders and Radford himself.

'Now, all we need to do is gain entry,' he said. 'Do you have the tools necessary?'

'Oh, of course,' she said and smiled as she stepped towards the black front door and crouched down towards three decoratively painted stones on the ground. She lifted each one until she found a set of keys. She stood up and held them up to Radford before opening the door and going in.

She sensed Radford behind her as she walked down the narrow, lilac-painted hallway, taking in the paintings on the walls, all of boats at sea.

She leaned closer to one and noticed Emma Ash's signature at the bottom. 'She was an artist. I never knew.'

'Not bad,' Radford said and followed her into a compact, light-grey carpeted lounge. There was a large brown leather sofa, armchair, small coffee table and shelves full of paperback books. More paintings of the wild sea hung on the walls, along with some excellent photographs of sunsets taken from a beach with silhouetted islands in the background. He tapped the framed photos. 'Where is this, do you suppose?'

Morris took a look. 'Erm… that looks like it could be the Isles of Scilly. I think. Nice place.'

He nodded. 'So I've heard.'

'Where do we start?'

Radford stared around at the place, his eyes seeming to find the rows of well-thumbed paperbacks of interest. 'I'll look at the books. People love to hide stuff in books.'

'What exactly are we looking for?' she asked, as Radford began systematically shaking out the books.

'Her darkest secrets.'

'They surely died with her?'

Radford stared at her. 'Oh, no, secrets don't die, Morris, don't make that mistake. They grow and they grow, consuming everything.'

The inspector nodded and smiled, pretending to know what the very odd detective was talking about, then headed to the mantelpiece over the fireplace. Her phone began to ring at that moment, so she took it out and saw Chief Superintendent Parsons was calling. She closed her eyes and braced herself for a telling-off, then answered.

'Hello, Chief Superintendent,' she said, grimacing.

'Where are you, Inspector Morris?' The Chief's tone was sharp.

'Making inquiries into Emma Ash's death, ma'am.'

'That's not your job now. You're to reassure the locals and tourists that this is just a one-off incident.'

'Two murders?'

There was a sharp sigh over the line. 'One accidental death, and now a probable terrorist attack. An Anti-Terrorism Unit is on its way from Southampton and they'll be overseeing Emma Ash's death. Also, the Home Office Pathologist is on his way. Dr Roy Shaw. I'm having him put up in one of the luxury shacks. Now, I thought it best to have a town meeting tonight, to reassure the locals that everything is being done to resolve this matter as quickly as possible. I want you there. It's starting at six tonight. Be there at the town hall. Is that understood?'

'Yes, ma'am.'

'Where's that idiot, Redford?'

'Radford, ma'am.'

'Whatever. Has he buggered off back to wherever he came from?'

Morris watched Radford searching every inch of the room. 'I think he'll be leaving soon.'

'Good. Six tonight. Be there.'

The line went dead, so she put away her phone and faced Radford. 'The Chief Super has an counter-terrorism unit on the way from Southampton, and she's called a town meeting to sweet-talk the locals. Oh, and she sends her love.'

Radford stared at her, looking confused. 'Oh, you were being sarcastic. Well, I think the town meeting is a good idea. I can get to know the locals and see who had the motive to murder both Gardener and Emma Ash.'

'That's the thing, I don't think the Chief Superintendent is going to appreciate you being there.'

'I'll be inconspicuous,' he said and smiled briefly.

'I don't think you *can* be inconspicuous. Anyway, she also said the Home Office Pathologist is on his way. Maybe he'll convince them that Ben Gardener's death wasn't just a misadventure?'

Radford made an unconvinced sound in his throat as his eyes jumped to the wood burner in the fireplace. 'Have you looked in there?'

'No.'

Radford walked over, crouched down and opened the burner. He then pulled a pair of gloves from somewhere and started to dig around.

'Ah,' he said and stood up.

'What is it?'

Radford held up a small, singed piece of paper. 'She burnt a letter, that's interesting. There's a name at the bottom.'

'What name?' Morris leaned in, trying to read the name. 'Peter Mayfield. The reporter. Her best friend. Why would she burn a letter from him?'

'Because it contained a secret. A secret they didn't want anyone to know.'

'We need to talk to him urgently.'

Radford nodded. 'Yes, we certainly do. As I

think his life is probably in great danger.'

Peter Mayfield watched the glass of white wine being poured by the young, pretty waitress, then smiled at her and waited for her to leave before lifting the glass and sipping it. It was light, crisp, and delicate. He looked back at the notes he had made that morning and then at his phone. He'd had three missed calls from Emma, but he wasn't in any hurry to answer them. He listened to one message she'd left and had been unnerved by the fact that she mentioned the death of Ben Gardener. Straight away he had called the office and was told by his new boss, the young upstart, that Ben Gardener had been simply killed by a rockfall. An accident. He sighed and took another sip of his wine.

Emma did like to worry, and when she had nothing to worry about, she tended to invent things. He had more important things to concern himself with, like the fact that the new housing development was being mostly financed by the Chief Super's husband. He had never been able to prove it, but he greatly suspected that his money came from disreputable sources. He would one day prove it all and have the last laugh. There was a deep-rooted establishment in the town and one that looked down on people like him. He would not stop until he brought it all down. They would wish their mothers had never been born at all.

He took another sip of the delicious wine, then felt the call of nature and hurried to the stale-smelling toilets. He went as quickly as possible, washed his hands thoroughly, and then went back to his table. He was about to make another note when he saw that someone had left a folded-up piece of paper under his wine glass. He looked round but all the other customers and staff were busy and not looking his way. He unfolded it and let out a harsh, shaky breath. He dropped it onto the table and stared round the pub again. No one looked his way. His heart raced as his eyes returned to the note. There, in big red letters, was the word, 'Coward.'

'Excuse me!' he called to the young pretty waitress.

'Can I help you? Is everything OK?' she asked.

'Did you see anyone leave this note for me?'

'No, I didn't. Sorry.'

He nodded, then looked round the room again. 'Then can I have the bill? I'll take the bottle to go.'

'OK.'

After he settled up, Peter Mayfield stepped out in the midday sun and put on his trilby, guarding his eyes and trying to remember where he parked. He'd only had one glass, so he was OK to drive. Oh, yes, he thought as he saw his Audi parked at the other end of the small car park. He carried the bottle, his mind troubled again by the note. Coward. The word kept playing over and over in his mind, his stomach constricting and his heart beginning to thud.

Coward. Yes, he had been a coward, once in his life, but not any more. Who had left the note? He needed to see Emma and discuss the matter with her. She was one of the few who would understand.

He was about to unlock his car when he heard a muffled tapping sound. He stood there for a moment, looking around the car park, trying to work out where the sound was coming from. Then his eyes went sliding over the silver bodywork of his car, landing on the boot. Yes, the sound, the tapping was coming from inside the car boot.

With great trepidation, he raised the key fob, pressed the unlock button, and listened to the loud click. He looked around again, swallowing hard and reached out to the underside of the latch. He pressed and saw the boot slowly open.

He frowned, seeing only his spare tyre, some tools and his waterproof coat. But there was something else, something unusual. There was a toy robot, slightly moving, its arms twitching. Where the hell did it come from?

Suddenly his mind raged, a burning light attaching to his spine, then his legs and every part of him as he jerked and spasmed, alive with pain. Something had been jabbed into his back.

He was being bundled into his own boot, and he had no strength in his body to fight back. Tape was wrapped around his mouth as he looked up and saw the silhouette of a man looking down at him. He wore a baseball cap, sunglasses and a face mask. Mayfield trembled at the sight of the mouth, painted on, but no less horrifying. A mouth of sharp teeth and blood dripping from them.

Just before the boot closed and the darkness came, he thought he heard his abductor mutter a single word.

'Coward!'

CHAPTER FOUR

The locals of Lyme Regis were making a raucous noise as they fought to get into the small town hall, which was pretty much a run-of-the-mill building that usually hosted jumble sales and small parties. Radford slipped through the crowd, keeping a low profile as Morris had suggested, and reiterated, that she thought it was a bad idea. She suggested strongly that he should stay away entirely and she would tell him later what had happened. But Radford's blood was up and he found it impossible to stay away, wanting to get a sense of what the locals thought of what was going on in their town. A town usually free of murder.

The crowd took to the plastic seats that had been put into neat rows across the polished parquet floor and facing the small stage where Radford laid eyes on Chief Super Parsons, Inspector Morris and a peppery-haired, thick-set man in a suit who seemed to be watching the locals intently. He decided to hide at the back as Parsons called for the chattering audience to quieten down.

'Ladies and gentlemen,' she said, raising her hands like a spiritual leader. 'Thank you for coming. I appreciate you've got busy lives, but I wanted to address any fears you may have because of the recent incident...'

'When you say incident, you mean brutal murder?' someone called out.

'Maybe we can charge the tourists to visit the site!' someone else said and laughed, but most of the crowd groaned.

'This isn't the time for jokes,' the Chief Super said with a huff. 'Now, obviously, there are lots of rumours going around about some maniac killer... but let me assure you, this was a very unusual incident...'

'Was this a terrorist attack?' a well-dressed woman near the front asked.

'Look, this is a difficult situation, Mrs Bartlett.'

'As you know, I run several establishments around here, and if this business scares away the tourists, then where does that leave me and my staff?'

'I appreciate you're...'

'Was this a terrorist attack, Chief Superintendent?' another person said and stood up. It was a young man, perhaps in his thirties.

'For anyone who doesn't know me, I'm James Headley. As you know, Chief Superintendent, I run the Lyme Hotel. I have done now for the last three years since I took it over…'

'We know who you are!' someone called out from the back.

Headley looked back at the rest of the audience, glaring before facing the Chief Super again. 'If this was a terrorist attack, then we can say goodbye to the tourists, goodbye to our livelihoods. So, I ask you, was this a terrorist attack? Yes or no?'

Parsons took a breath. 'I've been advised that, yes, this is terror-related…'

The locals erupted in shocked chatter, while the inspector and the Chief Super tried unsuccessfully to regain order. It was then that Radford saw the door to the hall open, and a wild-haired man came in, dressed in a dark suit. He seemed to look around the room with a strange kind of grin on his face, and then pull up a chair and sit down, still smiling as he crossed his legs.

'Quiet!' the man on the stage bellowed.

The crowd slowly quietened down.

'You don't know me,' the man said. 'My name is Colonel Jameson. I'm the head of Anti-Terrorism down here in this beautiful part of the world. Unfortunately, these kinds of random acts of violence are becoming more and more frequent. But rest assured, we are here to capture the person who committed this terrible crime. I will use every power I have to track down this terrorist and bring them to justice, so you can all rest easy and the tourists will keep coming back to your beautiful town. Just carry on and let us do our work. If you have any information, please let us know through your local police. Thank you.'

'Are there any more questions?' Parsons asked, looking around the hall.

Radford's eyes jumped to a petite woman, who raised her hand and mumbled something. But no one seemed to hear what she said.

'What about the rockfall?' one of the locals called out. 'I heard the terrorist caused that too!'

'That is quite ridiculous,' the Chief Super said. 'Unfortunately, and very sadly, one of our own happened to be by the cliffs when the rain and the wind... well, it was an unfortunate accident...'

'He wouldn't go there!' a woman's strangled, emotional voice rang out.

The entire crowd, including Radford, turned to see Mrs Molly Gardener standing halfway down the room, staring with red and wet eyes at the stage. 'I'm his wife if you didn't know. I'm Ben Gardener's wife...'

'We're very sorry...' the Chief Super started to say.

'Are you?' Mrs Gardener called out. 'Then why don't you look into why he was there?

He hated those cliffs. He knew that one day, something like this would happen. But not to him!'

Radford found himself pushing through the crowd, so he could be seen. He saw the Chief's and inspector's eyes jump to him, but he ignored them and turned to face the crowd. 'My name is...'

Everyone looked at him, their eyes filled with confusion and expectation.

His heart pounded, flashes of the dark tunnel, the rumble travelling up his body. Icy sweat coated his back and his palms. He wanted to run. He took a breath.

'I'm DCI Philip Radford,' he said. 'Mrs Gardener is quite correct. Ben Gardener would not have voluntarily stood or lain beneath those cliffs. This was no accident or a terrorist attack... this is two murders, both, I believe are connected. I promise you all that I will do my utmost to solve this case and bring peace back to Lyme Regis. You have my promise.'

The crowd roared again, more questions being shouted out and chatter echoed around the ceiling. Suddenly Radford found a hand under his arm as he was being pulled through the crowds that heckled him. He turned to see a red-faced, tight-skinned Inspector Morris directing him towards the exit. As they went, they passed the wild-haired man in the suit, who caught Radford's eye and smiled. Radford broke free of the inspector's grip and faced the man as he said, 'Who are you?'

The man delved into his pocket and brought out a business card that he handed to Radford.

'Dr Ray Shaw, Home Office Pathologist,' the man said, his smile fading a little. 'You should come and see me, DCI Radford. You too, Inspector Morris. We have a lot to discuss. Also, a fine wine to drink. So, you know where to find me.'

'Come on,' the inspector said and dragged him back into the evening air, where she turned to him, anger in her eyes as she pointed at him. 'What the bloody hell're you doing here? What did I say?'

'You know it's rude to point, don't you?'

Morris looked at her finger and then put it away with a heavy sigh. 'You know that you've got me in a lot of trouble, don't you?'

'What do you think Dr Shaw was alluding to?' Radford looked towards the building.

'I don't know. He's the Home Office Pathologist, so he'll be directed to stamp it as a case of misadventure and an act of terrorism. And there's nothing we can do to alter that fact.'

'I don't think so.'

The inspector walked away, shaking her head as Radford observed her.

'Are you upset, inspector?'

She spun around and stared at him. 'Am I upset? You are joking, right? Am I bloody upset?'

'You seem to be.'

'Of course I am. I'm just trying to keep my bloody job right now.'

'What about the two murders?'

Morris held her hands over her face for a moment, then looked up at him. 'I don't know. We still haven't found Peter Mayfield...'

'Because he's dead.'

'How do you know that? He's probably...'

'I'm quite convinced that Mayfield is the next victim. Emma Ash had a note from him that she burned. Now he's missing. He's either on the run or dead. I'm thinking dead.'

Morris puffed out her cheeks. 'OK, DCI Radford, what next?'

'We wait for Mayfield to turn up. Dead or alive.'

There was a glistening, blurry orange shape moving and dancing in the darkness as Mayfield opened his eyes. He blinked, taking stock of his body and mind, trying to recall what had happened. His mind raced as a sudden memory violently broke into his head, making his body tremble. The orange flickering shape resolved into a small fire burning in a fireplace. Slowly his eyes adjusted, allowing him to see he was in some kind of shed or small outhouse. He tried to move his arms, but they were bound, tied together behind the chair he was sitting on.

'Help!' he shouted, his voice echoing back to

him. He listened and thought he heard the sound of waves.

'It's no good shouting,' a deep voice said behind him, making him flinch.

'Who are you?'

'Vengeance. The hand of God. Justice. Whatever you want to call me.' There was the crunch of rubble and dirt underfoot as the figure moved behind him.

'I don't understand… please, I don't know why you've…'

'Yes… yes, you do know. If you don't… then that's even worse. If you've forgotten what you did…'

Mayfield hung his head as sickness filled every part of him, bile rising in his throat. Oh God, he thought, panic now rippling through him. This was it. It had all caught up with him. 'I'm sorry.'

'You're sorry?' The figure stood in front of him, a dark shape against the fire. Mayfield tried to see his face, but there was some kind of mask over his head. 'Is that the same kind of sorry that people utter at a funeral?'

Mayfield shook his head. 'No! God no, I'm so, so sorry…'

'For what?'

'For everything.'

'For what you did?'

Mayfield stared at him, then nodded, 'Yes, of course.'

'I don't think you're truly sorry...'

'I am... believe me. If I could...'

'Ben Gardener said he was sorry. He begged for his life, pleaded on his hands and knees. Sorry. A word, an empty, barren, pathetic... word.'

'Ben Gardener? But he...'

'A rockfall? Kind of. Fate sort of intervened. He was dead before the rocks hit him.'

'Oh God...'

'Emma Ash.'

Mayfield's eyes sharpened their focus. 'What? Why did you mention her? Please, leave her out of...'

There came a deep, hate-filled laugh. 'Too late.'

'What do you mean? Where is she?'

'In the morgue.'

Mayfield turned his head and released the vomit that poured down his shoulder and arm. He spat the rest of it out, his mind unable to take it all in. Dead. Emma. No. 'No. She's not dead.'

'I almost cut off her head, so I'm pretty sure she's dead. I mean, she might have lived a little while, knowing her head wasn't attached to her body any more...'

Mayfield vomited again.

'Are you sorry for what you did, what you didn't do, Mayfield, or sorry you're here, ready to die?'

'Please, please, don't kill me. Let me help

you.'

'Help me? How?'

'I don't know. There must be a way...'

'There is a way,' the masked man said and grabbed hold of Mayfield and the chair and grunted as he heaved it round to face the opposite direction, the sound of the chair legs scraping through the rubble and dirt filling the air.

Now Mayfield could see a low table in front of him and something large on it. He focused in and saw it was a tank. A large glass tank filled with water. He shook his head as he said, 'What's that?'

'Just some seawater.'

A hand grasped at his head, yanking him forward and pushing him towards the water. He fought to stay upright, growling, but it was no good. His head plunged into the water, his vision becoming misty as he jerked his head back and forth and side to side, fighting to keep his breath in his lungs. Then he was yanked backward, lifted from the water. He took a gasp of air.

'Thank you,' he said, panting.

Then he was being plunged again, screaming, pleading to be lifted from the water. But no hand came this time, no relief, and the panic overcame him, and he thrashed his head around, fighting to hold his breath. But then his chest ached, his lungs tightening, the air escaping. Water entered his mouth. He couldn't hold on any longer, and he started to pray as a grey cloud ebbed in, dulling his sight. Soon he could only see a deep mist and a kind of calm rushed in.

The bad weather had returned for the evening, the wild wind battering the shore and the cliffs, the torrid grey waters smashing against the absolute defiance of the rock faces along the coast, and spitting in foamy anger. Radford watched it all below, his mind reeling, trembling a little, imagining what it would be like to be plunged into those cold depths, sinking deep into the dark. For him, it wasn't just the water, the way it could fill his lungs and end him, but the unknown lurking beneath, waiting to lunge out of the depths. Radford's imagination conjured all of this as Inspector Morris drove them up a steep hill and around to another beach a little way up the coast.

Another narrower, private road took them down to a few luxury shacks that stood close to the cliff, all spaced quite far apart, with their own parking spaces and small gardens.

The inspector pulled up behind one of the shacks that stood closest to the jut of the cliff and turned off the engine.

'Are you OK?' she asked, turning to Radford.

He nodded. 'I'm fine. Why do you ask?'

'You were very quiet on the way here. Thinking about the investigation?'

'Thinking about death.'

'Oh, so something light-hearted.' She laughed. 'You don't like the water. I get it. People are scared of it.'

'I'm not scared of it. I have a healthy respect for it.' Radford climbed out and stood looking at the shack, the wind battering his body, pushing him backwards. Light rain tapped at his skin as he took a step towards the building.

The inspector climbed out and went ahead of him. As she reached the shack, the side door opened and a figure stepped out and seemed to watch them for a moment before whoever it was, came towards them and opened the small gate.

'Welcome, DCI Philip Radford,' Dr Shaw called out. 'Inspector, nice to see you again. Come in and have a drink. Or stay here and be mercilessly sucked down to the ocean's unwelcoming bosom.'

Radford heard him laugh a little wildly, then he opened the door for them. He followed the inspector inside to the plush, warmth of a large, well-decorated shack, much larger than Radford's. Alcohol was collected on a small dining table, some nibbles beside it. But it was the photographs on the walls that he stared at and that the inspector also seemed drawn to. Shaw had stuck a collection of post-mortem photographs on the walls.

'Are these our crime scene photos?' Radford asked and looked at Dr Shaw who was pouring a glass of red wine.

He grinned. 'Quite a few are, some are other cases I've worked on. Beautiful, aren't they?'

'Beautiful?' the inspector whispered to Radford. 'Is he OK in the head?'

Radford ignored her and stepped closer to him. 'You have had time to examine Ben Gardener's body, I take it?'

'Right down to business,' Shaw said and handed him a glass of wine.

'I don't really partake.'

'It's expensive and it would be a shame to waste it. I don't like to drink on my own. And when I drink, I become more talkative.'

The inspector appeared and snatched the glass of wine from him and sank it in one. 'I partake. Thanks.'

Shaw laughed and refilled the glass for her. 'That's more like it. Well done, Inspector.'

'What about Ben Gardener's body?' Radford asked.

Shaw picked up his glass, swirling the wine inside it. 'Don't worry, I'm dry when I'm in the autopsy room.'

'I'm sure you are,' Radford said.

'You worked for the Met, isn't that right?'

'I did.'

'Scotland Yard before that?'

'Yes. The body?'

Shaw sipped his wine. 'You've stared into jaws of death, haven't you, Radford? I can see it in your eyes. You've got the same look in them as the bodies I see on my table. The ones that have faced a violent and terrible death, that is.'

'I think both Gardener's death and Emma Ash's murder are linked,' Radford said.

'Do you indeed?' Shaw sat down on a dining room chair and sipped his wine. 'You're a man full of fear, Radford, I can tell. You fear life because you've faced death.'

Radford shook his head and looked at the inspector. 'Finish your wine and we'll go. Maybe you can get a copy of the report…'

'Do you know what I was before I was a pathologist?' Shaw asked.

'What were you?' the inspector pulled out a chair and sat down, the look of an enchanted child on her face.

'Look in my eyes, Inspector. Tell me what you see.'

She leaned forward. 'I don't know. You've got blue eyes…'

'*Daisy, Daisy,*' Shaw sang. '*Give me your answer, do, I'm half crazy, all for the love of you. It won't be a stylish marriage, I can't afford a carriage. But you'll look sweet upon the seat of a bicycle built for two…*'

The inspector looked at Radford and exchanged a look with him that said it all.

'*When the road's dark, we can both despise policemen and lamps as well. There are bright lights in the dazzling eyes of beautiful Daisy Bell,*' Shaw sang again, then was quiet for a moment, staring at the inspector. 'I was an army doctor. I was put with this secret unit, made up of mostly men from Special Air Service. The SAS, Inspector. Now those men were crazy, made me look like a sane individual. Anyway, we ended up in Iraq. The first time around, we ended up surrounded as we tried to sneak into the country and take out some of Sadam's highest-ranking officers. It didn't go well, we got spotted and all hell broke loose. We got pinned down. In the end, there were only a few of us still standing. One of them was hit by a sniper. Made a real mess of him, so I dragged him to cover and... I didn't have the right tools, but I managed to crack open his ribcage... took his heart in my hands and kept pumping, kept him alive until we were rescued.'

'Did he make it?' Morris asked.

Shaw looked at her and sipped his wine. 'He did. Married with three kids now. Still sends me a Christmas card without fail. Anyway, after that day I stopped caring what people think of me, stopped fearing anything.'

He looked up at Radford. 'I'll never be scared again.'

'That's wonderful, Dr Shaw,' Radford said. 'The bodies?'

'Ben Gardener was dead before the rockfall, in my opinion. Lack of blood around the wounds the rocks made, tells me that. His heart had stopped pumping by then. Also, the hyoid bone was broken. Not post-mortem. He was strangled to death. As for Emma Ash, well, of course, she was murdered. Two murders in one day in this town? Terrorist attack? Don't make me laugh. Then why didn't the killer kill more, and go on a rampage? No, this is a murder with a plain old, straightforward motive. Jealously. Hatred. Revenge. Take your pick, DCI Radford.'

'Peter Mayfield is missing,' Morris said, pouring herself another glass of wine.

Shaw nodded. 'Another one for me to cut up then. Business is good these days.'

Then came a muffled ringing and the inspector flickered to life and pulled out her phone.

'The station,' she said and answered it. 'Inspector Morris. Yeah. Oh, right, I'll be there as soon as I can.'

She ended the call and then looked up at Radford. 'They found Mayfield. Washed up on the beach. Drowned.'

CHAPTER FIVE

Radford stood on the cusp of the action, observing it all with his hood up, the wind digging into him, making him stagger a little as he watched the beach. The uniforms, all wrapped up in their waterproofs, guarded the area while the SOCOs did their best to preserve the scene against the elements. Mayfield's body had been discovered far up the beach, close to the row of static homes, the roaring waves quite far below his final resting place. Radford had noticed his clothes weren't soaked through, not like he'd been pulled from the sea, yet the doctor on scene had called it a drowning. It had all the hallmarks, Morris had told him before wandering off to question the people in the static homes.

Then Morris appeared along the pebbly beach, making her way back towards him, her face pinched tight in her hood.

'You should go inside!' she shouted against

the wind. 'There's not much to do here.'

'His clothes were almost dry, save for the rain,' Radford said close to her ear.

Morris nodded and looked towards the body that was now being moved. She looked at him again. 'You know what they'll say, don't you?'

'An accidental drowning?' Radford huffed. 'In almost dry clothes?'

She shrugged. 'It doesn't matter to them, as long as they can tidy it all away.'

'She cannot possibly tidy it away this time. Not this time.'

Morris sighed. 'Just you watch. Go on, go inside before you freeze to death.'

Radford looked towards the sea, then the body and gave an involuntary shiver. He nodded before turning and making his way awkwardly up the stony beach towards the car park and up the hill to the shack. He opened the door and went in, battling to keep the wind and rain out. He shook his coat off and hung it up, then turned to see Carr sat on the sofa as always, watching him with a smile.

'What a night,' she said. 'Looks like another storm.'

He looked out, towards where Mayfield was probably still lying. 'They found another body.'

'Another murder?'

'I think so. He was drowned, apparently, but when I saw him, his clothes were pretty much dry, too dry to be a drowning in the sea.'

'Accidental?'

'No. He was a close friend of the last victim, Emma Ash. We found the charred remains of what looked like a letter he had written to her. I don't know what it all means, why someone is targeting them...'

'But you'll figure it out, you always do in the end.'

He looked at her. 'But what if I'm too late again?'

'You won't be.' She stood up and came over to him and touched his cheek. 'You couldn't have seen all that coming, no one would have... I know you carry around the guilt of it all because you survived, but you can't live like that. You need to let it go.'

'I'm not sure I can.'

'Someone's coming,' Carr said, glancing towards the window. 'Probably here to talk to you. I'll make myself scarce.'

He stood there, watching her hurry into the small kid's bedroom and shut the door. There was a tap at the window and he turned to a windswept Inspector Morris looking in at him.

He opened the door and said, 'Come in and dry off, Inspector.'

'No time for that. There are marks on the victim's wrists, which look like from having his hands bound. They can't deny it now. I've called the Chief Super and she said she'd meet us at the station. Come on, let's go. Unless I was disturbing something?'

He looked towards the bedroom but shook his head. 'No, it's fine. I'll get my coat.'

'No, this just doesn't happen here,' Chief Superintendent Parsons snapped and shook her head as she sat at her desk. Radford and Inspector Morris were stood at the centre of her office, exchanging awkward glances.

'Not in this town,' Parsons continued, half muttering. 'In London or Manchester… that's the sort of incident that happens all the time, and terrorism… don't get me started. But not here, not in this town…'

'They found bruising on Mayfield's wrists,' Morris said, her voice a little strained.

'Who did?' Parsons stared up at her, her cheeks red.

'The SOCOs, the doctor who pronounced his death… they all saw it.'

'Well, if he drowned, then all kinds of damage can be done to a body…'

'His clothes were dry,' Radford said. 'At least too dry to have fallen in the sea and drowned.'

Parsons snapped her eyes on him. 'Oh, you're loving this, aren't you, Mr Radford…'

'DCI Radford.'

She stood up and pointed at him. 'I've been looking you up, Mr Radford, and do you know what I found? What do you think I found, Inspector Morris?'

Morris shrugged.

Parsons kept staring at Radford. 'He used to work at New Scotland. Used to be a detective chief superintendent, didn't you? That sounded pretty impressive to me until I dug around and discovered that your bosses couldn't wait to get rid of you. They didn't like you, did they, Phil?'

Radford sighed. 'They didn't seem to appreciate the way I did things.'

'No, they didn't. You seemed to have rubbed a lot of people up the wrong way. So they palmed you off on another station, another team, and guess what, Morris? It ended in disaster...'

'There was a hostage situation,' Radford started to say.

'Quite a number of your team died, didn't they?'

Radford tried not to let the images enter his head as he looked away, but he heard the distant sounds, growing louder all the time, the crying and begging. A gun went off in his mind and he flinched.

'Then comes the pièce de résistance,' Parsons said, a smile almost creeping onto her face. 'His last case with that team, the surviving members, involved some terrorist group... and what happened? They blew up the station, and only a handful survived, including our friend here, Mr Phil Radford.'

'DCI Philip Radford.'

'But you're not a police officer any more. Are

you?'

'I'm on gardening leave, while I recover.'

Parsons laughed and it was full of gloating. 'The terrorist attack happened over a year ago, and they made you take the leave because you didn't want to.'

'I didn't believe I needed…'

'You were suffering from PTSD. You probably still are, and God knows what else is going on in that head of yours. The bottom line is, you're not fit for duty, and certainly not fit to take charge of this investigation.'

The inspector cleared her voice. 'The fact remains, ma'am, that Mayfield didn't drown in the sea. He had marks around his wrist where someone had bound him…'

'He drowned!' Parsons said, her voice breaking, her face flushing. 'Emma Ash was killed by terrorists… who we will find!'

'Ben Gardener?' Radford said. 'Rockfall? Misadventure?'

'Yes!' She pointed at him. 'Yes. There's no… serial killer going around murdering people in this town. And you, Radford, are not going to somehow make your name or try and prove yourself by finding a killer who doesn't bloody well exist except in your messed up little mind.'

Parsons took a moment, and seemed to try and calm herself before she said, 'Now, we have a redevelopment happening not too far out of this town, with more housing, a new school…

and even a new hotel that will bring in more tourism.'

Radford laughed and shook his head, recalling a piece of information that the inspector had imparted.

'What is so amusing?' Parsons asked.

Radford looked at her. 'Correct me if I'm wrong, but isn't your husband behind this redevelopment?'

Parsons' eyes burned, her trembling finger rising again. 'How dare you! Now I get it, now I understand why nobody wants to keep you around. Now, get out. And hurry up and leave our town and go back to… wherever they will put up with you.'

Radford turned, realising that he had burned his final bridge and there was little reason to stay and try and argue the point. No one was going to listen to reason, so he decided in that moment, that perhaps it was time to pack his bags and leave a little early. He opened the door and waited for the inspector to go through.

'Hang on, Inspector,' Parsons said. 'I need a word with you. You can go, Mr Radford.'

Radford shut the door behind him and sighed, ready to go home and start packing. Where in heaven, or rather hell, was he going to go?

'Sit down, Inspector Morris,' Parsons said, sitting down at her desk, her face still scarlet. The inspector braced herself for the telling-off that she knew was coming, although a large part of her was moving in the direction of not caring. It had become blatantly clear that Parsons' motives lay with her husband's business and not with any kind of justice, but she smiled politely anyway.

'I'm not going to hide the fact that I'm quite disappointed that you've allowed yourself to be taken in by that charlatan,' she said. 'But I guess, he told you his background, made himself look good by mentioning his history with Scotland Yard, and of course, he seemed like he knew what he was talking about.'

'He does seem to know what he's talking about.'

'The man's mentally unstable, Morris.' Parsons' eyes took on the same look her mother's had when she gave her the 'this is for your own good' talk.

'I've been in touch with his superiors at the Yard and the Met. I feel sorry for him, I really do, but you can't trust him, certainly not his judgement.'

'But what about the marks on Mayfield's wrists?'

Parsons let out a heavy breath. 'Let's leave that to the crime scene people and the pathologist. Now, let's talk about what's going to happen next.'

'OK.'

Parsons sat back. 'As you know, the counter-terrorism lot have set up camp and they've already got their eyes on some possible suspects. One in particular. His name is Daniel Volkov...'

'Daniel Volkov. The Russian student? I've met him, he's just a...'

'Colonel Jameson has come to the conclusion that Volkov may be part of a team of radicalised young Russians who worship Putin and have wormed their way in here to try and destroy our democracy from within.'

'Volkov? Ma'am, I don't understand. I remember him criticising Putin's regime and calling him a fascist...'

'Of course, he's going to say that. Come on, Morris, you've got to realise these people are clever and sneaky. Anyway, I've volunteered you to join Jameson's team and to help him capture and question Volkov. What do you say?'

Morris' initial reaction was to tell her where to stuff her offer, but then she thought again, wondering if it might be better to be there in case anything got heated. Volkov a radicalised terrorist? She wanted to laugh but put on the face of a serious copper who wanted to do the right thing.

'Thank you, ma'am,' she said. 'I appreciate the opportunity. When's the operation happening?'

Parsons looked at her watch. 'In about two hours. They thought it better to catch him unawares. Right, the colonel's team are meeting here in about twenty minutes, so get your civvies on and get ready for the action.'

'OK.'

'Go on then, hurry up.'

Morris got to her feet, thinking it all over and quickly regretted her decision to say yes. Poor Volkov, she thought, the unsuspecting lad who had moved away from the fascist pressure of Putin's regime, only to be targeted here as some kind of terrorist. She sighed. But at least, she thought, if she was there, she could make sure the whole thing went smoothly, and Volkov could explain himself. Yes, she decided, she would help him, and she left Parsons' office feeling a tiny bit better about the whole situation.

The wind was rattling the windows of the shack as Radford put his suitcase on the lower level of the bunk beds. He opened it and stared into it for a moment, sighing, feeling a tinge of disappointment that what had started as a promising investigation had been stubbed out so prematurely, but he would be damned if he was going to stay and spend the rest of his leave arguing the toss. He had no way of knowing if the killer had finished his spree, or if more were to be targeted, but it was no longer his affair, so he started opening the drawers and neatly putting away his clothes in the case.

'Where are you going?' Carr asked, stood in the doorway, arms folded, eyebrows raised.

'Away from here,' he said. 'I'm not wanted.'

'What about the body on the beach?'

He let out a tired breath. 'Accidental drowning or at least that's how they will try and tidy it away. But it's none of my business any more.'

'Isn't it?'

'What can I do, Carr? I've tried talking sense to Chief Superintendent Parsons, but I believe her allegiances remain elsewhere.'

'Meaning?'

'Her husband is a local businessman and redeveloper. If this town gets bad publicity, and investors or the tourists think a crazed murderer is going around, then they lose money. It's as simple as that. They will not listen to reason until they find themselves up to their knees in blood.'

'So you're leaving?'

He stared at her, then stepped closer. 'We're leaving. You and I. I'm not sure where we can go...'

'I'm not going anywhere.'

'What do you mean? I thought we would...'

'Listen, Radford... Philip,' she said, and moved to him, looking up into his eyes. 'You know I can't go with you.'

'Yes, you can. I need your help.'

She smiled and shook her head. 'Oh, Philip,

you fool. You've got to snap out of it and realise I don't really exist.'

He closed his eyes tight, his heart beginning to thud and pound in his chest, the rise of panic deafening him for a moment as he found himself fighting for breath.

He was in the dark again, the air thick with black dust, filling his throat. He blinked, and saw nothing, just the endless dark. He was dead, he was sure of that, and somehow he felt peaceful… as if… yes, it was time.

Sirens started in the distance, fighting with the ringing in his ears. Then the panic arrived, the memory of running through the tunnel coming back to him as he lay there in the dirt, sprinting away from the bomb, the silhouette of DC Michelle Carr rocking in his vision, growing larger, getting closer.

'Run!' he recalled shouting.

His hands started scrambling in the dark as he called out her name, picking up rubble and throwing it out of the way until he touched her skin. Cool skin. Dust and dirt-covered skin.

'Carr?' he said, his voice echoing in the dark. 'Carr?'

He ran his hands up her arms until he found her neck and pressed his fingers to her pulse. Nothing. Not even a faint pulse, and he let out a sob as he started performing CPR. Somewhere in that dark time together, the rescue team found him and pulled him away from her. He would never lay eyes on her again, not until a few weeks later when she turned up at his door and he never questioned how she could be there. He was just happy she was.

'I'm not sure what I'll do now,' he said, wiping his eyes.

'You'll stay here and you'll find out what's going on. Someone murdered Ben Gardener, Emma Ash and now Peter Mayfield. You know it, so go and do something about it.'

He looked at his suitcase again, staring at his neatly folded clothes, running everything through his mind, all the deaths so far, trying to fight for his attention, images of their lifeless bodies flashing in front of his eyes. Where to start? There had to be a link between them, a reason they were being targeted.

'There has to be a motive,' he said. 'Some reason they were all targeted by the killer. He strangled Ben Gardener, tried to cut off Emma Ash's head and drowned Peter Mayfield. Very different modus operandi. Why?'

But no answer came as it usually did and he looked around to see he was alone. DC Michelle Carr was no longer there and she had never been there. The loneliness rose like the icy cold tide, and the feeling he would drown in it, made the panic start again. He had always prided himself on being an individual who didn't require the company of people and, in fact, despised them, but since he had found himself alone in the dark tunnel, with only Carr's lifeless body for company, there had grown in him this strange desperate need to interact. He still did not like most people, but compared to the horrid loneliness of the dark, he felt he could put up with them.

He put on his coat, ready to start his investigation again although once more he had no idea where to begin.

CHAPTER SIX

There was barely any light as Inspector Morris was rocked about in the unmarked police van that hurtled towards Charmouth, where there was a holiday complex at the end of a small village. It was gated, but they had already warned the owners of their imminent arrival. According to the gathered intelligence, Daniel Volkov rented one of the chalets at the very back of the complex, near the woods. Morris looked around at the team she was sitting with, all dressed in black, carrying handguns or MP5 submachine guns. The Colonel was up front, next to the driver.

'Right, you listen to me,' one of the armed officers said, pointing to Morris. 'You stay back and observe, you understand? I tell you to get out the fucking way and you do. Got it?'

'Got it,' Morris said, noticing some of the armed team laughing or grinning as they checked their weapons.

'Daniel Volkov,' the same officer said, looking at his people. 'Russian national. Been here for two years. We believe he could be a former soldier, but we can't be sure. You know how secretive the bloody Russians are these days. They like to sneak these people over and let them run amok right under our noses. Remember Salisbury? Let's not let that happen here.'

'Where did your intelligence come from on Volkov?' Morris asked.

The officer stared at her, looking like he wanted to slap her face. 'That's for us to know, Inspector. We've already got one poor woman with her head almost cut off. We don't want any more. I mean, we wouldn't want you to lose your pretty head, would we?'

Then came the laughter from everyone in the van, so she looked down, a horrible sense of doom filling up her stomach as the van slowed to a halt. The engine was switched off and they all sat in silence, the rest of the team staring at her.

Radford was on the point of turning back home as he fought his way along the dark high street, a sliver of deep mauve creeping up the horizon while the wind and rain kept pushing him in the opposite direction. He had no real idea of where he was going, but he found himself crossing the glistening wet street and heading to the narrow alleyway where Emma Ash had been discovered, almost headless. The police tape was still there, being whipped by the wind, a piece of it loose and flapping wildly. He stood there for a moment, staring into the darkness, his hands dug into his pockets, shivering. He looked up the darkened street, only the occasional vehicle passing him by. What did he hope to accomplish by visiting the scene? The SOCOs and the counter-terrorism unit had examined the scene and would have discovered any evidence left by the killer. He looked around, examining the street, the shops and the restaurants, suspecting that perhaps the killer was there somewhere among the population. Then something caught his eye, a movement further up the street. He stood frozen for a moment, seeing the silhouette of a hooded figure seeming to stare back in his direction. He was unable to see a face, so he took a step closer, staring at them and waiting to see what they would do.

They remained still, fixed to the spot as he took another step closer. He looked round him again, hearing only the wild groans of wind in his ears and feeling the rain hammering at his skin. He began to walk forward, watching the figure that was still staring in his direction. When he was a couple of metres from whoever they were, and he could make out they wore some kind of face mask, the figure swung round and lurched into the darkness of the next turning. Radford hurried along until he reached the turning and saw that the path led into the local gardens. There was very little light along the path that was lined with trees and benches. He took a few steps along the path, looking side to side, staring into the dark corners for the hooded person in case they were waiting to pounce. Radford was now breathing hard, almost panting, his body starting to tremble as he moved down the dark corridor until he reached the opening that he knew would lead down to the beach on the other side. Where had the hooded person gone, he wondered and realised that they had probably exited the gardens at the other end and then headed along the beach.

Radford turned the corner and saw the dark shape of a small van parked a few feet away, cutting off the path. Then the engine rumbled to life, the headlights beaming, blinding Radford for a moment as he held his hand in front of his face, shielding his eyes. The engine roared, the van jerking forward a little in a threatening way. Radford stepped back, his breaths coming faster, the slow burn of panic spreading up his chest. The van jerked forward again, the engine roaring louder. Then it was coming at him, and he turned on the spot and ran as fast as he could round the corner and the way he had come. The engine growled behind him, the headlights lighting his way as he ran, panting, his arms pumping as it got closer and closer. He could see the end of the gardens and knew if he could make it in time, he could swing out of the way of the van. He turned his head and saw the headlights burning out to him, the grille of the van right behind him now. He took a great breath and pumped his legs and arms harder than he ever had.

No, there had been a time not so long ago when he had run faster, the blast of the explosion chasing him through the darkness. Now it was back, death on his heels once more. He felt the van press against his calves, bumping him as he was barely a foot from the entrance of the gardens. He lurched sideways, gripping the stone pillar to his right and swinging himself around.

The van roared past, skidding out into the road and then taking a left turn and hurtling up the hill.

Radford had fallen to the pavement and stayed there a moment, his face pressed against the cold, dank ground. He pushed himself up to his knees with a grunt, then clambered up, holding onto the pillar for support as he turned and saw the tail lights of the van in the distance.

'I think I should go home now,' he said to himself and started walking awkwardly down the street.

'Daniel?' the mousey, grey-haired woman said as she pulled her anorak tighter around her, squinting against the wind and rain. Colonel Jameson and most of the team had been let in at the gates to the holiday park and stood on the gravel driveway of the main building. Mrs Winter, who ran the place with her large, balding husband, who was also there looking perplexed, shook her head, looking just as confused as she said, 'But he's such a nice lad.'

'Yeah, he is,' the husband said, scratching his scalp. 'Very helpful.'

'Is this because he's Russian?' Mrs Winter asked.

Inspector Morris watched it all unfold, buried in her coat, now with a bulky bulletproof vest underneath. She had observed how Jameson had gone storming in, waking everyone up and ordering them about as if the owners of the holiday park were part of his team. That was the kind of man he was, she guessed, the sort of man used to giving orders, to everyone jumping when he told them how high.

'Let us worry about the details,' Jameson said and signalled to the leader of the armed response team, who started ordering his people to get ready and check their weapons. Then they were starting to move, grouping up and spreading out, lifting their submachine guns or handguns as they tactically headed through the grounds.

'He hates Putin,' the husband said. 'Do you think he's some kind of sleeper agent or something?'

The Colonel ignored them both and looked

at the inspector, his eyes travelling up and down her with a look of derision. 'Right, come on, you. But stay out of the way, or you're liable to get your pretty head blown off.'

Then the Colonel hurried on, leaving the man and woman to stare at the inspector, confusion and questions in her eyes.

'I'm sorry,' Morris said.

'Is this something to do with that woman being killed?' Mrs Winter asked.

'Yes, I'm afraid so.'

'Well, he wasn't even around then. Where was he, Douglas?' Winter looked up at her husband.

'Bristol.'

Morris spun round and started jogging after the armed team, a horrible feeling of panic overtaking her, not unlike when she lost her mum in a big store when she was a kid. She moved faster, listening out but only hearing the wind and rain. Then there were shapes moving, black against the grey, stormy sky. Through the wind, she heard the crack of a door being battered and knocked in while commands were shouted. She ran closer, shouting, 'Wait! I don't think…'

But there was a cry from inside the building, a voice shouting out in a foreign language.

'He's making a bolt for it!' someone called out, torchlight beaming wildly around.

She followed as the team ran into the dark woods beyond the holiday park, the beams of torchlights bouncing around, catching the streams of rain. There was the roar of the wind in her ears now as she caught sight of a figure ahead, running for their life as the armed team gave chase.

'Stop fucking running!' someone shouted above the wind.

But the figure, undoubtedly Daniel Volkov, kept running deeper into the woods.

'Stop right there!' another voice cried out, and when the inspector caught up with the team, she found they had managed to surround Volkov, who stood with his hands slightly raised. In the torchlight, she saw his skin was pale, his eyes wide in terror. The armed response guys had positioned themselves so they had him in their sights, but careful not to get each other in the crossfire.

'Drop it!' one of the armed team shouted, and then the inspector looked down at Daniel's right hand to see he was holding something behind his trembling legs.

'Please, I can't go back,' Volkov said in broken English, almost in tears. 'They will kill me!'

'Who's that, Daniel?' the Colonel asked. 'Your terrorist mates?'

Daniel's eyes jumped to him. 'Terrorist? Me? I'm not...'

Then he raised his hands suddenly, the object in his right-hand lifting. The armed response team shouted for him to drop it, but then the first blast rang out. Volkov jerked, his eyes springing open further. His chest opened up, a spurt of blood bursting forth as he slumped to the undergrowth.

The inspector gasped in horror, frozen for a moment, the roar of the wind replaced by the pulse pounding in her ears. She stepped closer, staring down at the still body of Daniel Volkov.

'Stay back!' the armed response leader shouted, then looked at the rest of his team. 'The threat has been neutralised. Job done.'

Radford had only been back at the shack for a few minutes, his heart still rattling in his chest, the adrenalin pounding through his system, when there came a thump at the window. The sun was fighting to come up over the horizon, through the clouds, and he was able to just about make out who was standing outside the door. He stood up when he saw the shivering frame of Inspector Morris. Her face was spotted with rain, her skin pale. There was fear in her eyes.

He opened the door and she pushed past him, hurried to his sink and threw up in it.

'My God, Morris,' he said, turning away.

Still bent over the sink, she said, 'Sorry, but I've just... Jesus. They fucking killed him...'

She retched again and spat into the sink.

'Who killed whom?' Radford asked.

Morris straightened up, grabbed some kitchen roll and wiped her face. 'Those thugs, the anti-terror… thugs, that's what they are. Colonel Jameson had received some intel on a Russian lad living in Charmouth. They were trying to make out he was some kind of terrorist…'

Radford pinched his nose as the penny came crashing down. 'They were saying he killed Emma Ash?'

'Yep. But just before they went storming in, the woman who owned the place he rented, told me he'd been in Bristol that day. I tried to warn them, to stop them…'

Radford let out a breath, nodding. 'You did your best, Morris. Don't blame yourself, madness lies that way.'

Morris looked up at him. 'You've scraped your face.'

He touched his cheek. 'Have I?'

'Where have you been tonight? You've got your coat on and it's wet.'

'Well, maybe you could be a detective. I went for a walk and found myself face-to-face with a hooded and masked person. They ran and I stupidly ran after. Then they tried to run me down…'

'What the hell? Are you OK?' Morris grasped him by his arms and looked him over.

'I'm fine,' he said, pulling himself away from her grasp. 'The question is, what was he doing at that time? Was he planning another murder?'

'Has it occurred to you that maybe he followed you and was planning on killing you?'

Radford frowned. It hadn't occurred to him at all. 'Hmm, not sure about that. I gave chase and he ran off.'

'Then tried to run you down? Maybe the killer thinks you're getting close and wants you out of the way.' Morris shrugged, then went over and collapsed on the sofa.

'I'm sorry about what happened to you tonight.'

She huffed out a laugh. 'I'm sorry about the young man who died. I can't believe they did that. He ran away from them and they gave chase. He had something in his hand, they must have thought it was a knife or gun... it was only a screwdriver, hardly effective against submachine guns. He was terrified, kept saying he couldn't go back...'

Radford nodded. 'He was more than likely referring to Putin's Russia. He saw armed men coming for him and feared the worst.'

'Those bloody thugs. There'll be an inquiry.'

'Then you tell them what you saw.'

Morris suddenly curled up, grasping her face and beginning to sob. Radford stepped closer, hesitating, trying to work out what exactly was expected of him. Eventually, he sat down and, after raising his hand a couple of times, he patted her on the back.

'There, there,' he said.

She stopped sobbing and looked at him through her red, swollen eyes. 'There, there? Really?'

'I'm sorry, I'm not very good at this sort of thing.'

'No, you're not, are you?' She laughed, then sighed. 'This is probably a silly question, seeing as you're not a people person, but can I try and get some sleep here?'

Radford stood up and tried to smile. 'Yes, of course. That's a particularly uncomfortable sofa bed, so feel free to try.'

'What about you?'

'I don't really sleep these days. At least I won't tonight.'

She smiled. 'Thank you, Radford.'

When Radford started to collect together some bedding for her, Morris suddenly said, 'I take it there's no one special in your life?'

'No. No one can stand me for very long. Well, there was one person…'

'Where are they?'

Radford didn't know how to answer for a moment, his mind drawn back to the dark and dirt. 'They are… in a better place, they say, don't they?'

Morris nodded, looking sympathetic. 'I see. I'm sorry.'

'Goodnight, Inspector. Sleep well.'

'I'm not sure I will actually.'

Then Radford had a thought. 'Well, seeing that neither of us are going to sleep tonight, why don't we go and take a look at Peter Mayfield's house, and see what we can find out? If you can authorise it, that is?'

She stood up and stretched. 'I'm an inspector, of course I can. The way I feel right now, I can do anything I bloody want.'

CHAPTER SEVEN

Like the rest of the victims, Peter Mayfield had lived outside of Lyme Regis, and his house was on the way to Charmouth. It was a little grander and more modern than the other victims', with huge metal-framed windows that lined most of the front of the house. It sat alone on the edge of the woods, a tall wooden fence separating Mayfield's property from the woodland.

Inspector Morris drove them to the wooden farm-style gate where a large driveway led to the front door, then parked. Radford stared at the house for a moment, wondering how much such a place would cost to build or even buy.

'He was quite wealthy,' Morris said as if seeing into Radford's mind.

'How wealthy?'

'Pretty wealthy. I think his parents had some biscuit-making business and left it to him before they died. He sold it and made a mint. He had this place built about ten years ago. It's an eyesore if you ask me.'

As Radford climbed out of the car, a thought occurred to him. 'Who built it, exactly?'

The Inspector got out and stared at him over the roof of the car. 'You're wondering if Parson's husband had anything to do with it, aren't you?'

'It did cross my mind. If Parsons did build this house, then that would be a connection between Mayfield and him. Did they socialise?'

'Oh no.' Morris took out a set of keys and headed for the door, so Radford followed through the gate.

'Why not?'

'Mayfield was gay. Parsons doesn't approve of that sort of thing.' Morris unlocked the large glass and steel door and slid it open.

The house was cool inside and largely open-plan with an endless plain of polished wood flooring and '60s-style furniture that looked rather uncomfortable. Through a large, whitewashed arch, there was a clinically neat kitchen with every conceivable gadget and a wine rack that lined one wall, filled with a massive collection.

'Could sex be the motive?' Radford asked, examining everything he saw.

'Sex? Between Ben Gardener, Emma Ash, and Peter Mayfield? What, some kind of love triangle?' Morris gave a shiver. 'No, I don't think so and I never want to contemplate that ever again.'

Then Morris looked at him, seeming to examine him carefully. 'How did you end up here? I mean, not being funny, but you don't seem very keen on the sea, so…?'

'My doctor suggested it,' Radford said, slipping on some gloves. 'But the more I think about it, the more I'm convinced he was trying to get me to move away.'

Morris laughed. 'Well, I'm glad you're here.'

He looked at her, feeling surprised. 'Why?'

'Because of all this. Although, you should be suspect number one, seeing as all this started just after you turned up. It's like Murder She Wrote. I'd arrest Jessica Fletcher straight away.'

Radford chuckled. 'So would I.'

He walked across the miles of wood flooring, feeling the coolness of the building wash over him and the wind eerily whistling somewhere above him. Curiosity entered his mind and he looked over at Morris who was standing looking around the living room area.

'Are you married, Inspector?' he asked.

She laughed. 'Me? Oh God no. I'm a disaster zone. My last boyfriend turned out to be a nutter who started stalking me.'

'What happened?'

She looked at him strangely. 'I arrested him. Then got a restraining order. So, relationships and marriage and all that business… no, thanks. What are we looking for anyway?'

'Anything out of the ordinary. Something

that someone might kill for.' Radford left Morris in the living area and moved on down the whitewashed hallway until he reached a stairway that went up to a mezzanine level. At the very top was a set of large, church-style doors. He went up the steps and tried the doors, but they were locked.

'Inspector Morris!' he called out, his voice echoing.

Morris climbed the stairs to join him.

'They're locked,' Radford said. 'Is there a key on the bunch you have?'

Morris took them out and tried each of them in the lock but with no luck. She sighed. 'What do we do now?'

'Find a thin strip of metal and a screwdriver,' Radford said.

'You're going to pick the lock? I've got equipment in the car.'

'Yes, but that would mean making a mess, and we don't want anyone knowing we've been here, do we?'

'Not really.' Morris sighed again, then went back down the stairs and came back a few minutes later with what Radford had asked for. As he went to work, the Inspector asked, 'How do you know how to pick locks?'

'When I was at Scotland Yard, we worked with a former professional burglar who taught us some of the tricks of the trade. I knew that one day it might all come in handy.'

Morris nodded. 'Well, you could always become a cat burglar if you do leave the police.'

Radford ignored her as he heard the click of the lock he'd been waiting for, then turned the doorknob and went into the perfectly square, barren room. It was empty, apart from a landscape painting of a beach and a sunset.

'Why would you lock a room with a painting in it?' Morris asked as she followed him in.

'Perhaps it's stolen.' Radford folded his arms, turning his head, examining the picture.

Inspector Morris took out her phone and snapped a photo. 'Let's find out by doing a reverse image search on Google.'

'Good thinking, well done.'

Morris looked at him strangely, then shook her head and continued with her search.

'Ah,' she said after a moment.

'What have you found?'

'This is a painting of the beach at Samson Island, on the Isles of Scilly. It's quite expensive but not stolen. But why keep it in a locked room?'

'The Isles of Scilly?' Radford stepped back. 'There was a framed photo of the Isles of Scilly in Emma Ash's home.'

'Oh my God,' Morris said. 'I've got it. There was a trip to the Isles of Scilly, about four years ago. Some of the locals went.'

'Who, exactly?'

Morris stared up towards the ceiling.

'Emma Ash! Ben Gardener... and his wife. Mayfield. In fact, I think he might have a place over there.'

'Anyone else?'

'I can't remember. It's on the tip of my tongue... but, no, I'll have to look into it.'

'Very well, let's get out of here and have a last look around.'

'We should talk to DS Scott. He'd know who went on the trip. He drove them to the airport.'

'Good. Send him a text.' Radford went on down the stairs and back into the whitewashed and barren wasteland of the house. He turned towards the back windows where the early morning sun was beaming in. Now he could see the shape of a vehicle parked awkwardly at the end of the garden. He stepped closer, a feeling of dread creeping over him as he realised it was the same van that had tried to kill him only hours before.

'Morris!' he called out.

The inspector came hurrying down the stairs and joined him as he stared out the window. 'What is it?'

Radford pointed to the van. 'That's the same van that tried to run me over this morning.'

'You're joking?' Morris took out her Casco baton and snapped it to full length.

'I never make jokes.'

Morris made for the rear door, unlocked it, slid the door open and stepped out. Radford followed, watching the driver's side of the van for movement, half expecting the lights to come on and the engine to roar to life. It remained dark and quiet, with only the sound of seagulls and other birds singing and squawking somewhere above them.

'This is the police!' Morris shouted. 'Is someone there?'

Radford followed slowly, his heart rate speeding up as he watched Morris, her Casco baton raised in her hand as she moved around the van, looking in at the driver's side.

'Doesn't look like anyone's home,' she said. 'I'll check the back. You can stay here.'

'There is no way I'm letting you go alone.'

'OK, but stay back. You're not even supposed to be here.'

'Neither are you.'

She nodded, then looked back at the van and carried on, sweeping around to the back doors. She used one hand to pull a glove out of her uniform and awkwardly tugged it on before she tried the back door. It creaked as she slowly pulled it open. From Radford's position, he could see only the empty back of the van and the back of the front seats.

'Nothing,' Morris said. 'Apart from a black bag. The weird thing is, this is the gardener's van.'

'That makes sense since I was nearly run over in the gardens. Perhaps he's our killer.'

Morris made an unconvinced sound in her throat and frowned. 'Bob Brown? No, he wouldn't hurt a fly.'

'Was he on that trip to the Isles of Scilly?'

'Possibly. I'll check.'

Radford gestured to the back of the van. 'What's in the bag?'

Morris opened the back doors wider, the creak of them filling the morning air. Then she found a zip, slowly undid the bag and pulled it open. She jerked backwards, slamming into Radford and nearly knocking him flying.

'What is it?' Radford asked, trying to see over her shoulder as she backed away.

Then he saw it, the pale, slightly blue-skinned head poking out of the bag. But the eyes were empty, the sockets just a bloody mess.

'Who were they?' Radford asked.

'That's Bob, or was Bob, the gardener.'

Radford let out a shaky breath and turned away from the van. 'I suspect that Bob was on that trip to the Isles of Scilly.'

Morris didn't seem to hear him as she pulled out her mobile phone, and brought up a number.

'Who are you calling, Inspector?'

She looked blankly at him, her complexion having taken on a pale sheen. 'I'm calling it in. You'd better make yourself scarce.'

'I'm not leaving you here on your own.'

She sighed. 'Well, we'd better prepare for a great big bollocking, then.'

'Yes, we better have. But at least they cannot ignore it any longer.'

'No, I mean we've definitely got a serial killer on our hands.'

Radford pinched the bridge of his nose. 'No, Morris, this isn't a serial killer, serial killers tend to have a pattern and preference, like women or men, black or white. And more often than not, their crimes are in some way sexually motivated. There are no signs of that here.'

'Then who're we dealing with?'

'Four murders in two days, and they're escalating rapidly. This is a mass murderer and they seem to be driven by anger, some kind of need for vengeance. Whatever has driven them to such extremes, has formed some kind of psychosis. We're dealing with an extremely dangerous individual who will not stop until all the people who went on that trip, are dead.'

Morris let out a harsh breath. 'Well, there were more than four, I remember that. We'd better find them and warn them.'

Blue lights flickered, illuminating the side of the postmodern house as uniforms patrolled and set up the crime scene tape. Radford hung back, observing the dark shapes of Inspector Morris and Chief Superintendent Parsons standing on the driveway.

Every two seconds, they were lit up, and he could see the downcast expression on Morris' face.

The Isles of Scilly, Radford thought as he paced across the road by the line of trees.

The wind had calmed down as the sun was rising, spreading out the shadows. He kept seeing the lonely painting, trying to fathom what could have happened on their trip that would warrant someone going to such extremes of revenge and violence. He knew that it didn't take much, having spent many years witnessing the most horrific crimes committed for the smallest of reasons. But in the human mind, he knew, how those reasons could grow.

'Here you are again,' a voice said behind Radford and he turned to see DS Scott standing there, a subtle smile on his lips, his hands dug into his pockets.

'So, they put you in charge, DS Scott?'

Scott laughed, then looked over towards the chaos. 'God no. They've got a team coming from... well, somewhere, and they're a major murder team. No, I'm just here to lend support. I don't think you're in Parsons' good books, or the Inspector's for that matter.'

'No, I'm not.' Radford stepped closer to Scott. 'Tell me, do you recall a trip to the Isles of Scilly that some of the locals went on a few years ago?'

Scott looked at him strangely, then nodded. 'Yeah, I remember. Why do you ask about that?'

'In Mayfield's house, there's a painting

locked in a room all by itself. A painting of one of the Islands over there. We thought there might be a connection.'

'Oh, right. Strange.'

'Do you know of anything that happened while the locals were over there?'

Scott shrugged. 'No. I don't. I wasn't there. No one mentioned anything. I doubt it's got anything to do with this. I mean, Parsons thinks this is a terror attack, which makes sense. One person gets their head nearly cut off, now another has their eyes gouged out… sounds like a terror attack to me.'

'What about the poor lad who they shot dead in the early hours of this morning?'

Scott shrugged. 'I don't know. The anti-terror guys seem to think he was linked to some extremist Russian group with links to Putin. What were they meant to do?'

'Not shoot him?'

The detective nodded. 'Yeah, it's terrible. Apparently, they've contacted his parents and they're on their way from London. Poor people. The Chief Superintendent is giving a press conference tomorrow morning outside the police station.'

Radford heard his name being called and turned to see Chief Superintendent Parsons storming towards him across the road, the glint of anger in her eyes.

'Oh, there you are, Mr Radford,' she said,

folding her arms across her chest, while Scott took the opportunity to slope off. 'What gives you the right or authority to enter someone's home like this?'

'I am a police officer.'

'Not here you're not. You put Inspector Morris up to this, didn't you, filling her head with this ridiculous notion that some serial killer is going around knocking off our residents? It's absurd.'

'Mass-murderer would be more appropriate...'

'Terrorist. This latest murder backs that up. He's targeting anyone he can find and trying to make a statement, trying to get publicity.'

'What about the lad the counter-terrorism team shot dead this morning? I heard he was in Bristol when the murders happened.'

Parsons' jaw ground as she stared up at him. 'It doesn't mean he wasn't linked to this. It's a group, which means there is more than one of them. There will be an inquiry. But for now, I'm here to tell you that you're not needed. You've already got Inspector Morris suspended...'

'You're suspending her? Why? She was doing her job, investigating these murders.'

'Her search wasn't authorised by me. She needs to follow orders. Now, Mr Radford, please let us get on with investigating all of this. You can pack your things and return to London or wherever you go. Quite frankly, I don't care.

Goodbye.'

Radford was left standing by the roadside as Parsons turned on the spot and stormed across the road and back to the crime scene. He caught the Inspector's eye and she looked at him and gave him a sad shrug before she turned and walked away.

It was almost lunchtime by the time the press conference got underway and the small crowd of journalists gathered in the car park. As Radford watched them all, fighting to get closer to the main doors, barging each other out of the way, he wondered what the correct term for a group of journalists was. He knew the term *lobby* was used to describe groups of the press who strive to uncover political scandals, and that sometimes the term *crew* is also used.

Neither seemed appropriate—both felt too technical. Then he smiled to himself as he said under his breath, 'A pack of lies.'

'What did you say?'

Radford turned to see Inspector Morris beside him, having sneaked up, dressed in her civilian get-up of jeans and a hoodie.

'Nothing really,' he said, then tried his best to look sympathetic. 'I'm sorry you've been suspended.'

'I'm not sure I am. What's the point when you're trying to do your job, and your bosses are trying to stop you?'

Radford nodded. 'Indeed. They will not listen to reason.'

'What's next?'

'What do you mean? I'm supposed to be packing my things and leaving.'

Morris raised her eyebrows. 'But you're not going to, are you? We haven't found out what's going on. Someone's still out there killing people.'

'Did you find out who went on that trip?'

'No. I didn't get a chance to ask DS Scott. I saw you talking to him though. Did you ask him?'

'He seemed pretty vague about it. I had the feeling Parsons had got to him and now he's towing the party line. He fears for his job, me thinks.'

'I've got an idea.' She smiled. 'I think Scott quite likes me, if you know what I mean? Why don't I invite him over this evening and ply him with drink? Then you can show up and we'll get the info out of him. Is that a good plan?'

Radford flashed a smile. 'Yes, well, it's better than anything I can think of.'

'I'll text you my address. Come at eight. Hang on, he might know.'

Radford turned to see where Morris was pointing and saw a suited man in his forties, who had started to jostle his way through the reporters.

'Who is he?' Radford asked.

'Nathan Sharpe, he runs the local paper,' she

said, then called out, 'Mr Sharpe!'

Sharpe scanned the crowd, then nodded when he saw Morris and fought his way towards her.

'Inspector Morris,' he said, smiling and then looked at Radford and put out his hand. 'I don't think we've met. Nathan Sharpe.'

'DCI Philip Radford.' He shook his hand.

'Ah,' Sharpe said, 'then you must be here to sort out this awful mess? Can I get an interview for the paper?'

'I'm afraid not. I like to keep a low profile. But we were wondering if you knew anything about a trip some of the locals took to the Isles of Scilly about four years ago.'

Sharpe frowned a little. 'Four years ago? No, sorry, that was before my time. But I can dig around for you, I know a few locals that like to gossip.'

'That would be helpful.'

Then Sharpe pointed at him. 'You don't buy the whole terrorism angle, then?'

'No. Do you?'

Sharpe gave a brief laugh. 'A lot of old cobblers. If you ask me, someone's got it in for the locals.'

'At least someone believes us,' Morris said.

'I'll find out about this trip you mentioned, but you don't get something for nothing. When you find out who's doing all this, then I want that interview. An exclusive. Is that a deal?'

Radford looked at Morris and saw she had her eyebrows raised. 'Fine. It's a deal.'

They shook on it, then Sharpe said, 'I'd better go and find a better position. Talk later.'

Radford and the Inspector smiled and nodded at Sharpe then watched him elbow his way through the crowd as the doors of the police station opened and Chief Superintendent Parsons came striding out towards the pack of wild journalists. She was followed by Colonel Jameson and a few uniforms and they all stood facing the crowd who immediately started shouting questions.

'I'll be making a brief statement relating to the recent shooting incident,' Parsons said. 'But I will not be answering any questions.'

The pack of journalists took no notice of her warning and started surging and scrabbling and shouting more questions. The uniforms pushed them back as Parsons continued. 'As you know, there was recently a terror-related incident. Two valued members of our community were sadly and horrifically taken from us by an act of terrorism. A suspect was identified and, unfortunately, shot when he threatened our armed officers and they believed they were in danger…'

'You lie!' a voice shouted from the back of the gathered crowd and everybody turned to see where it had come from. Radford stared towards an angry man in an opened-neck shirt, his eyes red as if he had just been crying. The crowd parted, shoved out of the way by the man who kept shouting that Parsons was a liar.

'I'm sorry, we don't want any interruptions,' Parsons said. 'As I was saying…'

'You murdered my son!' he yelled, now in front of the reporters, jabbing a wild finger at Parsons and Jameson. 'You killed him, murdered him in cold blood. He was not here the day when the woman died. He was in Bristol!'

'I'm sorry, this man is disturbed,' Parsons said, looking round at the uniforms. 'Can we get this poor man some help?'

The uniforms merged into the crowd, heading for the man.

'You don't care! You want him to be a terrorist, you need him to be a terrorist! He was my boy! A good boy!'

The uniforms dragged him back through the crowd, but he fought against them, struggling back towards Parsons. Radford could only watch, seeing the man now with tears in his eyes, fighting and then screaming.

'They're going to arrest him,' the inspector said, shaking her head. 'The poor man.'

Radford found himself storming towards the crowd and the man who was now on his knees, struggling to break free of the uniforms that were trying to cuff him.

'Excuse me,' Radford said, pushing past the uniforms and crouching down in front of the man. The Russian man, the bereaved father, looked up at Radford, the anger and sadness shining in his eyes.

'My name is Radford, Philip Radford,' he said, looking him in the eyes. 'I know your son didn't commit the crimes he's accused of...'

'You lie, I know...'

'I'm not lying. I'm a police officer and I promise you, I swear to you, that I will find out who did commit those crimes, so everyone knows your son was innocent.'

The man stopped struggling and stared at Radford, blinking. 'You promise?'

'I do.' Radford looked over at Parsons. 'Let the man go.'

'Let him go,' Parsons called out and the uniforms helped the father to his feet. The man straightened his clothes and stared at Radford.

'You promised,' he said, then turned and pushed through the crowd.

'Did you just promise to find the killer?' Morris said as she came and stood by Radford.

'I did. And I will. With your help.'

CHAPTER EIGHT

Eva Morris poured more of the red wine she had bought that afternoon from the Co-op on The high street. It wasn't the more expensive Shiraz or Malbec she usually purchased, but she wasn't about to waste the good stuff on DS Scott. He wasn't a bad guy, but she didn't find him attractive, and the only reason she had asked him around was to pick his brains.

Scott picked up his glass, swirling the wine around while he looked around her small, untidy flat. He nodded, then said, 'So, this is where you live? It's nice.'

She sat back, picked up her glass and took a big gulp. 'Yeah, it's OK. The place is a bit lopsided, apples always roll off the kitchen table.'

Scott looked over and raised his eyebrows. 'Oh, yeah, the whole floor's out of whack, isn't it?'

'It is, but the rent is cheap and the bakery is right downstairs.'

'Nice. I'm glad you invited me round.' He smiled.

'Are you, Scott?'

'Yeah. I don't get to... you know, socialise much. I don't know that many people around here.'

'You've been here for... how long, five years?'

He shrugged. 'Well, you know, what with work...'

'It's been a tough day,' she said and sipped her wine.

'Tell me about it. That poor man. Did you see him?'

'Yep. But Radford sorted him out.'

Scott nodded. 'Yeah, thank God for him. Must be a shock learning your son's a terrorist... and dead, of course.'

'He wasn't a terrorist, Scott.'

'That's not what Colonel Jameson's saying...'

'Well, they can't say anything else now, can they? They shot and killed an innocent young man. You do know Putin will retaliate in some way?'

The buzzer rang out in the flat, making Scott nearly jump out of his skin. 'Jesus... fuck.'

'Don't worry, it's not Putin.' Morris got up, went over to the intercom by the front door and pressed the buzzer. 'Hello?'

'It's DCI Philip...'

'I know. Come up.' The Inspector sat down at the table again and picked up her wine, noticing Scott was looking from her to the door.

'Are you OK?' she asked.

'Was that Radford? Is he coming in?'

'Yeah, just popping in for a chat. Is That OK?'

'Fine.'

The door opened and Radford stood there for a moment, looking round the room.

'Come in,' Morris said. 'Sit down. Join the party.'

She looked at the almost empty bottle on the table and realised she had drunk a lot more than she thought she had. It had been a tough day, and the death of Volkov kept playing over and over in her head in a loop, her heart thumping mercilessly every time she pictured the scene.

'Hello,' Scott said to Radford as he sat down.

'Good evening, DS Scott.' Radford kept looking around the place.

'We thought you were Putin for a moment,' Scott laughed.

'Vladimir Putin?' Radford asked. 'Why? Oh, I see, you're afraid he might retaliate because they killed one of his countrymen.'

Scott shrugged. 'Well, it's a bit scary, isn't it? We don't want to go to war with him, do we?'

Radford stared at him as if Scott had suddenly dropped his trousers. 'War with Putin?'

'Yeah, you know, sending in our troops. I

heard they're going to start conscripting…'

Radford gave a short laugh. 'If we went to war with Russia, DS Scott, which is extremely unlikely, then no one would be sending in troops. If it's war, it would be thermonuclear war, mass and mutual destruction.'

'Jesus.'

'Not even he would come back from that.'

The inspector almost laughed, but held it in as she remembered why they were there. 'So, Scott, did you find out about that trip to the Isles of Scilly?'

'The Isles of Scilly? Oh, right, no, I haven't. It's a while back now.'

'Ben Gardener?' Radford asked.

Scott sipped his wine. 'Maybe.'

'Emma Ash?'

'I think so.'

'Peter Mayfield?' Morris asked.

Scott shrugged. 'I can't be sure, but probably. Why do you want to know all this anyway?'

'Because we believe that this trip to the Isles of Scilly is what links them together,' Morris said and sat back, sipping her wine.

DS Scott looked between them, narrowing his eyes. 'You're having me on, aren't you?'

'No, we are certainly not,' Radford said. 'I believe something terrible happened on that trip. I've even taken the time to look online to find out if there was anything out of the ordinary that happened that week. The only thing I have found is a missing Polish girl called Anna Bajorek. But she was reported missing a while after the holiday. Tell me, DS Scott, have you examined Mayfield's home?'

'No, I wasn't allowed in, the counter-terrorism lot took over,' Scott said with a sigh. 'Basically, I get to follow them around carrying their shit for them.'

'Mayfield had a painting of the Isles of Scilly locked in a room all by itself.'

'Could it be stolen?'

Radford shook his head. 'No, we checked. Why lock up a painting in a room where you're the only one who can see it?'

Scott shrugged again, sipping his wine. 'I honestly have no idea. But it's a bit of a stretch.'

'Apart from them all living in Lyme Regis,' Morris began, 'it's the only connection we can find. What about the Gardener, Bob Brown? Was he on the Scilly trip?'

The DS let out another heavy breath and then nodded. 'Yes, he was. I remember because of the loud Hawaiian-style shirt he was wearing. Awful, really awful it was.'

Morris fetched a piece of A4 paper and scribbled the names of the victims. 'So, Mayfield, yes, he was on the trip. Emma Ash. Ben Gardener and Bob Brown, the Gardener. All on the trip.' She sat back after ticking them all off. 'So what happened on that trip?'

Scott seemed to notice they were both looking at him and widened his eyes. 'You're asking me? How would I know?'

'No one said anything about the trip? Anything that happened?' Morris leaned towards him, looking into his eyes.

'I was new back then, so no one would've told me anything.'

'And now?'

'No, nothing.' He picked up his wine and took a drink.

'Who else went on the trip?' Radford asked. 'How many exactly?'

Scott looked at the table. 'If I remember rightly, it was nine.'

'Nine?' Morris looked at Radford. 'So, we've got another potential five victims. Shit. Who are they?'

'I only remember two of them. I didn't know people's names back then, or faces, so I couldn't tell you most of them. But, yeah, I can remember the other two. Adrian Parsons and Lynn Bartlett.'

'Parsons?' Radford said. 'As in Chief Superintendent Parsons?'

'Her husband, Adrian Parsons, the property developer,' Morris said. 'And Lynn Bartlett, who owns all those restaurants and bars?'

Scott nodded. 'The very same. They're all pretty cosy, that lot. But I never told you!'

'We won't let on,' Morris said. 'So, Parsons and Bartlett could be potential victims? Hang on, the day Emma Ash was murdered, Mayfield was off reporting on Parsons' latest property development. That's interesting, isn't it?'

'Maybe,' Radford said. 'We'll need to talk to both of them as soon as possible. Perhaps even tonight.'

Morris stared at Radford, hoping he was joking, but saw by his straight expression that he was not. He didn't make jokes, she reminded herself. 'You want to knock on Parson's door in the middle of the night? Are you crazy? She already hates you.'

'Then what about Lynn Bartlett?' Radford asked. 'Where does she live?'

'In this massive, eight-bedroom place in Ware Lane,' Morris said. 'But she wouldn't be there. More than likely she'll be at The Boathouse, it's a pub and restaurant she owns a couple of miles along the coast. It's her pride and joy. She's usually there overseeing things.'

Radford stood up. 'Then let's go and talk to her.'

'What about the Parsons?' Morris stood up.

DS Scott sighed. 'I suppose I could check up on them and make sure they're OK?'

'Great idea,' Morris said, grabbing her coat, but still not convinced that going to visit Bartlett at her restaurant was a great idea. 'Don't let on, though. Just… you know, say you were passing by.'

The detective got up, nodding. 'Yeah, I get it.

No problem. I'll keep my mouth shut.'

'Good. Let's meet back here after.'

'I'm not sure about this,' Morris said as she drove them along the narrow lane and then turned left and followed the signs until they found the car park and the gardens beyond it. The restaurant sat at the far end of the garden, where music and chatter emanated. Servers came in and out of the fake Elizabethan-style building, carrying food and taking away plates.

'We are only here to warn her,' Radford said as Morris parked up.

'And ask her about what happened on the trip?' Morris stared at him.

'That too.' Radford climbed out, so Morris got out and followed him through the garden and into the busy restaurant that was packed with customers. They were stopped by a young blonde woman in a short red dress who carried a tablet device in her hands, a professional smile of greeting on her red lips.

'Welcome to The Boathouse,' she said, grabbing two menus. 'Have you booked?'

The Inspector produced her warrant card from her coat pocket and showed the young woman. 'I'm Inspector Morris. This is DCI Philip Radford. Is Lynn Bartlett available?'

The young woman looked a little stressed for a moment as she glanced around, then back at them. 'She's around somewhere, but she'll be very busy. Can she get back to you?'

'Please tell Mrs Bartlett that this is a matter of life and death,' Radford said.

'Life and death?' the woman repeated, then waved a passing server over. 'Ryan, can you tell Mrs Bartlett that the police are here to see her? It's very important, they say.'

Ryan smiled and nodded, then went back the way he had come.

'Would you like to take a seat over there?' the young woman gestured to a sofa close to the entrance. 'I'm sure she'll be out soon.'

Radford walked over to the sofa and sat himself down, and Morris followed and seated herself a little way from him.

'What exactly are we going to tell her?' Morris asked.

'The truth. That someone is more than likely targeting her and her friends.'

'But if they all have some secret, the reason this killer is after them, surely she's not going to talk to us?'

Radford nodded. 'That is quite likely but I'd still like to gauge her reaction. People can often tell you quite a lot when they're trying to preserve the truth.'

'Thanks, Yoda. Hey, here she is.'

Radford was up on his feet before Morris and met the well-dressed, middle-aged woman in the flowery summer dress who came storming towards them, her face set in a stern mode.

'Thank you for talking to us, Mrs Bartlett.'

'It was very important, I was told,' she said, looking them both over. 'It had better be or you're both for the high jump. Now, talk.'

The house sat back from the road, just as modern and expensive looking to DS Scott as Mayfield's home was. They had way too much money, he decided, as he parked up on the driveway, close to the Range Rover, and then climbed out and headed to the wide glass and steel framed block. He went through the gate and to the entrance at the front of the building. There was a light on in what he knew was the lounge. He pressed the doorbell and waited, ensuring his face was visible to the camera mounted above the keypad by the door. He sighed and looked about him, staring out into the darkness. The wind had eased and the rain had let up for once, allowing spring to pop along for a bit. He turned round again, wondering why there had been no answer, so pressed the buzzer of the intercom but the thing didn't light up. Perhaps it's broken, he thought and decided to walk along the pathway around the side of the house and go into their extensive and perfectly kept garden. As he walked, he kept thinking about what Inspector Morris and the rather strange DCI Radford had said about the trip to the Isles of Scilly. He wondered what exactly they knew about the trip, and whether there was anything in their theories. His mind rewound to the day he picked them all up at the airport. None of them had said much to him, nor to each other, as they sat spaced out, staring into the distance. As he reached the back of the house, he started to wonder if the quiet people on that minibus were so reserved that day because something bad had happened.

The conservatory light was on, but he could see no one inside. He turned when he heard something behind him. There had been a change in the light too, as if something or someone had passed by the spotlights that had been set up at the end of the garden. He looked around, peering into the shadows as he held up his hand to protect his eyes from the bright beams of light. He blinked, moving his head, but he couldn't see anything, so turned to face the house again. Now someone was entering the living room and he could make out the familiar shape of Chief Superintendent Parsons. He braced himself, ready to face the music and knock on the glass. She wouldn't be best pleased.

The light behind him changed again, a shadow of darkness stretching out towards his back. He turned and flinched, jerking backwards as a dark figure stood close to him, the burn of the spotlights blurring the shape of him.

'What do you think you're doing?' Scott asked, reaching into his pocket to see what he had to defend himself with. There was nothing, so he moved backwards, now noticing the strange mask the intruder wore over their face. 'I'm a police officer and you're trespassing.'

The shape moved, his right arm lifting away from his body, something gripped in his hand. Scott immediately thought of the recent terrorist threat. 'Listen, violence isn't going to help your cause. I can contact people, get them to listen to whatever...'

But the shape didn't listen and moved fast towards him, lifting the object high in the air.

Chief Superintendent Parsons walked down the narrow hallway, the spotlights in the ceiling coming on as she moved. She'd only just finished her shower and felt a little chilly as she wrapped her dressing gown tighter around her body. She knocked on Adrian's office door and waited, taking a deep breath and trying to steady her nerves. Her blood pressure was up, but it always was when there was any kind of trouble. But this wasn't just trouble, some bureaucratic mess to tidy away, it was a complete disaster on a massive scale. She knocked again, trying not to think of the lad that had been killed, shot dead by those counter-terrorism idiots. She had only been following orders sent from above, the strict command to let the anti-terror team get on and do what they had to do. Oh God, what a balls up. And there was that busybody Radford to contend with and the terrible growing feeling that perhaps he had been right all along. No, why would a crazed killer be murdering their way through the town's locals? It didn't make sense.

She knocked again, but harder.

'What the bloody hell is it, Debbie?' her husband called out.

She opened the door to his office, stepped in and saw he was sitting behind his desk, staring at his monitor, not even bothering to look up at her.

'Adrian?' she said, stepping closer to his desk.

'Hmm?' he muttered, still fixed on his screen.

'We need to talk about this whole situation.'

His eyes jumped up to her. 'Talk about what exactly?'

'Talk about what? About everything that's going on. People are dying left right and centre.'

He sighed and sat back. 'You've got to let the anti-terror people deal with it. They're the experts.'

'They just shot and killed an innocent young lad!'

'Was he innocent? Do you know that for sure?'

'I don't know anything at the moment. I don't know which way is up. But I do know one thing…'

'What? What do you know?'

She gestured to the room. 'That you've hardly been out of this office since this all began.

That's not like you.'

'I've been busy…'

'You've been taking all your meetings on Zoom. You hated it when Covid hit and you were stuck in here…'

He let out a tired breath. 'Debbie, what's your point?'

'My point is, I want to know what's going on. Do you know who's doing all this?'

He stood up and laughed. 'Why would I know, darling?'

He came over, smiling down at her, putting his hands gently on her shoulders. 'This is either a terrorist or just some mentally disturbed person who imagines we've slighted him in some way.'

'Why did you say that?'

'What? About slighting someone…'

They both stopped speaking and turned to face the open doorway when they heard a bang against the window.

'What the hell was that?' Parsons said.

'Probably a bird flying into the glass, nothing to worry about,' he said, but there was nothing in his tone to convince her it wasn't cause for concern.

She started towards the corridor, taking careful steps and edging out to look around.

'Debbie, where the hell're you going?' Adrian snapped. 'Get back here!'

She ignored him and went into their

bedroom and found her Casco baton and pepper spray, then she moved quietly down the hallway again, the lights following her.

'We should shut ourselves in the office,' Adrian said, now just behind her.

She shushed him and kept on moving down the corridor, then stopped on the corner, ready to sweep into the lounge. She threw her arm out to her side and flicked her baton out, ready to swipe at whoever was there. She took a deep breath, ignoring the tremble that had overtaken her body. Then she lunged out, her eyes darting all over the room. No one. There was no one there.

'Thank God,' Adrian said, sneaking into the room. 'Must have been a bird after all.'

But something had caught her eye outside. She stepped closer to the windows. The spotlights outside were burning into the room, making it hard to see, but when she got closer, she could make out a leg and a shoe.

'Someone's out there,' she said, pointing the baton to the window.

'What?' Adrian came over, staring at the leg.

'Someone's been hurt.'

She went to open the window, but Adrian grabbed her arm. 'Don't!'

'Why?'

'Because he's probably waiting out there.'

She looked at him strangely, hearing the fear heavy in his voice. 'Who's waiting out there? Who is he? Adrian, who the bloody hell, for God's sake is out there?'

'I don't know.'

'Yes, you do. What is this all about?'

'I'll tell you later, let's just call someone...'

She shrugged his hand away. 'I'm going to help whoever that is.'

Adrian moved back as she unlocked the sliding door and opened it, ready to step out. She glanced down, now able to see the figure sprawled on the grass. She looked back at her husband. 'It's DS Scott. He's got blood on his head.'

She stepped onto the grass, crouching down to take a look at Scott.

'Debbie, come back in and we'll call an ambulance!'

'You call an ambulance!' she shouted and looked down at Scott and saw he was still breathing. 'Scott, can you hear me?'

'I'm shutting the door!' Adrian called out and slid the door shut. She shook her head, realising what a selfish coward he had become. Her husband stepped back from the window, retreating into the safety of the house.

Parsons let out a harsh breath as she saw someone move into the room, passing by the window. They were inside. The hooded figure was inside the room with her husband. She jumped to her feet, grabbed hold of the handle and tried to open it. It was locked. Adrian had locked it. She looked into the room to see Adrian backing up, stumbling over the furniture as the hooded figure moved towards him, a knife gripped in their hand.

She banged on the window, then looked around and saw her baton lying on the grass. She grasped it and swung it at the glass but the window stayed intact. She did it again, swiping hard at the window. Only a couple of cracks appeared as the hooded figure approached her frozen and terrified husband.

'Run!' she yelled, pounding the glass. 'Adrian, run!'

But he didn't move and only held up his hands, cowering as the hooded man lifted the knife, then lurched towards her husband. Adrian doubled over, then straightened himself, his face pale. His hand reached down and brought back blood on his fingertips.

'Adrian!' she yelled again, smacking the glass.

The figure lunged again and again, and spatters of blood hit the window.

'No!' she screamed, tears filling her eyes. She could only watch as Adrian slipped to his knees, then fell to his side, his eyes staring out at her.

She flinched when the figure turned around and seemed to fix their eyes on her. She scrambled to her feet and moved backwards, stepping over DS Scott. She wanted to turn and run, but she couldn't. It was a nightmare, the one she'd had as a child where she couldn't run from someone chasing her.

Now it was all too real, as he unlocked the door and opened it. He gripped the knife in his hand, lifting it as he stepped out onto the grass. He moved faster then, starting to jog towards her, the knife catching the spotlights and glinting. As he got barely a foot from her, she knew she would die and she braced herself for the pain as she trembled. He reached her...

He ran past, sprinting towards the spotlights.

She was still standing there, staring at where he had been.

Then she was falling, her legs giving way beneath her. The grass felt cool against her cheek as she passed out.

CHAPTER NINE

'We believe your life might be in danger,' Inspector Morris said, thinking that her words might warrant a shocked response from Bartlett, but she simply looked at her with annoyance in her eyes.

'Yes, I'd already ascertained that,' she said, sounding bored. 'Is this to do with this whole terrorist threat?'

'It is, sort of,' Morris said. 'Thing is…'

'It's not terrorists committing these acts,' Radford interrupted.

'Oh, he talks,' Bartlett said. 'So, who is responsible?'

'Someone intent on revenge, I believe.'

The restaurant owner looked at him carefully. 'Revenge? For what?'

'We're not sure at this moment in time, but

we will find out. By the way, have you ever been to the Isles of Scilly?'

He saw it, the quiver in her skin, the hint of pink appearing in her cheeks, and the flash of fear in her eyes. 'Once. Ages ago, what's this got to do with this ridiculous revenge theory you've cooked up between the two of you?'

'We believe there is a link between the victims and that link is a particular holiday that took place four years ago.'

He saw the subtle tell, the twitch at the corner of her mouth before she managed to put her poker face back in place.

'Well, I don't know anything about the holiday you're referring to, and actually, I'm very busy, so I'll thank you for your time.'

'Whoever this person is who bears this grudge,' Radford said, 'will not stop until all of you are dead. If you know why someone might want each of you dead, then you'd best speak up now.'

She stared at him, and for a moment Radford thought she might be considering telling the truth, but then the dark cloud moved over her head again and she huffed and shook her head before storming off.

'Well, that went really well,' Morris said. 'Now what?'

Before Radford could make a suggestion, Morris' phone started ringing in her pocket.

She took it out and said, 'Inspector Eva

Morris.'

Then he could only watch as the Inspector sat again, listening, her mouth slightly open. 'Jesus. Where is she now? She's what? OK, we'll be there soon. Thanks.'

She ended the call but kept staring straight on for a moment before she slowly looked up at Radford. 'There's been an incident. Chief Superintendent Parsons' home was broken into and... her husband was killed. Stabbed to death. DS Scott was attacked too, but he's OK.'

'What about the Chief Superintendent?'

'She's at Dorset County Hospital. In shock, I think. She's OK, but weirdly, she's asked to see us.'

'Then let's not waste any more time and go and see her.'

Inspector Morris hurried through the corridors of the hospital after showing her ID to the staff at the main reception desk. Radford followed, managing to keep up with her using his long strides as she headed for the cubicle they had placed Chief Superintendent Parsons in. She saw a constable on guard outside the curtained-off bay and showed her warrant card to him.

'How is she?' she asked, lowering her voice.

The male PC looked towards the green curtains and raised his shoulders with a frown. 'I'm not sure, boss. I mean, she's unharmed but she's in a helluva state.'

Morris thanked him, then pulled back the

curtain, making Parsons jump and crawl back up the bed. She was wearing a hospital-issue gown, her hair tied back. She looked ever so pale and vulnerable, and for the first time, Morris found herself feeling sorry for her usually abrupt and rude boss.

'It's OK, ma'am,' Morris said and pulled up a chair. 'You're safe now.'

Radford stepped into the cubicle and remained in the corner, watching.

'Adrian!' Parsons sat bolt upright, her eyes wide.

'We're here,' Morris said and took her boss's trembling hand.

'Oh, God, he... Adrian...' The Chief Super clasped her hands over her mouth. 'I couldn't. I didn't... I didn't know. How could I know?'

'You couldn't.' Morris looked up at Radford and shrugged.

'They said, didn't they?' Parsons stared at her. 'They said follow orders... it was them who...'

'This attacker who broke into your home...'

'It's not my fault. I didn't want anyone to be hurt. I wanted everyone to be safe...'

'We know, but we need you to try and concentrate...'

'I have to think of the town, of policing the town... and it doesn't happen here, it just doesn't happen here.'

'Did you get a look at him?' Morris asked,

touching Parsons' hand.

'It'll be summer soon and we need the tourists...'

'Ma'am... Chief Superintendent Parsons...'

'Parsons!' Radford shouted, making her jump and snap her eyes to him. She blinked up at him as he came closer, then pulled up a chair.

'Look at me, Parsons,' he said and snapped his fingers in her face. 'We need you to tell us about your attacker. Did you see him?'

She swallowed, then nodded. 'He had a mask covering his mouth and a baseball cap on. Oh, God, I went outside because Scott was there... oh, God, Scott!'

'He's all right. Now concentrate, did your attacker say anything?'

She shook her head. 'I was outside, and somehow, he was... he got inside and he was alone with... and I couldn't. I couldn't...'

Parsons grasped Radford, burying her tear-streaked face in his suit jacket.

Radford looked horrified, but gradually started to pat her back as he said, 'How did you get away?'

She let go and looked up at him. 'I didn't. He came out of the house and... I tried to run, but he just came at me, but I couldn't move. I froze...'

'You're telling me he walked right past you?' Radford said.

She nodded. 'I don't understand. Why did he... why is Adrian gone and I'm still here?'

'Did you go on the trip to the Isles of Scilly four years ago?'

She looked confused. 'What? The Isles of... no, I couldn't. I had work commitments. What are you talking about?'

'DS Scott didn't go either,' Morris said. 'That's why he's still alive.'

Radford nodded. 'He left you alive, Chief Superintendent, because you were not there when this bad thing must have happened.'

'What bad thing?' Parsons asked. 'I don't know what you're talking about.'

Morris leaned in as she said, 'We believe that something happened on that trip involving Mayfield, Ash, Gardener, Brown and... well, Adrian. Whoever this killer is, he's targeting people who went on that trip. We need to know what happened.'

Parsons kept looking at her, staring through her. 'I don't know. I know Adrian wasn't himself lately... he was always shut in his office as if he was scared to go out. This must've been why.'

'Did he ever mention the trip?' Radford asked.

She shook her head. 'No. He never really talked about it. I remember trying to talk to him about it, but he didn't seem to want to... oh... that's why, isn't it? What happened out there?'

Morris sat back. 'We don't know.'

'Do you know who else was on that trip?' Radford sat down and took out his notebook and pen.

'Who else? Lynn Bartlett, I think. Yes… and Freddie Wells, the man who owns the antique bookshop, and… let me think… Anthony Jones, he's the barman in the Wheelwright Pub near Charmouth. Oh, and Molly Gardener.'

The inspector and Radford exchanged confused looks.

'No, Molly didn't go,' Morris said.

'Yes, she did,' Parsons said. 'She got a flight out a couple of days later. She gets seasick, so she doesn't like the boat.'

Radford turned and headed out of the cubicle before Parsons had even finished speaking.

Morris jumped up, turning to her boss as she started to hurry out after Radford. 'Thank you, ma'am. We'll be back!'

She jogged down the corridors, searching for Radford, trying to catch up with him as her heart pounded, the panic having invaded her system already. He was obviously thinking what she was thinking, that Molly Gardener was all alone in her home, and the killer was possibly going after her next.

After catching up with Radford at the main entrance, the inspector called it in and arranged for an incident response car to meet them on the way to Molly Gardener's house. Morris drove fast down the dark, narrow lanes, watching out for the headlights that beamed out to them from the blind corners. She could see Radford gripping his knees, and pressing his foot down on an imaginary brake pedal every few seconds.

She slowed down when they reached the turning for the narrow lane that led to Molly's cottage. But darkness had come in, swallowing up the area, bathing it in a sinister hue. They parked a little way from the house, then walked the rest of the way, joined by the uniforms that they sent around the back. Radford tapped Morris' shoulder and pointed out what she had already observed; the front door was slightly open, and there seemed to be distant voices talking somewhere. As she clicked her Casco baton to full length, she passed Radford her taser. Then she moved in, listening to the voices that grew a little louder, but still muffled, contained somewhere deep in the small house. The house was mostly in darkness, and she could see only some electric blue light flickering at the end of the hall. Radford was behind her all the way, and she could hear his heavy breaths as he pointed the taser into every corner.

It was at the very end of the hallway that Morris found the source of the light and the voices. At the back of the cottage was another living area, where a TV was on, the volume low. There was no sign of Mrs Gardener.

'Where is she?' the Inspector asked Radford, but when she looked at him, she could see he was staring towards another door further along that had been opened fully into the room. He pointed at the door, and it was then Morris noticed some rope had been wrapped over the door and the handle. It took her a couple of seconds to realise what was possibly on the other side of the door, a cold set of fingers caressing her spine as she stepped closer. Morris put her Casco baton away and slipped on some gloves, then gently reached out for the door and pulled it towards her. It was heavy and moved slowly.

She looked down and saw a pale and small foot. There was a fluffy pink slipper on the floor, dragged towards Morris by the bottom of the door that scraped along the carpet. She took a deep breath and pulled the door around. She stared for a moment, hardly able to take it all in, the breath leaving her lungs as her eyes took in the small shape of Molly Gardener hanging on the door, the rope wrapped around her throat, cutting into the grey flesh of her neck. One of her hands was caught in the rope as if she had been desperately struggling to undo it. Her other hand hung loose, the nails all broken.

'We've searched the house, but we can't…' one of the uniforms said as he stuck his head in the room.

'It's OK, we've found her,' Radford said. 'Can you let them all know?'

The uniform was staring at the door where he would be able to make out the profile of Mrs

Gardener. Then he was gone, and the beeps and squawks of his radio started up.

Morris took her eyes away from the body, walked to the doorway, put her back against the wall and stared up at the ceiling and the blue light from the TV that still danced over it.

'Let's wait outside,' Radford said, gesturing to the door.

'I can't leave her,' Morris said, feeling tears pricking her eyes.

'She's gone, Inspector,' he said. 'She's not here.'

'I know, but I still can't leave her.'

Radford nodded, and she thought he was going to walk out, but he rested his back against the wall beside her.

'What now?' Morris said, enclosing her palms over her face.

'We go back and talk to Chief Superintendent Parsons.'

'Do you think she'll listen to us now?'

'Yes, I'm sure she will.'

There came a knock on the doorway close to them and they looked up to see Dr Shaw standing there.

'Hello, Doctor,' Radford said. 'You got here fast.'

'I was at the station and saw the uniforms rush off,' he said, his eyes jumping to his left. 'I knew there was trouble afoot. Who lives here?'

'Mrs Molly Gardener,' Morris said. 'She's over

there.'

Shaw stepped into the room, his hands dug into his pockets and they watched him as he strolled across the room and then stared at the body of Mrs Gardener. He turned his head, side to side, as if he was examining a painting in a gallery, then stepped closer, taking a careful look at her.

'*There is a flower within my heart,*' he sang quietly. '*Planted one day by a glancing dart. Planted by Daisy Bell. Whether she loves me or loves me not. Sometimes it's hard to tell...*'

'What do you make of it, Doctor Shaw?' Radford asked, walking over to him.

'Nothing to her, was there?' Shaw said, taking out a stick of chewing gum and popping it in his mouth. 'A hundred and twenty pounds, give or take. Heaved her up with the rope with no trouble. She scrabbled around for a while, then gave up the ghost. Pardon the joke.'

'Jesus,' Morris said and huffed as she faced the window, shaking her head.

Shaw watched Morris, then looked at the body again. 'Second one tonight, wasn't it?'

'It is. The Chief Superintendent's husband was stabbed and killed a couple of hours ago.'

Shaw nodded. 'Mrs Gardener's been deceased for about six hours, I'd say, judging by her colour and the lividity.'

'We've got three more potential victims,' Radford said aloud but stared over at Morris.

The Inspector looked back at him. 'We need to get them somewhere safe.'

'I don't think they'll listen to us. But I think I know someone they might listen to.'

Lynn Bartlett waited by the entrance, pacing a little and looking out into the garden where the rain had started to fall again, the wind driving it towards the windows and making it hard to see if anyone was out there. Now and then she saw a shape and thought it might be him, but then nothing. She didn't want to go out there, into the darkness just in case. Her mind kept turning over what the police had said, that someone was targeting the locals who had gone on that trip. She felt sick to her stomach, the same way she had that night, four years ago. Most days, when she was busy, she could put it out of her head, pretend it had never happened, but then the night came and she would lie there staring up at the ceiling, flashes of that night flickering and jarring. Sleeping pills helped a little to get through the nights, and of course the busy work days too... but now what? She wanted to call their theory, their wild claims that some maniac was hunting them all down, ridiculous, but when she thought back to that night and what had happened, she felt this icy feeling inside her, deep down in her bones. It was true, it was real.

A shape appeared at the doors and she gasped and jerked backwards. Then the door opened and Freddie Wells came in shaking rainwater off his umbrella. He wore his long, dirty raincoat as always, the one she had offered to replace but he wouldn't spend money on frivolous things like clothes, and wouldn't allow anyone else to either.

'I can't believe you'd make me come out in this,' he said and hung his umbrella on a chair, pulled out a handkerchief and blew his hooked nose on it. 'I'll have a cold by the morning.'

Lynn stepped towards him, trying to smile, glad as always to see her friend. She braced herself.

'What's got into you, you silly woman?' he said, then smiled. 'You need a holiday, and not to be running yourself ragged with this place.'

As he said holiday, she felt herself go weak and a tremor pass over her flesh.

'God, you look like death. Sit down, Lynn.'

He made her sit down and then sat himself down and stared at her. 'Do you need a brandy?'

She shook her head. 'No, thank you, Freddie. The reason I asked you here… is because of what's been happening lately.'

'What's been happening? You're being very cryptic.'

'The murders, that's what I mean.'

He stared at her as if she had announced she was going to turn her beloved restaurant into a pie-and-mash shop.

'The terrorist attack? Awful business…'

'It's not terrorists, Freddie, that's the thing.'

'It's not?'

'No. Ben, and Emma, Peter Mayfield and Bob Brown, the gardener and now I just heard Molly, Ben's wife is dead...'

'What? No, that can't be... I talked to her the other day...'

'It's true. It's the holiday. It's what happened.'

He stared at her, then gave a tired, almost irritated laugh. 'Don't be silly, Lynn.'

'It is. Listen to me, Freddie, someone is killing... murdering the people who were on that holiday...'

He looked towards the doors. 'No, it's got to be a coincidence. Why after all this time would someone...'

'We've got to go away. Perhaps abroad...'

He looked at her as if she had lost her mind. 'Leave the bookshop? Good God no. Oh no, I'm not going anywhere.'

'He'll kill us. It's not like we can go to the police, is it?'

Freddie stood up, tapping his nose, staring into space.

'I can't sleep at night,' she said, her stomach twisting and knotting. 'Do you sleep at night?'

He turned to her, a strange look in his eyes. 'I haven't slept since. Not really. How could I, Lynn? Every time I shut my eyes I see that poor girl's face.'

Lynn bent her head, putting her hands over her mouth. 'I know. I know.'

'We've got to stand our ground. We can't run. Come to my place, you don't want to be alone.'

'What about Steve?'

'You're always telling me that he's never home, that you're always lonely. Come on, let's go.'

Freddie had his hand out, looking impatient… and scared, she thought. He always looked so serene, so calm, sitting behind the cumbersome old, battered desk in his dusty old shop, surrounded by shelves stacked high with old books. Nothing ever seemed to flap him and now he had the same look that she saw in her face in the mirror, the underlying guilt and shame.

She stood up and took his hand and they headed out of the restaurant and through the darkened gardens towards the car park. There was only one light working, a distant street light beaming down a golden glow towards the dark asphalt. Lynn saw his car parked a few metres away as Freddie kept pulling her fast towards it.

She stopped dead, yanking him to a stop.

'Come on, Lynn, we've got to go,' he said, sounding like an impatient parent.

But she couldn't move as her eyes scanned the darkness. She could sense something, something wrong.

'What is it?' he asked, looking to where she was staring.

'The lights. There's only one light. There's usually more. He's done something to the lights.'

'They're probably just broken.' He grabbed her hand again and started pulling her across the car park, but she could see him turning his head back and forth, keeping an eye out. His hand was trembling in hers.

The car was only a couple of metres away and Freddie fumbled in his coat pocket, trying to pull out his car keys.

There was a crunching sound like broken glass being stepped on.

They both stopped, staring towards where the sound had come from. There was another crunch and slowly, moving into the half-darkness, a figure emerged. Whoever it was, stood watching them.

'Who's there?' Freddie called out, searching for his keys again.

Sorry to scare you,' the man said as he stepped forward into the light.

Lynn let out a sigh as her eyes took in the police uniform the young man was wearing, his face still in the shadows and hard to make out. 'I was sent to make sure you got home OK.'

Freddie found his keys and unlocked his car, nodding and smiling at the young constable. 'Thank you, we appreciate it. That's very kind of you.'

'Get in, Lynn,' Freddie said and opened the passenger door for her. She climbed in, smiling and waving to the uniform who stood watching them. Freddie shut her door, hurried around, got in and started the engine. He struggled to put the car into gear, and when Lynn looked at his hand, she could see it was trembling.

'It's OK, Freddie,' she said and patted his hand. 'We're safe. Let's go.'

But Freddie was staring at the uniform. 'Do you think he was a real policeman?'

She looked over and saw that there was no sign of the constable. 'Where did he go?'

'I don't know, but I'm not hanging around. I don't trust anyone any more.'

When Morris and Radford arrived back at the hospital, they found Chief Superintendent Parsons dozing on the bed in the cubicle. A uniform was still on guard.

'She's asleep,' the Inspector said, almost feeling a bit sorry for her.

But Radford grabbed Parsons' shoulder and shook her until her eyes snapped open and she fought to clamber away from him.

'Oh God!' she cried. 'You scared me to death. I thought he was back.'

'Molly Gardener is dead,' Radford said, straightening up and letting the words sink in.

'How?' Parsons asked.

'Does it matter?'

She looked down and shook her head. 'No, I suppose not.'

'He's not going to stop,' Radford said. 'And you'll be the Chief Superintendent who sat back and let it happen.'

She snapped forward, her face red, her eyes filling with tears. 'My husband... is dead! Dead!'

'I know. And I'm sorry, but we need to do something. Now.'

The Chief started muttering, almost to herself, as she said, 'The counter-terrorism team, they can... they can...'

'They've already killed one innocent person.'

'Then what do we do?' Parsons looked up at him, a look of pleading in her eyes.

Radford looked deep into her eyes. 'First, you hire me...'

'Hire you?!'

'Yes. Then you give me the power to do what I can to stop this maniac.'

Parsons stared up at him and Morris could see the calculations going on behind her eyes before she nodded. 'OK, you're hired. Do it. Do whatever it takes to make this town safe again.'

Radford reached out a hand to pat her shoulder, then hesitated and withdrew it. 'Thank you.'

Morris followed Radford as he turned and started moving at speed back down the corridor.

'What do we do?' she asked.

'We find a house away from the town, but not too far. Somewhere isolated.'

'Then what?'

He looked at her. 'We wait for him to come to us.'

CHAPTER TEN

The minibus rumbled outside the station as the sun slowly rose. Inspector Morris was sitting behind the wheel, looking as if she was having second thoughts about the whole affair, Radford thought. Quite frankly, he didn't blame her. One of the uniforms, a dark-haired young woman called Nash carried a few bags of supplies, placing some under the front passenger seat and others at the back of the bus. The house they were heading for had belonged to Adrian Parsons. It was situated along the coast, overlooking the beach and the sea beyond.

There wasn't much else around, just nature paths and a scattering of trees, the perfect place for them all to hole up. They would be able to see the killer coming from a mile away. Even though the whole arrangement had been given the green light by Parsons, it had come with some caveats. The first condition was that they take at least one armed officer, which of course Radford had agreed to. As much as he wanted to apprehend the killer, he did not want to walk blindly into the jaws of death either. The whole point was to drag him out, make him come to them and then the trap would be unveiled.

'Where do I sit on this half-arse mystery tour?'

Radford turned round, flinching a little.

Dr Shaw was stood there, grinning, a rucksack on his back.

'You don't, Doctor. I think we have enough passengers.'

'I don't just deal with the dead, Radford, you know. I am qualified to treat the living. You may need me. Oh, and in case you're worried that I'm the killer, I was hundreds of miles away at the time all this started. You can check.'

'I have already checked, Doctor.' Radford sighed and looked over at Inspector Morris.

'A medical doctor might be good to have along,' she said.

'Very well, Doctor,' Radford said. 'You had better get on board.'

Shaw laughed and climbed aboard while singing 'Daisy, Daisy' to himself, and Radford immediately regretted agreeing to him coming along. A doctor would be a sensible addition, he had to agree, but he was not convinced that a half-mad, singing one was.

'We'd better get moving,' the Inspector said, looking at the sky. 'Let's pick up the other passengers before it gets light.'

'Agreed,' Radford said and was about to climb into the passenger seat when he heard a car coming towards the car park. It stopped and they all stared towards it. Radford's heart began to thud as the car sat there, whoever was driving staring their way.

Then the door opened and Parsons climbed out, wrapped up in a waterproof jacket, her hair a little wild but tied back as she slowly came over.

'You should be resting,' Radford said.

She nodded, her eyes still full of fear and shock. 'So they say, but I wanted to see you all off.'

'Thank you, but we are fine, Parsons.'

Her eyes jumped to the minibus. 'You're taking Dr Shaw with you?'

'Yes, he kindly volunteered.'

'You know he's quite mad, don't you?'

'I'm getting that sense. But I feel his heart is in the right place.'

She nodded and looked up at Radford. 'I'm sorry...'

'For what?'

'Not listening to you. I didn't want it to be true. I didn't want our little town...'

'I understand.'

'Now... now Adrian is... he's gone.'

She started to sob, her hands gripped to

her face. Radford stood there for a moment, wondering what was expected of him. He reached out, his hands trembling a little, thinking perhaps he should embrace her. He started to put his arms around her, but her head sprang up and she looked at him strangely.

'What are you doing, Radford?' she asked, her eyebrows raised.

'I… I don't know.'

'Just go. Hurry up and catch this bastard.'

The bus coughed and spluttered as it made its way up the steep hill, heading for Freddie Wells' house, where Radford had been informed Lynn Bartlett was staying. They pulled up outside the yellow-brick terrace house and Morris climbed out and rang the bell. It was seconds before both Wells and a rather forlorn-looking Bartlett came out and stared towards the van. Bartlett seemed to give it the once-over with a look of disapproval, but then let out a heavy breath and climbed on board. Wells brought their bags that they stowed at the back.

Their last stop was at a row of shops on the way to Charmouth, where the rotund, balding publican, Anthony Jones, lived in a small flat.

Again, it was Inspector Morris who climbed out and buzzed the intercom next to the door that was situated between two shops.

The man came out in a lumberjack shirt, a holdall in one hand, looking none too happy. But

Radford could only wonder if it was the thought of being cosied up with the rest on the bus for a couple of days, or the potential death because of what they had or hadn't done. What he did manage to witness was the publican casting a dark look at Wells and Bartlett before he climbed on board and took a seat far away from them.

'I just hope this place has five stars,' Anthony Jones said, looking around the bus as Morris started it up. 'I don't get why we're slinking off to some house somewhere anyway. Bleeding ridiculous, if you ask me.'

'No one asked you,' Bartlett said with a huff.

'Oh, did the Queen say something?' Jones sang. 'I'm so sorry I didn't hear that, your Majesty, would you say it again in your bleeding annoying voice?'

'Please don't speak to her like that,' Wells said, piping up, even though his voice remained broken and quiet.

'Listen,' Radford said, standing up at the front of the bus and facing them all. 'I quite understand why you all have reservations about this whole arrangement, but it may just save your lives.'

The passengers all stared at him in silence for a moment but then it was broken as Jones said, 'Who is this weird bird man? Who are you, mate?'

Dr Shaw started laughing, and they all turned to look at him, but he was staring out of the window.

'His name is DCI Philip Radford and he's trying to save your life,' Morris called over her shoulder as she drove them towards the house. 'I'm not sure why we're bothering really. I mean, do you want to stay and take your chances?'

No one replied, but Radford saw them all look away, avoiding his and each other's eyes as the minibus rumbled on, climbing another steep hill. The wild grey sea was clambering over itself, rolling and spitting like a mad thing as it appeared down below the cliffs that were on their right. The house stood a short distance from the cliff. He could see it already, a small cottage with a little land around it, a scattering of trees. In the summer he imagined it would look picturesque, quaint even, but now it had an eerie air, a haunting quality as it sat against a grey, rain-soaked sky.

The bus shook and fell silent as Morris parked it by the side of the house, then they all grabbed their luggage and barged past each other to disembark from the vehicle. Jones managed to elbow his way off first, leaving Bartlett and Wells to tut and shake their heads.

Morris unlocked the house, and then the armed uniformed officer, who had come from the armed response unit stationed in Bournemouth, went into the house and did a quick search while everyone waited impatiently outside.

'You know, the people in Lyme Regis are very nice people,' Morris said.

'I know,' Radford said, 'I've met a lot of nice, kind people since I've been here. They have been very welcoming.'

Morris nodded. 'Just none of them are here.'

'No, none of them are here.' Then Radford paused as he went to walk towards the old house, a little voice telling him he was about to make a faux pas. He looked at Morris and said, 'I'm including you in the nice group.'

Morris smiled. 'Thank you. That means a lot. Especially coming from you.'

'What do you mean?'

'Because you don't like people.'

'Normally I do not and they generally don't like me.'

'I like you.' She smiled and blushed a little. 'Anyway, let's get these rude sods settled in.'

The cottage had been partly redecorated, with a couple of second-hand sofas sitting in the long living room that opened onto a small kitchen. There was a fireplace and a wood burner that everyone agreed should be lit immediately. The other uniform fetched the logs from the metal box outside, put some in the burner and started the fire, while Lynn Bartlett, surprisingly, offered to make everyone a drink.

'Don't put poison in mine,' Jones called out as he fell onto the sofa. 'Two sugars, plenty of milk,' he added.

Bartlett was about to say something but Wells touched her arm and shook his head as they stood in the kitchen.

Radford watched it all, observed their movements as the wind and rain picked up, dashing the windows and rattling and whistling around the roof. Outside it was grey and he could see the sea roaring up and spitting plumes of white cloud into the air. The armed officer put on his waterproofs and braved the elements, taking a walk around the perimeter of the building.

'There's some jigsaws here,' Wells said as he investigated a sideboard in the living room.

'Oh, bleeding fantastic,' Jones said, then craned his neck over to the kitchen. 'Is that bloody tea coming? I'm parched.'

'I'm not your slave, Mr Jones,' Bartlett said, her eyes narrowed at him.

'I'll make the dinner tonight,' Shaw announced as he stood looking out the lounge windows. 'I'm pretty good in the kitchen. Well, I say good, but let's put it this way, none of the people on my table died because of my cooking.'

The rest of the room stared towards him in silence, but eventually Jones sat up and said, 'Who is this fella? Sorry, who are you?'

'I'm the Home Office pathologist.' Shaw turned round and faced him. 'If this killer gets hold of you, then I'll be the one dissecting you. Are you as beautiful on the inside as you are on the outside, Mr Jones?'

The publican stared towards Radford. 'He's joking, isn't he?'

'Don't wet yourself, Anthony,' Bartlett said with a huff.

'It's Tony,' he snapped. 'To my friends, but to you, it's Mr Jones.'

'How come you lot went on holiday together in the first place?' Morris asked to the room and Radford saw them turn away, the air becoming decidedly frosty.

The door rattled open loudly and the armed officer came in, shaking the rain off his coat, then looked around the room and saw everyone looking his way.

'Sorry,' he said. 'It's wild out there. But there's no one around for miles. All clear.'

Everyone seemed to relax a little at that, and more so once cups of tea had been handed out.

'*Daisy, Daisy,*' Shaw sang. '*You'll take the lead in each trip we take. Then if I don't do well, I will permit you to use the brake... my beautiful little Daisy Bell...*'

'Well, at least we have some entertainment,' Wells said, fetching a jigsaw and putting it on the kitchen table.

'The awful singing or the boring jigsaw?' Jones said, laughing to himself.

They all froze as a heavy thud echoed from upstairs, and then raised their heads, looking towards the ceiling. Both uniforms moved towards the stairs, the armed officer taking out his firearm.

'What the hell was that?' Jones said.

'Seagulls,' Shaw said and pulled up a chair and sat down.

'Seagulls?' Jones clambered to his feet. 'That must be a bloody big seagull!'

'Have you ever met a seagull?' Shaw asked. 'They're not known for being small. Some of them are as big as a medium-sized dog.'

'You're barking mad.' Jones went to follow the uniforms who had started up the stairs to the top floor and disappeared. Their creaking footsteps crossed the floor slowly as the rest of the group all looked up to the ceiling, following their steps. Then nothing.

'What's happening?' Wells asked. 'Oh my God, he's up there, isn't he?'

'If you mean a great big seagull, Mr Wells, then you'd be right,' Shaw said, taking a small metal flask from his coat pocket and pouring some liquid into his tea.

'What're you doing?' Morris asked.

Shaw stared up at her. 'Turning my tea into an Irish tea.'

'I'm pretty sure you can't have an Irish tea,' Jones said. 'I'm a publican, I should know. It's an Irish coffee.'

'Well, there's no coffee in this, only tea.' Shaw sipped his drink. 'Delicious.'

The footsteps started again and the uniforms came down, smiling a little.

'What was it?' Jones asked.

'Just a massive seagull,' the armed officer said. 'You should've seen it. Weird thing is, it looks like it got in through an open window, but I'm sure it was locked last time I checked.'

Morris watched them all look at each other with accusations burning in their eyes.

'Who was it?' Jones demanded. 'Who opened the bloody window? Do you want us to be murdered?'

Shaw laughed.

'Was it you?' Jones pointed at him.

'No, it wasn't me. I was laughing because this is like one of those murder mysteries. You know, where all the people in the old house get bumped off, one by one.'

The room fell silent again, the wind blowing outside and bringing a driving rain with it. Morris didn't like it. She watched Radford to see if he was shaken at all, but he had fetched a copy of a Charles Dickens book from one of the shelves and was reading it. She looked round all the faces and saw them all avoiding each other's glances – the guilty secret was there, as if it was just another guest in the room.

The time ticked away slowly as everyone became silent, the clock on the table gently chiming every hour. Slowly, it became darker, the weather even more grotesque, the occasional seagull riding the wild and grey sky and disappearing to the cliffs below. Morris watched it all through the window, scanning the horizon. No one had been outside for a couple of hours as everyone considered it too dangerous. Wells and Bartlett were sitting at the other end of the lounge, putting the jigsaw together which seemed to be some kind of painting of a ship. Radford had taken a look and declared it was the Fighting Temeraire and then sat back at the table, reading his book.

The silence was broken when Jones stood up abruptly with a grunt and stared round at everyone.

'What the bloody hell're we actually doing here? I mean, do we just stay here until this killer gets bored, or what? Is anyone looking for him back in Lyme Regis? The police? Oi, birdman, did you hear me?'

Radford sighed and put down his book, then looked up at the publican. 'No one back home is looking for him, as far as I know.'

Jones stared at him, then gave an incredulous laugh. 'You're joking? You are bloody joking?'

'No, I'm not, Mr Jones. I'm quite serious. You see, the killer is intent on murdering every one of you. For whatever reason that may be. So, it occurred to me, that the best course of action was to bring him out into the open.'

The three potential victims all froze and looked at each other.

'Hang on,' Wells said, getting to his feet. 'This is some kind of trap? We're not here to keep ourselves safe?'

'You're perfectly safe,' Radford said, picking up his book. 'We have an armed officer with us.'

'You're using us as bait?' Jones growled, and when Radford didn't look up from his book, he grabbed it and threw it across the room.

'Try and calm yourself,' Radford said.

Morris stood up, feeling like she could swim through the tension in the room. 'OK, I understand you're all probably very scared.'

'Wouldn't you be if some crazy person was trying to kill you?' Bartlett said, glaring at her.

'Yes, I probably would be. But like DCI Radford said, you're all perfectly safe. We're not going to let anything happen to any of you.'

The room fell silent again, apart from the quiet mutterings of Jones who paced the room, occasionally staring out into the growing darkness.

'I'd better start dinner,' Dr Shaw announced as he got up, grinning as if he was enjoying the whole evening far too much. 'I take it there are no vegetarians among us?'

No one said anything.

'Good,' Shaw said. 'I'm cooking a roast.'

After a moment, Wells said, 'The fire's going out.'

'Then go and get some logs,' Jones said.

'You go out there and get some logs.'

'Bugger off. I'm not going out there.'

Wells walked up to him, smiling. 'Why not? Are we scared?'

'No, it's pissing down and I'm likely to get bloody blown off the cliff!'

'You?' Bartlett laughed. 'Blown off? I don't think so.'

Tired of all their bickering, Morris stood up. 'I'll go.'

They all looked at her as the wind rattled the windows.

'OK, she'll go,' Jones said, happily.

'I'd better go,' the armed officer said, getting up.

'No, it's fine,' Morris put on her raincoat. 'It's only at the end of the garden. I'll be fine.'

'Come straight back,' Radford said, raising his eyes from his book.

'I will.' Morris zipped up her jacket and pulled on her hood, then walked back through the house and along the hallway to the front door that was being rattled by the wind. She took a deep breath, then unlocked the door. Immediately, the wind pushed the door against her, and she fought with it, struggling to get around it and out into the now dark night. She managed to shut it behind her, then turned to look into the void. She could see nothing and could only hear the wind howling in her ears and the occasional angry roar from the sea below.

She took out her phone as the wind pushed and tugged her. She turned on the torchlight and shone it out into the black night, forming a small spot of light that travelled over the path and the garden wall. She stepped forward, then stumbled sideways as the wind pushed her again. She moved the torchlight, shining it over everything until it ended up on the metal box that contained the logs. She took another few awkward steps, still keeping an eye out, her heart pounding. She got closer and closer to the box. All she had to do was get the box open, grab some logs and hurry back to the house. As she got to the box, she turned and swept the light over the ground around the garden gate, and up the path. There was no one, only the shape of the swaying trees and the edge of the cliff where the sea spat up into the air. Then she turned back to the metal box with a sudden horrifying realisation that she would have to put her phone away to open the box and carry the wood inside. She shone the torch to the front door, estimating how long it would take her if she hurried and how quickly she could get the door open, her arms full of wood.

Shit. This was just like being a kid again, she thought, terrified of the dark but busting for the loo. When she was little, she would have to run to the toilet, cross the landing, quickly shut the door and hit the light. The same back again, her heart hammering until she got to the safety of her room and her bed covers.

She swept the phone light over her surroundings again, checking the coast was clear. Nothing. Just the outline of the trees.

She took a shaky breath, turned off the light and plunged herself into complete unfathomable darkness. She hurried, chest tight, the pulse in her ears pounding louder than the wind as she grasped for the box and yanked it open. Her hands blindly grasped for the logs, piling them up in one arm, balancing them awkwardly until she felt she had enough. She shut the box and hurried back towards the cottage.

But something moved. Out of the corner of her eye, as her vision adjusted to the dark, she thought she saw movement. She swung round and backed up a little, staring out at the grey darkness.

Her phone was in her pocket, but the logs were in her arms. Shit. She tried to balance most of the logs in one arm, while she used her free hand to try and take the phone from her pocket. Some of the logs clattered to the ground, but she managed to get the torchlight on and beam it out along the garden. She went from the skeletal outline of the trees, along the cliff and back to the garden gate. She could see nothing. There was nothing there.

'Great, I'm imagining things,' she said to herself. 'Why the bloody hell did I say I'd fetch the shitty logs?'

Then the darkness moved, the shape of a hooded figure stepping into her line of vision. She jerked backwards. The man was only a couple of metres away from her, staring in her direction.

CHAPTER ELEVEN

'I'm a police officer,' she said, the wind swallowing her voice as she stared at the hooded figure.

The shape moved, its right arm lifting, a hand appearing, a knife gripped in it.

Morris stepped back, still watching the figure, her heart racing. It looked like a man. She kept backing up until she bumped into the door, then dropped all the logs. She gripped the handle of the door, watching him as he stepped closer, the knife gripped tight in his gloved hand. He took a few more fast steps towards her, so she turned, pulled open the door, jumped into the house and slammed it behind her.

'What the bloody hell was that?' Jones shouted out to her.

Morris backed up towards the open doorway to the kitchen, where everyone had turned to face her.

'Are you OK, Morris?' Radford asked.

She was still staring towards the door, then slowly looked round at the others. 'He's out there right now!'

They all got up and rushed to the window, elbowing each other out of the way as they stared into the night. Radford stayed at the table, now returned to his book.

Morris stared at him, watching him calmly reading while the killer was outside. 'Radford, did you hear what I said?'

He looked up at her as if she had told him dinner was ready. 'I heard you. It's OK, Morris, because we have the advantage. We have a well-trained armed officer with us.'

'Then where is he?' Bartlett asked. 'I haven't seen him for a while. Has anyone else?'

They all backed away from the window and glanced around the room, confusion written on their faces. Wells hurried up the stairs and was gone for a while before returning, looking a little frightened as he said, 'He's not up there.'

'Where is he?' Morris asked. 'Did he go out?'

'I think he went to patrol the grounds,' Bartlett said.

Radford turned to the female uniform. 'Did he go out on patrol again?'

She nodded. 'I'm afraid so. A while back. He's usually back by now.'

The air in the room suddenly turned chilly and each of them seemed to look downcast as they turned towards the window. He was out there now, having tracked them down.

'How did he bloody well find us?' Jones asked, staring at Radford.

'He was probably following one of you and then saw us all climbing aboard the bus,' Radford said matter of factly.

'Oh, bloody hell!' Jones shouted. 'That's great. That's really bloody great. So we've got a killer out there, and the armed officer's disappeared?'

'He's probably killed him,' Bartlett said, her eyes wide as she covered her mouth.

It was Wells who stepped towards Radford at the table, pointing at him, eyes narrowed. 'You knew this would happen, didn't you? Was this the plan all along, to use us as bait?'

Jones stormed over. 'Is that bloody well true? Did you use us as bait?'

Morris watched Radford as he put down his book and looked at them all in turn. 'It was the most effective way to draw out the killer.'

'Oh, Jesus!' Jones turned away, grumbling to himself.

'I think you all need to sit down at this table,' Radford said, his voice now changed, a more commanding element to it.

'Why should we listen to you?' Wells asked.

'Because I'm your only chance of leaving this house alive.' He stared at Wells.

The three of them all looked at each other

and then sat down at the table.

'I'll keep dinner warm then, shall I?' Dr Shaw said, but no one replied as they all waited for Radford to speak.

'The killer is out there,' he said, his voice low, his eyes set on them all in turn. 'The killer who, for whatever reason, is determined to murder you all. And probably in the most gruesome fashion.'

'Please!' Bartlett said, looking a little pale.

'I'm giving you the facts,' Radford said. 'Chances are our armed officer has fallen foul of that same killer. All we have is each other and the walls and doors keeping him out.'

'Just bloody great!' Jones huffed.

'Let's call for backup,' Morris said and took out her phone. There was no signal. She looked up and saw them all staring at her, hope in their eyes. 'No signal.'

Jones buried his face in his arms. 'We're all going to die.'

'No, you're not,' Radford said. 'I'm not going to let that happen. You have my word.'

'What are you going to do against this... killer?' Bartlett asked, her voice strained.

Radford sat back. 'I worked a particularly difficult case back in London. There was this psychopath who believed he was some kind of angel of death...'

'What happened?' Morris asked, sitting down at the table.

Radford looked at her. 'He wanted to kill as many people as he could, any way he could. That's what he believed his fate was. What we didn't know was he had taken on the identity of a solicitor we were already working with and was able to gain entry to the station...'

'Oh, God, what happened?' Bartlett asked.

'He managed to get hold of a gun and started shooting my colleagues and anyone else who was in the building. I saw them fall one by one. But I knew the only way to stop him was to talk to him...'

'Talk to him?' Jones said. 'A psycho?'

Radford nodded. 'Even a psycho has reasoning and sometimes all they want to hear is someone justify their reasoning.'

'That's what you did?' Wells asked. 'You walked up to him and just...'

'I told him that I could see his point of view. I discussed with him everything that had happened to him in his life and all the murders he had so far carried out. Then, after a while, he surrendered his weapon to me.'

'Just like that?' Jones said. 'And you're going to go and talk to this nutter waiting outside for us?'

'It might be our only chance. But...'

'But what?' Bartlett said, and they all waited for his next words.

'For it to work, I need to know the truth of the matter.' He looked at them all, and so did

Morris and she saw them all look away, their collective shame and guilt rising again.

'Whatever happened, however terrible,' Radford said, 'it's the only thing that will save you.'

They looked at each other, then down at the table. It was Bartlett who suddenly said, 'Maybe it's time to talk about it.'

'No!' Jones snapped. 'We can't.'

'If you don't tell him, I will,' Wells said. 'It might save us.'

Jones got to his feet and went over to the window. 'Fine. Tell him. I'm not bloody listening.'

Wells stared at the back of the publican and then turned to Radford, his face tight, looking decidedly sick.

'Well, as you know, we all went on holiday to the Isles of Scilly,' Wells said. 'Me, Lynn, Jones, Gardener, Brown, Emma Ash, and Mayfield. It was Adrian Parsons' idea. You see... we'd all ended up with money to invest. I'd come across a rare first edition of... anyway, we all had our windfalls. Parsons got wind of it and let us know he had this investment opportunity. Normally, when people say stuff like that, I assume they're some kind of scammer or opportunist, someone who's going to part you from your money...'

'But it was Adrian Parsons,' Bartlett added. 'He had his fingers in so many pies... sorry, Freddie, you tell the story.'

'Yes,' Wells continued. 'Adrian Parsons, it seemed, was a man to be trusted. So when he suggested we all go on this trip to the Isles of Scilly, none of us could think of an excuse not to go. I mean, he was paying for the whole thing, anyway.'

Wells looked away for a moment, then swallowed before he said, 'He wined and dined us the first night. Gave us a lot of spiel about this investment opportunity he was putting together and we listened... I wasn't really interested, but he was buying so... anyway, on the second night...'

Morris watched as Bartlett hung her head. She looked over at Jones, the publican, and saw he was almost doing the same thing. There was silence for a moment, only the sound of the wind outside whistling eerily through the rafters.

'The second night,' Wells said again, hesitantly, 'he invited us to this hotel, on one of the other islands. We got picked up by boat and there was champagne... he'd laid on a private party in the basement bar of this plush hotel. The Dungeon Bar, it was called. Parsons had invited another person along. A man in his late thirties, a real piece of work, flashy and arrogant. He wore an expensive suit and talked like he knew everything. I only caught his surname. Farah. With him... he'd brought along this young woman, maybe in her twenties, probably younger. She had an accent...'

'I think she was Polish,' Bartlett said quietly, looking down at the table. 'She was quiet and shy.'

Wells nodded. 'Yes, she was. I don't know what she was doing with him. Farah drank quite a lot and he kept disappearing off to the toilet with the girl and it became apparent that they were taking drugs. He was getting more and more out of control. The young girl didn't seem really into it, but he just kept on trying to entertain us all. By that point, we were alone. The staff had gone, leaving us alone there as they knew and trusted Parsons. He went there on holiday a lot, apparently. Then came the final, awful part of the evening.'

Bartlett sniffed, and Morris saw there were tears in her eyes.

'I'm not sure what happened,' Wells said.

'He must've put a mickey in her drink,' Jones piped up, but still staring out of the window.

'More than likely,' Wells said, nodding. 'But whatever happened, or whatever he did, the girl ended up in a right state. She was freaking out, obviously having a bad trip or something. We tried to calm her and for a while, we thought she was getting better but then... she just sort of collapsed. In the toilet.'

'What did you do?' Morris asked.

'We tried everything,' Wells said, his voice now a little shaky. 'CPR...'

'You didn't think to call the police?' Radford

said, looking between them.

It was Jones who swung around. 'We would've bleeding called the police, but... that psycho went and did what he did!'

'What psycho?' Morris asked.

'Farah.' Wells took a deep breath. 'She was gone. The girl was dead. It was too late for an ambulance... we all realised that. Next thing we know, Farah, who is out of his tree by this point, starts suggesting the most messed up, crazy stuff. He wanted us to make it look like she was attacked by some madman. He wanted us to get a knife and stab her and... the rest is too horrible to talk about. But we didn't know what to do, so we all sat there and talked about it, trying to decide if calling the police was the best option.'

'But you didn't?' Morris said.

Wells shook his head. 'No, we didn't. Because no one had realised that Farah had sloped off...'

Bartlett buried her face in her hands as she sobbed. Wells looked at her for a moment, hesitating again, then looked at Radford. 'That psycho... that monster had gone and found a knife...'

'Oh, God!' Morris said.

'Yes, that's what I thought,' Wells said, looking sick to his stomach. 'That horrible person... had... I can't describe what he'd done. But then we were left in a hole. We could've called the police before, but then... we were all screwed.'

'You could have still called the police,' Radford said, irritation filling his voice.

'That's the thing, we couldn't,' Wells said. 'He appeared out of nowhere, covered in blood, the knife in his hand, and he stuffs the knife right in Lynn's hand. She ends up with blood all over her.'

Bartlett let out another sob, so Wells put his arm around her and hugged her to him, then looked at Radford. 'Maybe we should have called the police. Maybe we're bad people, but we didn't. Parsons had a reputation and deals on the table, so he talked us into making her disappear. Farah told us she was some girl backpacking around, from Eastern Europe. Said she didn't have many family, and that she would hardly be missed. We shouldn't have listened, but we just panicked.'

'You weighted her down,' Radford said. 'Then took her body out in a boat and dumped her at sea?'

Wells nodded. 'Parsons had a boat. And there's no one to check up on you there. We all thought her body would turn up one day but it never did.'

'Anna Bajorek,' Radford said, quietly.

Bartlett looked up, staring at him, her eyes red. 'Was that her name?'

'Yes. She was reported missing about three weeks after your holiday. Her father tracked her down to there, but he never found any other trace of her and the police didn't know what had happened to her.'

'It's him,' Jones said, his eyebrows rising. 'The father! He's out there now! It's him, he's the psycho doing this.'

'Are you going to talk to him? Wells asked Radford. 'Reason with him?'

'No.' Radford looked back at him blankly. 'That would be suicide.'

'But you said...' Wells started to say.

'I lied. I said that so you would tell me the truth, which you did. There is no psycho out there, outside this cottage, I mean. Wherever the killer is, he's more than likely back in Lyme Regis waiting for you to return so he can carry on picking you off.'

'But I saw him,' Morris said, her mind spinning, pointing at the window. 'Out there!'

'No, you didn't,' Radford said. 'Who you saw was DS Scott. I asked him to dress up in a hood and mask and make himself known, so one of you would see him and think the killer was outside. It just happened to be you, Inspector Morris.'

'Where's the armed officer, then?' Bartlett asked.

'In the minibus, reading a book,' Radford said and stood up and stretched.

'You did all this to trick us?' Jones growled, pointing one of his thick fingers at him.

Radford looked at him with a heavy sigh. 'I

did this to help you. To get to the bottom of all this, I needed the truth. And that was something none of you were willing to surrender easily, so I had to be a bit… crafty.'

'Crafty?' Bartlett cried. 'This is… some kind of entrapment, isn't it?'

Radford looked at the remaining uniformed officer. 'The constable will make a statement according to what happened here. Then that will be used to start the legal process against the three of you.'

'You bastard!' Jones shouted, his face reddening.

'Dinner's almost ready,' Dr Shaw said, oven gloves on his hands, smiling. 'Shall we eat?'

'Would be a shame not to eat the meal the doctor has cooked for us,' Radford said. 'Why don't you all take a seat, then we can eat and then go back to Lyme Regis.'

'Where we'll be arrested?' Wells said, his eyes wide.

'More than likely,' Radford said. 'But if you all testify to what happened, then I think you will all fare quite well. I think the guilt you have been carrying has been quite heavy on your shoulders. I'm sure it feels a little better to have that weight lifted somewhat, doesn't it?'

Morris sat down, feeling exhausted and looked over at the three guilty people in the room. She saw them look at each other, slowly losing the anger that they felt towards Radford as they sat down at the table.

'Shall we eat, then?' Shaw said, then started serving up the dinner as the front door opened and the armed officer and DS Scott came strolling in.

Morris looked over at the sheepish-looking Scott, who was carrying the outfit he had been wearing outside. He looked at her and shrugged as he said, 'Sorry.'

She huffed, even though her annoyance was fading away too. She looked at Radford, who had picked up his book again and seemed to be happily reading as the dinner was being placed on the table. She suddenly understood why so many people didn't like Radford or his little ways.

'He's still out there,' Wells said suddenly, looking down at the table and the plate that had been placed before him.

'He is,' Radford said, looking up from his book. 'But we'll find him.'

'I wonder what happened to that psycho Farah,' Bartlett said.

'Undoubtedly dead,' Radford said, matter of factly. 'He was probably the first person he tracked down, then he probably tortured him to find out about all of you.'

'Oh, God.' Bartlett put her head in her hands, then she looked up. 'It must be her father. Find him and you've got the killer.'

'Perhaps,' Radford said. 'We'll see. Let's eat and then we'll return to Lyme Regis and try and find our killer.'

CHAPTER TWELVE

After they had eaten, mostly in silence, everyone had climbed aboard the bus and taken their seats, ready for the journey back to Lyme Regis. Radford had noticed a strange kind of calmness had come over the three guilty parties as if admitting to what they had done had truly lifted the weight off their shoulders. They would sleep tonight, probably better than they ever had since that terrible night. He looked over at Inspector Morris, who was driving them along the dark and narrow road. She had hardly said anything to him since he had revealed his trickery, and for some reason, he found it bothered him that she might be upset by what he had done.

'Are you quite all right, Inspector?' he asked.

He saw her briefly look at him from the corner of her eye. 'Fine.'

'You didn't approve of my plan?'

'Not really.' She was quiet for a moment. 'I thought you might've told me what was going on.'

'Whoever saw him needed to be genuinely scared...'

'Oh, I was genuinely scared, don't worry about that. I'm starting to understand why some people take a dislike to you. But I suppose in your subtle way, we learned the truth.'

'We did. I've been in contact with some old... colleagues at the yard and managed to find out that the young businessman, who Parsons brought along to their party, was probably a Farah Greene. At least there was a Farah Greene who arrived on St Mary's that week. He has previous, which includes ABH, possession of drugs, and thievery when he was younger. Then he somehow became a man of the city, investing here and there. His parents had money, you see, and they allowed him to invest some of his trust fund. There were also a couple of suspected sexual assaults and one rape, but those charges went away. I'm guessing the aggrieved parties were hushed up.'

'I won't lose any sleep over him, then. So, chances are he would've done something terrible to that poor Anna girl?'

'Undoubtedly. He probably spiked her drink and it went bad from there.'

'So where is Farah Greene now?'

'He went missing from his London flat just over three years ago. He has not been seen since.'

Morris looked at him with wide eyes before facing the darkened road ahead. 'Three years ago? Are you thinking our killer caught up with him?'

'I am. He probably found out what he wanted to know from him and then disposed of him.'

'Three years ago? And now he's here? Why did he wait so long?'

Radford had been thinking that over, imagining the hatred and blood lust the aggrieved killer would have felt, and how much patience he had. 'He wanted to take his time, get to know them, learn every detail of their lives before he killed them. He wanted to watch them, and savour the moment. Imagine the amount of patience it took not to take a knife and plunge it into their hearts as soon as he saw them.'

Morris shook her head. 'I can't. I can't imagine what's been going through his head. I wonder who it is. Her father or brother or even a boyfriend?'

'That I don't know, but I believe he's living among us. He would have arrived in Lyme Regis about three years ago, so we need to examine the lives and movements of any of the residents of this town who match that description.'

'OK. There can't be that many. When we get back, we'll take a thorough look.'

The wind was a little calmer as he trudged back to his car and climbed in. The rain hit the windscreen, so he turned on the wipers and listened to them scrape and squeak back and forth. Beyond the glistening wet glass, he watched the old cottage and the group of people who had left. He had gripped the steering wheel when he saw them walking free, unpunished as they were delivered to the interior of the vehicle before it rumbled to life and headed back to Lyme Regis. He assumed it had been some kind of trap, a way to draw him out, which meant they still had no idea who he was. They might know who he used to be by now, he decided, but obviously not who he had become. He had found himself staring at the bus and the dark silhouetted passengers as it moved away, the rage bubbling up inside for what they had let happen to her.

There was something strange about the whole scene as it played out. He found it almost amusing as he watched the three of them, those scumbags, walking from the house. It was the fact that there were only three of them when he knew there should have been four. Which meant that they did not realise one was missing from their line-up. He even found himself laughing a little, the tears blurring his vision as they poured from his eyes. The laughter turned back to shouts and cries as he pounded his fists on the steering wheel.

She came to mind, her face, her gentle smile... *Anna*.

The bus had driven away. But he stayed there for a while, thinking and planning. It was time for the fourth person to face justice. He started the engine and drove towards Lyme Regis.

They delivered the minibus back to the police station and all three were booked in for further questioning and to get their statements. Radford watched them all being processed, the strange calmness hanging over them, then he returned to the quiet of the shack and the four walls that yawned at him as he entered, no ghosts waiting for him to return. A hollow sadness washed over him as he showered, dressed in his pyjamas and dressing gown, and stood looking out at the dark sky. He now knew the truth, knew that the murders were committed out of the oldest motive in the book. Revenge. Now all they had to do was note who had arrived in the town in the time period they had identified and question those individuals. It was almost an anticlimax that soon the murders would be solved and then he could move on. That was the thought that had begun to plague him since the realisation that the investigation was coming to an end. Where would he go now? He looked round the empty room again, wishing that he still had Carr to share his thoughts with. No, not actually Carr, and not even her ghost, just an image of her created by his troubled mind.

He pushed away his own problems and thought about the man they would be searching for, imagining the pain and loathing that had been contained in him for three years. He thought of his rage, his own hatred for the people who had blown up the police station and murdered so many of his colleagues.

Carr.

He sat down and stared towards the TV, nodding to himself, understanding exactly what drove the killer. It wasn't only Carr's death and his colleagues' that helped him understand, because he had another horrific moment in his life when death had come and taken someone he loved from him.

He saw his mother, smiling at him when they would visit a specialist dental hospital in London, where he would have his braces readjusted. Afterwards, as a treat, she would take him across the road to a small cafe and buy him a cheeseburger, fries, and a banana milkshake. The memory was always warm and comforting for a bit, until the rest of it played out. Days after that last visit to the dental hospital, she was shot and killed in a robbery gone wrong at the building society where she worked.

He understood pain, but it would not stop him from doing his duty and finding their killer. He was out there, undoubtedly watching and waiting.

There came a knock on the window which made Radford jump and dragged him away from his dark memories. Stood outside, wrapped up in a raincoat was the journalist, Nathan Sharpe. He smiled and waved.

Radford gave a heavy sigh, got to his feet and opened the door, the wind blustering in.

'Sorry, I didn't mean to disturb you,' Sharpe said, looking him up and down.

'You didn't. Come in.'

Sharpe stepped in, looking the place over. 'You look ready for bed.'

Radford sat on the sofa. 'What do you want, Mr Sharpe?'

'Nothing really. I was just checking you were OK. I haven't seen you lately, or Inspector Morris for that matter. I hope everything's OK?'

'Your journalist's nose has smelt something, is that it?'

Sharpe smiled. 'Let's just say I got a little curious. Especially since I noticed three of the locals had disappeared too.'

'Well, I cannot discuss that at all, so you have wasted your time coming here.'

The journalist nodded and looked around the room. 'Thing is, DCI Radford, there's been no more murders. Is it over, do you think? My readers have their concerns.'

'I'm sure they do. You know, you might be able to help me.'

Sharpe raised an eyebrow. 'Really? How?'

Radford stood up, then took his kettle and filled it up, thinking that the journalist might be privy to information that he might not so easily come by. 'Do you fancy a cup of tea?'

'Coffee would be nice. So, what do you need help with?'

Radford pulled out the table and the two chairs. 'Sit down.'

Sharpe did so, narrowing his eyes at the detective suspiciously. 'Are you about to shine a light in my eyes and ask me a series of questions until I break?'

Radford found the coffee that had been left in the shack by the owner and made a cup for Sharpe. 'No, I'm just wondering how many people have moved to this town in the last three years.'

Sharpe picked up his coffee and blew on it. 'You mean to live?'

'Yes.' Radford sat down.

'Well, I can name one. Myself.'

'I see. When did you move to Lyme Regis?'

'I think... yes, it was about three years ago. Before then I was in London, working on a broadsheet, but I didn't like the fast pace of the city, so here I am.'

'Anyone else you know who moved here about the same time?'

Sharpe sipped his coffee, eyeing Radford carefully. 'Now, I can understand you want information from me, and of course, I want to help, but I must ask…'

'What's in it for you?'

'Exactly. I mean, I've been looking into you, DCI Radford and you have quite a history. An interview with the detective who solves this case and who survived a terrorist attack would be quite the scoop.'

Radford nodded. 'I'm sure it would. OK, very well. When this case is closed, then I'll meet with you and I'll give you your interview.'

'Good. Now, why are you so interested in people who moved here three years ago?'

'I'm afraid I cannot answer that.'

Sharpe sat back. 'Let me think. You think the killer moved here three years ago, am I right?'

'I cannot comment on that.'

'OK, well there's me… James Headley who runs the Lyme hotel… oh, and Adrian Parsons' former business partner.'

'Former business partner?'

The journalist took another sip of his coffee. 'Yes, Nigel Oldroyd. He moved from Manchester, I think or somewhere up north.'

'Was there any animosity between them?'

'Well, they fell out over money, but I think they buried the hatchet.' Sharpe narrowed his eyes at Radford. 'Do you think it could be Oldroyd? Parsons upset him and now… no, that doesn't fit, does it? Why would he be targeting all the others?'

Radford's eyes were drawn to the night outside when he thought he heard the gate opening. After a moment, a silhouette appeared, and he recognised it as the familiar shape of Inspector Morris. It was Sharpe who got up and opened the door for her, letting in the light rain that came with her and had covered her raincoat.

'I can see you're busy, Radford,' the journalist said. 'I'll leave you to it unless the inspector here has a quote for me?'

'Nice try,' she said, taking off her coat.

Sharpe laughed and headed out the door and disappeared into the darkness.

'What did he want?' Morris asked, sitting at the table opposite him.

'What do all journalists want?'

She nodded. 'You know he arrived here a few years ago?'

Radford nodded. 'We were just discussing that. You had better check him out. He said he'd been living in London before he moved here.'

'OK.' Morris got up again and retrieved a bottle of wine from the inside of her coat and held it up. 'That's why I like this coat. Deep pockets. Fancy a drink?'

'I don't drink.' He watched her as she found a wine glass in one of the cupboards and sat back down and poured herself a drink.

'What do you know about Nigel Oldroyd?'

Morris sipped her wine. 'Adrian Parsons' former business partner? Not a great deal. I know they fell out a while back.'

'I've been informed he's from Manchester.'

'From up that way. I see where you're going. He came down about three or four years ago. But that would mean he came down here and became business partners with one of the people he wanted to kill. Well, I suppose that might explain why they fell out. Maybe it wasn't just about money for Oldroyd.'

'Perhaps not. I think we need to go and see him tomorrow morning and then visit James Headley.'

Morris emptied her glass of wine, then wiped her mouth with the back of her hand. 'OK, that should be fun.'

'You might not want to drink any more tonight.'

She stared at him. 'I was only going to have a couple of glasses.'

He was about to say something else before a ringing came from Morris' coat and she started scrambling at it to find her phone. She managed to pull it out and stared at it. 'Oh dear, it's DS Scott calling me. Can't be good.'

She answered, 'DS Scott, how are you? Dressed up as a killer and scared anyone lately? What? What did you say? Where?'

Radford watched her go to the window, staring off into the night. 'You're joking. Someone just called it in? All right, I'm coming.'

She ended the call and started putting on

her coat.

'What's happened?'

She looked at him as she zipped herself up. 'Someone called the station and said there's a package waiting for us at the end of the Cobb.'

Radford stood up, his heart hammering. 'It could be a bomb.'

'You said this wasn't a terrorist attack.' She opened the door.

'It's not. But if this is our killer, we know he's capable of… but…'

'But what?'

'If he has left it for us, he wouldn't put a bomb inside it, because he has no grievance with us.'

'Good.' Morris went to go out.

'Unless he wants us to think that, but we are getting close to the truth and he wants us out of the way?'

Morris let out a frustrated breath. 'Right, I'm taking a look.'

'Hang on, let me get dressed.'

'Hurry up!' she said, then seemed to think for a moment before she added, 'Boss.'

Radford found himself being battered by the wind and rain as they made their way along the promenade, past the closed-up food huts and restaurants and towards the sea wall. He could see the light flashing close to the small aquarium that sat at the end of the Cobb. The wind had certainly picked up again in strength and was once more hurling the sea at the wall, sending great plumes of foamy waves into the air. Already, as they reached the steps up to the Cobb, Radford was covered in a cold sweat and his hands were trembling while his heart pounded in his ears.

He found himself stopping dead.

Morris must have sensed he was no longer behind her and turned to look to see where he was. She came back and shouted, 'What's wrong?'

'I'm sorry, but I can't go any further,' he said, breathing hard.

She nodded. 'It's OK, stay here. I'll take a look.'

'Be careful,' he called out, but she was already up the well-worn steps that were slippery with rain and seawater. He watched her disappear as she made her way along the Cobb.

He thought of the bomb that he had found in the tunnel underneath the police station and felt the panic beating through him, making him dizzy. He took an unsteady step forward, then another as he rested his hand on the wall, steadying himself. He looked at the steps and saw a surge of wild and angry foam breaking over the Cobb. He breathed hard, trying not to listen to the voice in his head telling him to turn and run back to the shack.

He put a foot on the first step, then

immediately put it back down. He couldn't do it.

He closed his eyes and heard the wind and rain and his pulse in his ears. He opened his eyes and took two steps upwards. He forced himself on, trying not to think what he was doing. Somehow, he found himself standing at the end of the wall, which now seemed so much narrower. The waves crashed against the wall, spraying into the air. They were like clawed hands, trying to grasp anyone stupid enough to walk along it and pull them back into its terrible gloom.

He could see Morris now halfway along the wall, heading for the light and the small box left for them. His heart hammered every time a wave crashed and almost swept her away. He couldn't let her retrieve the box by herself. He couldn't. He took another shaky step, the wind pushing and pulling him, trying to force him closer to the edge. His knees trembled as he took another step, breathing hard, mumbling under his breath, telling himself he was crazy.

Now he could see the inspector crouching by the box, slipping on gloves and looking the object over. He held his breath as she reached out to it, putting her gloved hands on either side, ready to lift.

'No!' he shouted, but the wind and waves swallowed the sound.

She lifted it. Nothing happened. She stood up and started carrying the box carefully back along the wall, pausing only when another massive wave smashed against the Cobb wall and tried to grasp her. Then she moved faster, hurrying towards him.

'What are you doing?' she said, her eyes wide, staring at him.

'I was coming to help you,' he said, his body now trembling all over.

'But you're scared of the water.'

'No, I'm scared of drowning.'

'Well, come on, let's get this to the station.'

'I'm pretty sure I can't move,' he said.

Inspector Morris sighed, took his arm and pulled him back down the steps.

CHAPTER THIRTEEN

Inspector Morris moved slowly across Chief Superintendent Parsons' office and placed the small damp box on her desk. Parsons, dressed in her neat uniform, stared at the box, then up at Morris and Radford, her eyes widening.

'Has it been examined by the bomb squad?' Parsons asked, her voice shaking.

'No,' Radford said and stepped forward, 'but it's far too light to be a bomb.'

Parsons stared up at him and then pointed. 'You'd better be right!'

'I am right.' He looked at Morris and saw she didn't look convinced either. 'I am right, Inspector.'

'Who's opening it, then?' Parsons asked, looking between them. 'Because I'm not.'

Radford sighed, then slipped on a pair of

gloves and approached the desk.

'Hang on,' Parsons said and got up and went over to the door. 'OK, go on.'

Radford stared at her for a moment, then looked back at the box. There was only a small piece of black electrical tape holding down the lid, so he gently took the end of it and peeled it back. The lid jumped up and he took a deep breath before he carefully opened it. He looked inside and paused, trying to make sense of what he was looking at.

'What is it?' Morris asked, coming closer. 'I guess it isn't a bomb?'

'No, it is not.' Radford reached in and took hold of the dress that had been neatly folded and placed in the box. He lifted it up and let it unfurl.

'A dress?' Parsons said. 'So, this isn't from our killer, it's just someone's idea of a joke.'

'I'm not so sure,' Radford said. 'I think someone's trying to tell us something.'

'Well, whose is it?' Morris asked. 'It couldn't be the dead girl's, it's too old lady for her.'

Radford nodded. 'You're right, Inspector. It's an older lady's dress. And it smells of perfume that an older lady would wear. The more I look at this dress, the more I feel like I've seen it before somewhere.'

'Where?' Parsons asked.

'I have no idea.' He turned around so they could get a better look. 'Do either of you recognise it?'

Parsons and Morris looked at each other, then at the dress, and shrugged.

'It does look familiar,' Morris said. 'But no, I don't know whose it is. Maybe another victim?'

'But we have the remaining potential victims downstairs making statements.' Radford carefully folded the dress up and put it back in the box.

'Have we?' Morris asked. 'What if we've been wrong about what this is about? Maybe it isn't this Polish girl. Maybe it's something to do with...'

She stopped speaking when Radford glared at her.

'What is it?' Parsons asked, narrowing her eyes. 'Something to do with what?'

Radford realised that they were better off telling the truth and seeing if their boss knew anything about her husband's old business partner. 'We believe that perhaps the killer is living among us, or rather among all of you, and has been for about three years...'

'What?' Parsons looked as if she had been slapped. 'You're saying it's one of us? No, it can't be.'

'Someone who is connected to the girl who died on the trip to the Isles of Scilly,' Radford added.

Parsons shook her head. 'I don't believe any of that! Adrian wouldn't have...'

'I'm sorry, ma'am,' Morris said, putting on

a look of sympathy, 'but we have three people downstairs signing statements.'

Parsons was red in the face and looked close to tears. 'There must be some mistake… anyway, what were you going to say or ask?'

Radford moved closer to her. 'What do you know about Nigel Oldroyd?'

The Chief Superintendent looked at him quizzically, then walked back to her desk and sat down. 'He came here two or three years ago, give or take… so you're thinking he's murdered all these people? Nigel? Really?'

'Do you think he's capable?' Radford asked.

'No. He's just a plain old, boring… businessman.'

'The thing is, ma'am, just about every murderer starts off ordinary or even boring… until hate enters their heart.'

She huffed. 'Oh, don't get all poetic on me, Radford. Just go and do your job and talk to Nigel and anyone else who might know who that dress belongs to. Go on, hurry up and leave me in peace.'

'I feel a bit sorry for her,' Morris said as she drove them out to Nigel Oldroyd's house on the outskirts of Charmouth.

Radford turned to her. 'Why?'

Morris laughed, then looked at him and realised he wasn't joking. She should have known. 'Because her husband was just murdered?'

'Oh, yes, of course,' he said. 'Very sad. You don't recognise the dress?'

She shrugged. 'Not really. I mean, I definitely feel like I've seen it somewhere… what if the killer's messing with us, making us think there's another potential victim when there isn't? I mean, why go to the bother of sending it to us?'

'Because the killer is making a statement. He's communicating with us, with the world, showing us how he's dealing out justice, telling us how we've failed him and that young girl.'

Morris looked at him, realising there was a touch of tenderness in his voice, which made her question whether Radford was as cold as he made out.

'Well, we've got his potential victims held at the station,' she said as she signalled and took a right turn into a narrower road lined with rambling hedges. 'So, the killer's out of luck.'

'But we can't hold them there forever. The CPS will have to decide if they have committed a crime that is worth charging them for…'

'But surely they will. They can't let them get away with it.'

'I'm afraid, my dear naive Morris, that often the CPS either feel that they don't have enough evidence, or that it's not in the public's interest to charge the suspects. In this case, we have little evidence. The girl is missing, there is no body, no real evidence of a crime.'

Morris stared at him, unable to take in what he was saying. 'Jesus. So, they'll get to walk out, free as birds?'

'Free as a flock of birds...or in this case, a murder of crows.'

Morris could feel her anger rising as she turned off the road and reached the gated drive to Nigel Oldroyd's house. She pulled up, opened the gate while Radford watched from the car, blank as always, then climbed back in. She drove them onto the gravel drive and towards a house that looked quite modern but was designed to look like a much older mansion. There was a Land Rover parked close to it, and she noticed the licence plate: N1G3.

'He seems to be doing OK for himself,' Morris said, pointing to the personalised number plate. 'Breaking up with Parsons doesn't seem to have done him any harm.'

'No, apparently not,' Radford said as he approached the large, almost ecclesiastical, arched front door. 'But money begets money.'

'The rich get richer and all that?'

'Exactly.' Radford pressed the bell, and it was only a moment later that a young woman with bobbed brown hair appeared dressed in a red, one-piece swimming costume and looked them over with her eyebrows raised.

'Hello, can I help you?' she asked, in a well-spoken voice.

'We are looking for Nigel Oldroyd,' Radford said and produced his warrant card and held it up. 'I'm DCI Philip Radford, and this is Inspector Morris. Who are you?'

'Amber,' she said, looking suspiciously at them. 'Amber Marsh. I'll go get him. He was on the phone in his office, the last time I checked.'

'Is he your father?' Morris asked, smiling at her, slightly jealous of her slender figure. She never liked the look of herself in bathing costumes and seemed to bulge in all the wrong places. 'I didn't realise he had kids.'

The young woman looked at her, then gave an empty laugh. 'No, not his... kid. But that is funny. I'll tell him you're here.'

She went off laughing to herself and Morris thought she heard her repeat the word kid.

'Do you think she's his...?' Morris said, unable to bring herself to say the actual word.

'Lover?' Radford said, making a face that suggested he found the whole situation just as torrid. 'Probably. But we probably shouldn't judge.'

'Probably shouldn't. But I am. It's weird. He's got to be fifty-odd, and she's what? Barely twenty?'

'She's twenty-five,' a gravelly voice said from the doorway and Morris turned to see a grey-haired man in a white flannel shirt and khaki trousers. He put a cigarette between his lips and lit it as he stepped out and looked them both over. 'I know what people think, but I don't give a stuff.'

'Good for you,' Radford said. 'We are here to talk about Adrian Parsons.'

Immediately, Oldroyd's face fell into what seemed a practised look of glumness. He nodded solemnly, then took a long thoughtful drag of his cigarette. 'That was a terrible business, wasn't it? I still can't believe it. Do they know who did it?'

'No. We are still looking into it, Mr Oldroyd,' Radford said, waving cigarette smoke from his face. 'Where were you that night?'

'Where was I?' the middle-aged businessman took on a look of annoyance. 'Where was I the night my business partner was murdered?'

'Former business partner,' Morris added with a smile.

Oldroyd stared at her, then took another drag. 'Yes, former, but I never lost respect for him.'

'Why did you fall out?' Radford asked.

'That's none of your business.'

'It is, if it has any relation to why he was murdered,' Radford said.

'Why was he murdered?' Oldroyd stepped closer, lowering his voice. 'Was it to do with some dodgy business deal?'

'I'm afraid we cannot discuss that,' Radford said. 'Have you ever been to the Isles of Scilly, Mr Oldroyd?'

'Let me think,' he said, looking up and blowing out some smoke. 'I've been to a lot of places. Maybe once years ago. I can't really remember. Why?'

'You didn't go there on a business trip with Adrian Parsons? Roughly four years ago?'

'Four years ago? I don't think I was even living here then, so no. Come on, what's this got to do with him being murdered?'

Radford looked at Morris. 'Show him the photo.'

Oldroyd looked over at Morris as she dug out her phone and let him see the photo of the dress that had been left for them in the box.

'Ever seen this before?' Morris asked.

'No, I haven't seen it before. Looks frumpy though. Sort of thing an old dear might wear. Are you going to tell me what's going on?'

'We need you to let us know where you were at the time of each murder,' Radford said in his usual blank manner.

'You are bloody kidding?' Oldroyd said. 'Why would I go round killing them?'

'Parsons had some business investment that he was trying to get them to put their money into,' Morris said. 'Were you involved in that?'

'I don't know anything about it and I didn't kill anyone,' Oldroyd said and let out an exhausted breath. 'I'm a businessman, that's it. Not a murderer. Now, can I please get back to work?'

'Yes, you can,' Radford said. 'But we still need you to give your whereabouts on the days of the murders.'

'Fine. I will.' Oldroyd shook his head as the young woman came back, slapping her bare feet across the floor again, now wet, her hair dark and pulled back.

'Coming for a swim, Nigel?' she asked, smiling.

'Do you live around here?' Morris asked her, thinking about the dress again.

'I do. Why?' the young woman asked, looking suspicious.

Morris showed her the photo of the dress. 'Recognise this dress?'

'I have a photographic memory,' she said.

'There's no such thing,' Radford stated. 'There are only good memories and bad memories. No one has a photographic memory.'

She sneered at him. 'Well, I have a photographic memory and yes, I know who owns a dress like that.'

'Who?' Morris asked.

The girl looked particularly pleased with herself as she said, 'Sue. The frumpy one. She was at the meeting the other day. In fact, she was wearing that dress.'

Radford let out a harsh breath. 'Of course. The woman who put up her hand and everyone ignored her.'

'That's it.' The young woman nodded.

'Sue who?' Oldroyd said, looking irritated.

'I don't know,' the young woman said, with a shrug. 'My photographic records only have a photo of her and a name. Sue.'

She didn't know where she was, except it looked like an old barn. It smelt damp and she thought she could hear the sound of the waves hitting the beach. The wind was rattling the doors where a little dull light managed to get through. She was trying to keep herself calm, breathing deeply. She remembered a yoga class she had joined and the relaxation techniques. She tried to move her arms again, but they were held behind her back, strapped together so she couldn't even move from the chair she was tied to.

She was trying to keep a thought from her mind that had been trying to burrow in since she woke up with a splitting headache. At last, it popped in, and the panic began to fizz in her heart.

It was the killer, the mad person who was killing her friends. No, not friends, she couldn't really call them that. Most of them didn't even know her name, even though she had lived among them for nearly fifteen years. You, thingy, Sally sometimes, all kinds of labels apart from her real name.

A door behind her creaked open, and there were footsteps travelling towards her. She moved her head, trying to get a glimpse of who was there.

'Hello?' she called. 'Help me! Please, can you untie me, please?'

The footsteps stopped for a moment. Then they continued until a shape emerged in the gloom of the barn. She looked up and saw a hooded figure standing there, a mask covering the lower part of his face. She jerked backwards as he stepped towards her. The chair didn't move.

'Please don't hurt me,' she said, her voice breaking up.

He didn't say anything, just stared at her, watching her for a while. He wore dark glasses over the face mask.

'I'm going to kill them all,' the figure said, stepping closer again.

She snapped her eyes shut as a sob burst from her lips. 'Please… please don't kill me.'

'They don't even see you, do they?'

She slowly opened her eyes.

'Sue Bishopp,' he said, his voice low and strange sounding. 'Sue Bishopp, with two ps. They forget you're even there, don't they?'

She looked away, tears running down her face.

'Don't you get angry that they don't see you? At the town meeting, you clearly had your hand up, but they ignored you.'

She looked down, the memory of that day coming back to her. She sobbed again, partly out of fear and partly because what he said was true. Nobody ever noticed her. Even the ones she called friends, talked over her.

'You were there that night,' he said, and she could hear something horrible and dark in his voice.

She looked up slowly, ready to say she didn't know what he was referring to, but she had never been a very good liar. There could only be one night he meant. She nodded.

'You know the night I mean?' he asked. 'The night she died and you all stood around and did nothing.'

'I wanted to!' she said, the tears coming again. 'I said... we've got to call the police... I begged them.'

'But they didn't hear you?'

She shook her head.

'Because they never hear you.'

She sobbed, the burst of tears exploding from deep inside. 'I'm so... so... sorry.'

'At least...' he began, his voice seeming to soften a little. 'At least you tried.'

'I did. I swear.'

He didn't say anything, just looked towards her. She couldn't tell what was going on beyond the mask and the hood, but she had this awful feeling reaching out to her, beating through the air, poisoning everything.

'I sentenced the others straight away,' he said, his voice quieter. 'I couldn't stand to be around them longer than I had to. They didn't deserve to breathe the air that she should've been breathing.'

'Please… will you let me go?'

He lowered his head for a moment, then shook it. 'I can't. I'm sorry, but I can't.'

'I tried to get them to call…'

'I know. I'll give you time. It's all I can give. Think about her, imagine what she could be doing now.' Then he pulled something from his pocket and she saw it was it was a piece of material.

'Please…' was all she managed to say before he wrapped the material around her head and gagged her mouth. She pleaded through the gag, staring up at him, now able to see his eyes. There was something familiar about them, she had definitely seen those eyes before.

He stepped back. 'I'll be back with food and water. Think about her. Think about her until it's your turn to die.'

CHAPTER FOURTEEN

Radford opened the door to the interview room for Inspector Morris to go before him, then he watched as she pulled up a chair opposite where their three potential victims were all seated around a table, drinks in front of them. They all blinked tiredly, having spent the last few hours answering the same questions several times. Radford could not bring himself to feel sorry for them as he stood with his back to the wall, looking them over one by one.

'I take it you have all made your statements?' Radford asked.

Jones, the publican, stifled a yawn then said, 'Yes, I don't know how many bloody times. What happens now?'

'You get to answer more questions,' Morris said and Radford saw her trying to hold in a smile.

'More?' Bartlett said, her voice a little shrill. 'I need some beauty sleep.'

'You'll need a few years' worth then,' Jones said and laughed to himself until Bartlett glared at him.

'When you told us who was there that fateful night,' Radford said, 'you forgot to mention someone.'

They all looked at him, their collective brows furrowing. They looked at each other, confusion overtaking their emotions.

'No, we didn't,' Jones said. 'The rest are dead, which is very sad, but here we are. The survivors. Listen, I'm not proud of what we did…'

'It's what you didn't do that's the problem,' Morris said.

'Sue,' Radford said, raising his voice so they all stopped and stared at him.

'Sue?' Bartlett said. 'You're saying we need to sue someone?'

'No, the other person you neglected to mention, is called Sue.'

They all stared at each other again but remained looking lost.

'Sue who?' Wells said.

'Short, aged around fifty, grey-blonde bobbed hair,' Morris said, reading from her notes. 'Ring any bells?'

'No, sorry,' Wells said, while the others shook their heads.

Radford took out his phone and brought up the photo of the dress and showed it to them all. They leaned in, staring at it.

'There's something familiar about it,' Bartlett said. 'I'd always remember a dress that hideous.'

'I've no idea.' Jones sat back and folded his arms.

'Oh, God,' Bartlett said, looking at Wells. 'Sue. Don't you remember me pointing her out in this dress and saying how hideous she looked?'

Wells looked at the dress again, then the lights in his eyes came on and he put a hand to his mouth. 'Oh, yes, I'd forgotten about... what's her name again?'

'Sue!' Morris said, sounding exhausted. 'None of you have ever noticed her, not unless you're critiquing her dress sense.'

'I observed her at the town meeting,' Radford said.

'She was there?' Bartlett asked.

Radford sighed. 'Yes, she was there. She even put her hand up to speak, but no one even saw her. Or if they did, they chose not to see her.'

'I remember now,' Wells said, staring off into space. 'That night. She was there. Oh God. She tried to...'

'What did she try to do?' Morris asked.

Wells looked at Morris, a dark look coming over his face. 'She tried to get us... she wanted us to call the police. But we didn't listen.'

The other two potential victims looked down.

'Do any of you know where Sue might live?' Radford asked. 'She is in great danger.'

They all looked blank until Wells' eyes widened.

'My shop,' he said, sitting up. 'My ledger. She got me to order these weird romance, vampire books, I think they were. I'll have her name and address in my ledger. It was about a month ago. It'll be in there.'

'We will need the keys to your shop,' Radford said, holding out his hand.

Wells searched his pockets, then brought out a chain with four keys on and handed them over. 'The bottom lock is temperamental. Give it a twist and a shove.'

'Come on, Morris,' Radford said and hurried to the door.

'What about us?' Jones called out.

Radford looked at them all, a tiny part of him happy about what he was going to say next. 'You will have to stay longer and amend your statements.'

'Well, he was right about these locks,' Morris said, fiddling with the keys as they stood outside the old bookshop on the corner, not far from the Lyme Regis Museum. Even from there, Radford could see into the dark windows and make out the stacks of well-worn books that filled the many shelves lining the walls. He already knew what the place would smell like.

'This last lock won't budge,' Morris said crouching down towards the bottom of the door.

'If you move out of the way,' Radford said, 'I know an old police trick.'

Morris stood up. 'Really? What?'

Radford turned his body and pressed his shoulder against the door. He pulled himself back, then slammed his shoulder hard into it, close to the locks. He shunted the door and it opened.

'Oh,' Morris said. 'I don't think Wells will be pleased about that.'

'What a shame, I'll send him my condolences.' Radford stepped into the narrow and gloomy hallway of the building which had old black and white photos of the town on the walls. Inside the dark and musty shop came the waft of old books, the ancient pages and pleasurable words. Morris flicked a switch and the strip lights above them flickered on, revealing the many shelves and the hordes of volumes that were crammed into them. If given the time, Radford would have loved nothing more than thumbing the dry pages and reading something of the classics, but he had to shake himself out of his dream and find the ledger. There was a large, antique desk near the back of the crammed and untidy shop. He looked through the drawers as Morris watched on, and eventually he found a battered ledger. He opened it and flipped through the pages.

'Have you found it yet?' Morris asked, pacing a little.

He looked up. 'Have a little patience, Inspector.'

'I don't get these people,' Morris said and gave a sharp exhale. 'They want to unburden themselves of their guilt, but they also expect us to treat them like victims and give them a hug. Don't they realise they can't have their cake and eat it?'

Radford stopped reading the names and addresses, the irritation biting at the back of his mind. He tried to resist the urge, but could not fight it. 'They cannot eat their cake and have it too.'

'Sorry?'

Radford sighed and pinched his nose. 'That is the correct expression you're looking for.'

'No. I meant you can't have your cake and eat it.'

'Yes, you can. You can have your cake and eat it. But you cannot eat your cake and have it. You cannot have it both ways. The expression has been so horribly misquoted over hundreds of years that it now doesn't make logical sense…'

'Have your cake and eat it,' Morris said, looking up towards the ceiling. 'You can't eat your cake and have it. Oh, yeah, makes sense.'

'It's how they caught the Unabomber. He

wrote a manifesto, but he tried to come across as a not-so-educated man. Unfortunately, he used the correct expression, something only an educated man would use, giving himself away. Ah, here we are.'

Morris came over and joined him as he looked down the page and found an entry for Sue Bishopp.

'Sue Bishopp?' Morris said, straightening up. 'With two 'ps'. Is that even a thing?'

'I believe it is. Right, we have her address. We'd better get a move on.'

Sue Bishopp's home turned out to be a two-bedroom flat in Fairfield, just off Charmouth Road. The building was a beige block with a brown roof and balconies. Radford picked the lock to the top floor flat, then they went into a compact, tidy flat with all the signs of comfort that a middle-aged woman might need. There was a flowery reclining armchair, a matching sofa and a large TV. Women's magazines and crossword books were neatly stacked in a unit by the armchair. Morris looked around the place, looking out for some signs of a struggle but saw none. Everything was neat, the bed made. There were photos of other adults smiling with small children, but Sue Bishopp didn't seem to be in any of them.

'Look at this,' Radford called from the front room.

Morris found him as he was looking through a cupboard in the kitchen. He was holding a pack of photos, most of which seemed to be of beaches and sunsets.

'The Isles of Scilly,' he said, sounding victorious.

'Where did you find those?'

'Strangely, tucked at the back, along with tins of fruit that were gathering dust.'

Morris picked up the small stack of photos and started going through them, each one a shot of the beach or some other view of the islands. Then she saw some taken on a boat, in which Wells and Bartlett were also travelling.

'Look,' Morris said. 'Wells and Bartlett, on a boat that Sue was on.'

'They probably didn't even know she was there.' Radford sighed, then turned to look at the photos again. 'Lay them out. Put them on the work surface and let's take a closer look.'

Morris did as requested, even though she was unsure of what exactly he was expecting to see. When they were all laid out, Radford started peering at each one. Then he stopped and looked at Morris, his eyebrows raised.

'What have you found?'

'Look at this one, taken in some pub, I think.' Radford passed her the photograph. 'Look at the girl in the background.'

The photograph was of Mayfield, Wells and Bartlett all smiling at the camera as they were sitting at a table mid-meal, a couple of the party raising their wine glasses. Morris focused in on the background where she could see the darkened entrance to the pub and a young woman walking past. Morris looked at him. 'Is that her? Is that Anna Bajorek?'

'Let us find out,' Radford said and brought up the image of the missing girl on his phone. 'Yes. It's her. What do you think?'

Morris looked from his phone to the photo, then nodded, realising that it was the same girl. But she also noticed someone on the other side of her, although they were obscured by one of the pillars in the pub. 'She's with someone.'

Radford nodded. 'She is. Anna Bajorek was reported missing by her family back in Poland. I've checked and her immediate family are all still in Poland.'

'A boyfriend?'

'They say she didn't have one and was rather shy.'

'Could that be Farah beside her?'

'It's possible, although I did find out that Farah arrived at the island only a day before the fateful night. We need to check when these photos were taken. Take them with you and let's collect any photos the victims had and, of course, any belonging to our potential victims.'

'You know they are going to have to release them soon while this is all investigated? The team dealing with this will be coming here to ask them all questions.'

'Good.' Radford straightened his tie and then seemed to examine the flat once more.

'Good? They'll be out there, wandering around…'

'I doubt that very much. They'll probably be at home. Wells and Bartlett will probably… how do they say? Shack up together?'

She gave a laugh, a bubble of a question rising to her mouth, unable to hold it in any longer. 'I'm sorry, but I have to ask…'

Radford raised his eyebrows as he stared at her. 'What do you have to ask?'

'The way you sound when you talk… I love it, don't get me wrong, but you sound like you come from the Victorian age or something. I don't mean to offend.'

'I'm not offended.'

'OK. I take it you were sent to some boarding school…'

'No. A comprehensive in North London. If you want to hear what my accent used to be, then watch Eastenders.'

'But how come you sound like this now?'

'I decided to teach myself to talk properly.' Radford started examining the piles of magazines.

'Why?'

He looked at her blankly. 'I don't remember why.'

'OK. Weren't your parents a little…

confused?'

'At first, but they soon grew accustomed to my new accent, or rather lack of one.'

Morris smiled and shook her head as she started to collect the photographs together. 'You are a very interesting and surprising person, DCI Radford.'

'Am I?'

She turned and saw he genuinely looked perplexed. 'Yes, you are. You might be the most interesting person I've met for… well, a long time.'

Radford straightened up. 'What about you, Morris?'

'What about me?'

'What is the chain of events that led you here?'

Immediately she regretted having given her new boss the third degree, as she definitely didn't like having anyone interrogate her. 'There was nothing major. My dad was a policeman down here, after leaving the navy. I followed in his footsteps, went off to train and then came back home. That's it really.'

'In my experience, that is rarely just that.'

She shrugged. 'Well, I must be the exception, because I've led a pretty boring life… well, until now. Right then, shall we get these snapshots back to the station?'

'Yes, but first we have to visit James Headley at the Lyme Hotel and find out where he was when the murders were committed.'

She could hear the sea growing louder, the crash of the waves echoing around the interior of the barn. She could smell the seaweed, the salt in the air and that horrible scent of long-dead fish. She had been thinking the entire time her captor was gone, her mind rushing this way and that with blind panic. Then her mind drifted, focusing on the others, the cowards who hadn't listened to her when she tried to get them to call the police. The poor girl. She felt sick and rage bubbled up in her. It hadn't just been the death of the girl that had made her hate them so; it was the way they dismissed her or didn't seem to see her. She didn't feel ashamed in the slightest when she came to the conclusion that they deserved to die.

The door behind her opened and the footsteps came closer. Out of the corner of her eye, she saw him moving, just a dark hooded shape. Then he moved again and walked out in front of her, his mask still in place as he opened a bottle of water. He came closer, pulled the gag down and held the bottle to her lips, so she started to drink. After a few gulps, he took the bottle away.

'Are you hungry?' he asked. 'Chicken sandwich all right?'

She nodded, even though she didn't have any appetite, but she knew she needed to eat. It was a good sign too, wasn't it, that he was feeding her? She told herself that it was, that if he wanted to kill her then he would have done it already. Her captor opened the sandwich, broke off pieces, and held them out for her to eat. This went on for a while until she shook her head as he offered her another piece.

As he went to walk away, she said, 'I can help you.'

He stopped and looked at her. 'Help me how?'

'I can...' She panicked, her mind running in every direction. 'I can tell you all about them... I can make sure you know how you can get hold of them...'

'I already know all about them. I've been watching you all for a long time and none of you knew. It would have been so easy to kill you when I first arrived, but I wanted to take my time, learn everything about all of you.'

'There must be something I can do. I can... what if after you let me go, I help you to trap them?'

'The police have them.' He kept staring but she could see he was thinking about it. 'But they'll have to let them go while they investigate.'

She nodded. 'What if I went to them and arranged something, like a dinner party or... I don't know...'

'They don't know you're alive. Why would they come to your dinner party?'

She didn't know what to say. For one thing, he was right, they didn't know she existed and the ones who might, didn't even care. She hated them all, and the more she thought about it, the more she found herself fantasising that they might all die.

'But,' he said. 'Now you're missing, they probably do know you're alive. I've put you on the map.'

She tried to smile.

'What do you say?' His voice became strained.

'Thank... thank you.'

'If I let you go, you'd go straight to the police.'

She shook her head. 'I wouldn't. I don't want what we did getting out, do I? I won't go to the police, I swear. Please, you've got to trust me. I hate them too. What they did, the way they wouldn't listen to me... I tried to get them to do the right thing. But they're not good people...'

'No, they're not. They deserve to die.'

She nodded.

'Say it,' he said, staring into her eyes. There was something familiar about his eyes.

'They do. They all deserve to die.'

He nodded. 'OK, I'll let you go.'

Her heart pounded, partly with hope, partly with fear that he might be toying with her. 'Really?'

'Yes.' He stepped closer and stared deep into

her eyes with a look that made her want to run and scream. 'But listen to me. Pay attention. Because if you betray me, if you go and tell the police what you know, then I'll kill you. I'm one of you, I'll be close, close enough…'

He reached into his pocket and brought out a long thin knife. 'Close enough to gut you before anyone blinks. Do you understand?'

'I do. But the police will talk to me, they'll ask me questions.'

He raised the knife and brushed it gently against her neck. 'Then you lie and make it convincing. Tell them you were in a shed like this, but you don't know where. You begged for your life and then I let you go. You don't know why. It'll confuse them.'

'OK, I'll tell them that.'

He kept staring for a moment before he walked around behind her. She began to shake. He had lied and now he was going to stab her or cut her throat. A bag went over her head, too thick for her to see anything.

'When the time is right, I'll contact you. Understand?'

She nodded, trembling all over.

'Good. Time to go.'

CHAPTER FIFTEEN

The Lyme Hotel was more of a restaurant than it was a place of accommodation, Radford realised as they walked down the damp, glistening streets through the centre of the town as the wind tried to blow them back the way they had come. The hotel was a whitewashed building with black timber beams. Its bottom floor was made up of a fish and chip shop and a restaurant called The Lyme. It was the top two floors that housed all the rooms to rent.

'Headley is just about the last of the newcomers who arrived in the past three years,' Morris said as she opened the glass doors of the entrance and let Radford into the small reception area.

'Well, I'm sure one of them is our killer,' Radford said as he took a long stride to the dark wooden reception desk where a curly-haired brunette woman, decked out in a grey trouser suit, was standing with a bright welcoming smile.

'Welcome to the Lyme Hotel,' she said looking at them both. 'Are you wanting the restaurant or the hotel?'

'Neither,' Radford said and watched as the Inspector showed her warrant card. 'We'd like to talk to the owner, Mr Headley.'

The woman lost her smile. 'Oh, I see, well, he's away at the moment. He'll be back in a week's time.'

'Where's he gone?' Morris asked.

'That, I don't know,' the receptionist said. 'He just sent an email saying he was going on holiday and would be back in two weeks.'

'Does he usually notify you by email?' Radford asked.

'No, actually he doesn't. He'd usually have a little meeting with me first, you know, have a handover. I did think it was unusual…'

'I think he might be in danger,' Radford said. 'Where does he live?'

The woman stared for a moment, open-mouthed at Radford before she said, 'In danger? Really? Oh, God. He's got a house in Charmouth but most of the time he stays in his apartment here.'

'We'll need to have a look,' Morris said.

The woman looked unsure as she opened a

drawer and took out a set of keys. 'I'm not sure Mr Headley would want me to let you in there…'

'The man is in peril,' Radford said. 'There may be something in his room that helps us stop him from being murdered. We can wait for a search warrant but it could be too late. Do you want to be responsible for his death?'

The woman shook her head as she pushed the keys across the desk. 'Maybe I should show you the way?'

'Very well.'

'In peril?' Morris asked as they walked behind the receptionist along a red-carpeted corridor on the top floor of the hotel. She was still trying to come to terms with Radford's strange olde-worlde speech. At least now she knew what it would be like to hang around with Shakespeare.

'Yes, in peril.' There was no hint of humour in his face. 'What have I said?'

'Nothing. I just would have gone for in danger or something like that. But it's fine.'

'Here we are,' the receptionist said, trying to smile as she reached the last white door in the corridor. Her smile seemed to wither as she started to unlock the door and then paused with her hand on the handle. 'I'm not likely to get in trouble, am I? I don't want to lose my job.'

Morris smiled at her reassuringly as she gently nudged her out of the way. 'It'll be fine. It's on our backs, not yours.'

Morris pulled on some gloves before pushing the door open. She stepped into a narrow magnolia-painted hallway that had an archway at the end of it. Beyond the arch was a large lounge area that had a wall of glass at the end and a beautiful view of the wild and stormy sea. There was expensive, antique furniture dotted around the room and a writing desk near the windows, on which sat a laptop. To her right, Morris saw an open doorway to a large bathroom and an equally sized bedroom. Everything looked neat.

'Is this the home of a sociopath with a vendetta?' Morris asked as she turned to see Radford walking in, his hawk-like eyes taking everything in. Then she had a strange thought; was she Watson to his Sherlock Holmes? And wasn't Watson supposed to be stupid?

'What is the matter?' Radford asked, staring at her. 'You have a very peculiar look on your face. Let's get searching.'

'What are we looking for?'

'Anything that points to James Headley being our killer.' Radford went into the bedroom for a moment then came back and stood in the doorway. 'Did the receptionist say Headley lives here most of the time?'

'I did!' a muffled voice called from the doorway before the receptionist's head appeared. 'He never really stays at his house. He should sell it really, I think.'

'All his clothes seem to be here,' Radford said. 'At least there doesn't seem to be any missing.'

'There isn't?' The receptionist hurried through the apartment and disappeared into the bedroom. When she came out, she looked at Morris. 'He's right. That's very strange.'

'We need to check he's not at his house,' Radford said. 'Please write the address down and my colleague will send some uniforms there to look for him.'

While the receptionist grabbed a piece of paper and a pen, Morris started looking at the books on the shelves and through any drawers she found. She pulled one out and saw some photo albums and a few letters. The first album she opened had a few holiday snaps in, taken at some beach in a hot country by the looks, she decided. Then she stopped dead when she reached the next photo which was of a man who she took to be James Headly. He had his arm around a young woman. A familiar-looking young woman. She turned around and showed the photo to the receptionist. 'Is this James Headley?'

The receptionist took a closer look at the photo. 'Yes, that's him. I don't know who she is.'

'Radford,' Morris said, dragging him away from his examination of the room. She handed him the photograph and watched as he examined it. 'Isn't that the victim, Anna

Bajorek?'

He nodded. 'It seems to be. James Headley knew her.'

'He must be our killer.'

'You think Mr Headley killed someone?' The receptionist's eyes opened wide as her head shook. 'You must be mistaken. Mr Headley wouldn't kill anyone.'

Radford lowered the photograph and looked at the woman. 'Apart from his other home, does Mr Headley own any other properties? Perhaps somewhere remote?'

The receptionist stared off towards the windows and the wild sea beyond as she said, 'The only place I can think of that he owns is this old boatshed thing down the coast a couple of miles. He used to rent it out to some local artists so they could exhibit and sell their work, but not lately I don't think.'

Morris turned to Radford and saw his eyes were ignited.

'I think we should take a look at this boatshed,' Radford said. 'Could you please give us directions?'

By the time Inspector Morris had driven along the coastal road, going higher and around towards where the old boatshed was located, the rain, wind and mist had wrapped itself around Dorset and was refusing to let go. The road ahead of them was darkened by storm clouds that had come in low and brought the hammering rain. The mist seemed to be rolling in, cutting off their view of anything further along the road.

'I can't see a thing,' Morris said, leaning over the steering wheel and staring out at the road. A little way behind them was an incident response car with two uniforms inside it. Radford's theory was that James Headley might just be the killer and his boatshed could be where he took some of his victims. He looked across the cliffs and saw the sea raging and huge sprays of foam shooting up from the rocks. He shuddered a little and turned back to look at the road blanketed by a thick mist.

'Stop!' he shouted and Morris stepped on the brakes and swerved away from the figure that had appeared out of the mist and was standing in the middle of the road.

Radford opened the door and climbed out, the rain and wind digging into his skin as he stared at the woman in the sodden clothes, her wet hair stuck to her face.

'Mrs Bishopp?' Radford called as the rain lashed at his face.

She nodded, staggering slightly as the strong wind shoved her.

'Where is he?' Radford hurried towards her as he heard the incident response pull in behind them.

She turned and pointed along the road. 'He… he kept me in a shed, or some kind of…'

'A boatshed?' Radford asked as Morris climbed out and came over.

Mrs Bishopp nodded. 'I think so.'

'Is he still there?'

'I think... yes, I think so.'

Radford turned towards the uniforms who were climbing out of their car as the rain and wind hammered them. 'Take Mrs Bishopp to the police station!'

One of the uniforms hurried to Sue Bishopp and started to help her towards the incident response car. Radford climbed back into their car and watched Morris join him and start the engine again and take it along the misty road.

'Where is this boatshed?' Morris said driving slowly and looking towards the wild sea below them. Then Radford saw something, a dark stone shape below them where the sea raged and spat foam high into the air.

'Stop!' Radford called out as he saw a short and steep path to their left. When Morris had slammed on the brakes, Radford pushed open the door and rushed out of the car and towards the path as the wild rain pelted his face and body while the wind tried to stop his progress. He fought on and jogged down the path. At the end of the path, he saw a set of ragged stone steps that travelled down to the building and the sea that roared and clawed at the land, seeming determined to drag everything into its icy and tumultuous lap. He froze as his heart started to pound and the sweat turned to ice along his sides. He felt dizzy as he tried to take another step closer. Even from there, he felt the salty spray in the air.

'What are you doing?' Morris shouted behind him.

'I don't think I can move!' he called back.

'Let me pass then!' Morris elbowed him out of the way as she tried to get past him on the narrow steps. Radford's pulse pounded in his ears as he tried to get a grip and not fall to the wild sea below.

Then he saw Morris taking the rocky steps two at a time and almost disappearing into the mist.

'Morris!' he called out. 'Wait for me!'

His legs didn't move, even though he told himself that the sea wasn't that close, that there was a little land and the boatshed between him and certain death.

'Come on, Philip Radford,' he said to himself. 'It's not the Cobb. It's merely some steps.'

His leg moved, his foot hitting the next slippery step as the sea crashed down on itself and the boatshed. He took another step and another. His heart quietened a little and he found he could move more easily.

He froze when he saw a dark figure rush away from the boatshed and disappear into the mist. It didn't look like Morris.

'Morris!' Radford called out as he forced

himself down the steps until he was standing close to the boatshed and watching the sea through the blanket of mist. The figure had gone to his left, so he followed, hurrying over the rocks, his shoes slipping and sliding as he went. There was another set of rocky steps that faded into the grey above him. There was nowhere for the killer to have gone apart from upwards, so he reached the steps and started to climb. He clasped at the earth and roots that protruded from the cliff to steady himself as he reached the top. He scrambled up and stood up on the grass and searched the horizon as far as the darkening sky and the mist would allow. Then he saw something or someone through the curtains of fog. Someone was standing a hundred yards ahead, not moving, as if they were frozen to the spot.

'You!' Radford called out. The mist had parted slightly, and he saw the figure wearing a dark hooded coat. 'There's nowhere for you to go! I know you want revenge, but this is not the way.'

The figure seemed to turn a little as if he might be listening. Then he burst into a run again and headed into the rain and mist. Radford gave chase into the cloud of mist that enveloped him. There came a roaring sound and he realised that the sea was rampaging not far below. When the mist lifted a little, he could see he was a hundred yards from the edge of the cliff and just ahead was the man again, standing with his back to Radford. It seemed he was waiting for him to catch up, wanting him to give chase, but Radford found he was welded to the spot. He couldn't move. The sight of the sea so close filled him with a terrible sense of dread.

To his side, he heard a cry and turned to see Inspector Morris running past, calling for the man to stop. But the figure didn't, he ran on towards the cliff, vanishing into the mist.

Radford was left alone, listening to the roar of the angry sea, the rain pelting him mercilessly.

'Morris?!' he called out, his heart racing again. 'Are you there?'

Then he saw a dark figure against the wave of sea mist that drifted towards him. Someone was coming. He tried to move his legs, but they were stuck. The figure was getting closer, running towards him.

'Morris?'

The inspector broke out of the mist and stopped in front of Radford as she panted for breath. 'He's... gone.'

'Gone? Where?'

'Off the cliff, I think. He was there one second, then gone.'

CHAPTER SIXTEEN

Radford was wrapped up in a thick police jacket that Inspector Morris had found in the boot of her car. He was standing by the old boatshed, watching the sea charging at him, seeming to get closer with every crash of the waves. The seagulls were screaming a little way above him as they headed inland. They were not stupid, he thought as he moved out of the way for the SOCOs who had arrived and were carrying equipment carefully down the slippery steps behind him.

More of the forensic team was around the corner, wading in the water while a police diver searched for whoever had run away from him and Morris before diving off the cliff. He took a couple of steps closer to the water but soon retreated in a panic when the waves roared in.

'You can do it,' the familiar voice said behind him.

Radford turned and saw Carr, smiling as always. 'I don't think I can.'

'I was referring to the case. You can solve it. Don't doubt yourself, Radford.'

'Supposedly our killer is dead.'

Carr looked over at the water. 'Is it ever that straightforward?'

'No, never. Do you think the killer is still out there?'

She laughed. 'Do *you* think the killer is still out there? That's what's important.'

'Excuse me!' Another SOCO appeared, coming down the steps carrying a metal case. Carr had vanished.

When the SOCO entered the boatshed, Morris slipped out and came over to him.

'Why don't you go and sit in the car and put the heaters on?'

Radford looked out to the raging sea. 'I'm waiting to see if the divers retrieve a body.'

'I saw him go,' she said, looking at him like a mother trying to placate a child. 'He just…went.'

He nodded. 'So you say. But I want to know who it was.'

'Our killer, that's who. It's over. He killed the others out of revenge, and then, when he realised we'd caught up with him he… well, he jumped.'

'But don't you want to know who the killer was?'

She nodded. 'Of course. But it could take them a while, if they find the body at all. Come on, let's get back up to the car. Don't forget we need to talk to Sue Bishopp and get her side of the story.'

Radford looked behind him at the ragged steps. In all the excitement he had forgotten about the poor woman who had been held captive by their killer, just like the others had easily forgotten about her. He didn't feel guilt, as his mind didn't allow him to fixate on that little detail and urged him on to the big question.

'Why did he let her go?' Radford said aloud as they started up the steps.

'I don't know. She's the only one who tried to talk sense to them, so perhaps that's why he let her go? I have no idea, but in a while, you can ask her.'

'He's dead?' Chief Superintendent Parsons said, eyebrows almost jumping off her forehead as she sat back in her chair. Radford was pacing the room a little which Morris was finding rather distracting as she sat and briefed her boss.

'We just got the call from the search team,' Morris said. 'They found a body caught on the rocks. It's in a right state, but they found his ID on him. It appears it was James Headley. Luckily, he wasn't washed away.'

'Headley?' Parsons sat up, shaking her head. 'I've known him for a few years... well, not that well, but he always seemed… well, OK and not a psychopath.'

'He's not a psychopath,' Radford said as he stopped his pacing. 'He was exacting revenge. He had a motive, he was not randomly killing strangers. And psychopaths are rarely killers, not unless they have suffered abuse or…'

'OK, OK,' Parsons held up her hands. 'That's fine, Radford, but what I want to know is, was James Headley the killer, because if he was, then he's the bastard who murdered Adrian!'

Morris had momentarily forgotten how deep things ran for Parsons and found herself feeling sorry for her superior officer when she saw tears in her eyes. 'Yes, he was…'

'I don't know.'

Parsons and Morris stared over at him.

'What?' Parsons said as she wiped her eyes. 'What do you mean you don't know? Was he or was he not?'

'He ran out of the boatshed when we turned up!' Morris said, looking at Radford, hardly able to believe what she was hearing. 'And he happened to be away, conveniently, and there's the photo…'

'What photo?' Parsons looked between them.

Morris sat back. 'We found a photo of Headley with Anna Bajorek, the Polish girl who died on the Isles of Scilly. We don't know what their relationship was, but it looks like we've got a motive.'

'I'm not convinced,' Radford said as he pinched the bridge of his nose.

'Why?' Morris stood up, getting a little angry with him for the first time as she started to realise why people found him disagreeable. 'I chased him and he ran and jumped off the cliff! Why would he do that if he wasn't guilty?'

Radford stared at her, a strange lost look in his eyes. 'I don't know.'

'Well, let's talk to Sue Bishopp and see what she knows, then Dr Shaw will perform the post-mortem and then we can make up our mind.'

Morris waited for PC Galston to open the interview room door, then took the tray of coffees inside. Well, it was two coffees and one water, because, of course, Radford didn't drink coffee or tea like any normal person.

Sue Bishopp was sitting opposite Radford, fidgeting and looking generally worried. Radford was sitting upright, arms folded, staring accusingly at her.

'Here's your coffee,' Morris said, smiling and putting Sue's mug of coffee next to her. Perhaps Radford was being the bad cop, so she decided to be extra nice as she took a seat.

'Thank you,' Mrs Bishopp said as she wrapped her hands around the mug. 'I need something to warm me up. Might treat myself to a brandy later.'

'James Headley,' Radford said, his voice quite rigid.

'I'm sorry,' Sue said, looking perplexed. 'What about him?'

'Do you know him?' Radford asked.

'Well, I know of him. He owns the Lyme Hotel... what's he got to do... oh no, he's not been... you know?'

'He's dead.' Radford stared at her.

Morris leaned towards her. 'Don't worry, Sue, just drink your coffee. We just need to ask you a few questions and get things straight, that's all. Just procedure.'

She nodded and tried to smile.

'He jumped off a cliff, not long after we found you on the road,' Radford said. 'Very conveniently.'

'I don't understand.' Mrs Bishopp stared at Morris. 'He grabbed me outside my home and drugs me or something and I wake up in this... this barn thing...'

'What did he say to you?' Morris asked. 'I know you've been through a lot, but if you can try and remember anything he said...'

'You did little to help that young woman,' Radford said. 'Anna Bajorek. The young woman that none of you protected...'

'I tried!' Bishopp said, tears appearing in her eyes. 'I begged them to call the police! But they never listen, they just pretend I'm not there. What could have I done?'

'Nothing,' Morris said and patted her hand. 'We understand. Is that why he let you go?'

Bishopp nodded as she sipped her coffee. 'Yes, I told him how I begged and begged them to call the police, but it was like I was invisible.'

'They have never seen you, have they?' Radford asked. 'They will never see you. How does that feel?'

For a moment, Sue Bishopp stared back at him, her face reddening with what seemed to be embarrassment, her mouth opening a little. 'I've always had to just... well, put up with it.'

'But perhaps you no longer could put up with it.'

Sue looked at Morris, her eyes wide. 'What's he mean? I don't know...'

'It's OK,' Morris said. 'We just need to get to the bottom of it all, and seeing as you were one of his intended victims...'

'He just let me go, that's all.' She looked from Morris to Radford and back again. 'I don't know why. He must've... just... felt sorry for me. I don't know. Am I in trouble?'

There came a knock on the door and it opened to reveal Chief Superintendent Parsons, her face set in an expression of annoyance. 'Sue, you're free to go.'

'We have not yet completed our line of...' Radford started to say.

'Yes, you have.' Parsons walked up to the desk and folded her arms as she stared down at

Radford. 'I've been watching on the monitor. Sue is a victim in all this, not a suspect. The killer, James Headley is dead. He killed himself instead of facing justice. End of story. Everything you've got will be handed over to the coroner. Now, I'm going to take Mrs Bishopp home. Come on, Sue, let's go.'

When the two women had left, Morris said, 'You were pretty hard on her.'

'And you, Morris, practically dipped her in treacle.'

'I thought we were doing good cop, bad cop. Weren't we?'

Radford got to his feet. 'No, I definitely was not. Don't you find it strange that our killer, who has ruthlessly slaughtered all his victims so far, suddenly decides to let Sue Bishopp go?'

Morris shrugged. 'I don't know, perhaps he thought she'd suffered enough what with them lot ignoring her all these years.'

Radford sighed and shook his head. 'Something is not right here.'

Morris stood up. 'Well, Headley is dead. So, the murders should stop, shouldn't they?'

Radford looked at her. 'In theory, yes, they should. I think we should put a surveillance team on all three of them.'

'The Chief Super will never agree to that.'

'Yes, I think you're right. I'll have to do it myself.'

'But Wells and Bartlett are in one house, and

Jones, the landlord is staying God knows where.'

Radford sighed, then hurried out of the room and along the corridor until he caught up with Parsons and Sue Bishopp as they headed for the stairwell.

'Mrs Bishopp!' Radford called out as Morris caught up.

Parsons turned on him, her pissed-off look stamped on her face. 'Don't you dare, Radford...'

'I just need to ask her something,' he said. 'Who else knew Headley well? Who were his friends or associates?'

Bishopp stared at him and then sighed. 'I guess... Freddie Wells... and the one who runs the paper... can't think of his name.'

'Nathan Sharpe?' Morris asked.

Bishopp nodded. 'That's him. They hung around together, I think.'

Radford turned to Morris. 'We should go and talk to the both of them.'

CHAPTER SEVENTEEN

Radford and Morris came out of the wind and rain that was still mercilessly attacking the streets of Lyme Regis and stepped inside the offices of the local paper. Radford spotted the figure of Nathan Sharpe standing at one of the small desks near the back of a long narrow room. The journalist seemed to be busy talking to a young female reporter before he looked up and saw Radford and Morris and nodded. After a moment, he left the reporter and came smiling towards them.

'I take it you've come to give me an exclusive?' Sharpe asked as he looked between them.

'No, not yet,' Radford said. 'We came to ask you some questions.'

'About what? I've just heard that you may

have caught your killer?'

'Not quite,' Morris said. 'He's dead. At least we think the killer's dead.'

'You think he's dead?' Sharpe narrowed his eyes as he looked between them. 'That's not much of a quote. What do you mean?'

'We cannot discuss the finer points of this investigation,' Radford said, 'but as I said, we have a few questions for you.'

The journalist rested his backside on one of the desks and folded his arms. 'All right. Go ahead. What do you want to know?'

'How well do you know James Headley?' Morris asked, staring intently at him.

'Headley?' Sharpe frowned. 'Jim? Quite well. A few of us get together now and then and have a few drinks and put the world to rights. We even play poker occasionally. Why are you asking about Headley? Does he have something to do with all this?'

'Has he ever mentioned Anna Bajorek?' Radford asked and watched the journalist's reaction but saw only confusion.

'Wait a minute,' Sharpe said and shook his head. 'Now I'm wondering if you think Headley was the killer and whether he knew Bajorek or was related to her or something.'

'Did he know her?' Morris asked.

Sharpe shrugged. 'I don't know. I don't think so. I don't think he ever mentioned her. But Headley? Really? A crazed killer?'

Radford took out the photo they had found at Headley's home and showed Sharpe. The journalist took it and examined it. He looked up suddenly. 'Jesus. I've seen this before. We were at his place, at the hotel, I mean. He showed me this photo… he said it was a girl he'd met or that she had worked for him or something. I can't remember, but he'd said they'd had a relationship. This is the missing girl, isn't it?'

'Headley and this girl had some involvement?' Radford asked, taking back the photo and ignoring his question.

'I think so.' Then Sharpe pointed at Radford as his face darkened. 'But you're wrong if you think Headley's the one who's been murdering these people. There's no way.'

'I didn't say he has,' Radford said. 'Please, no mention of this in your paper.'

'No. But I want an exclusive, remember?'

Radford nodded. 'I remember. You'll get it. Come on, Morris, we need to go to the post mortem and then we need to pay a visit to Mr Wells.'

Mrs Bartlett walked through the darkened main corridor of the old house, the scent of freshly burnt wood still thick in the air as she went and stood in the doorway to the long and wide kitchen. Freddie had told her the place used to be a baker's a long time ago. The walls were bare stone and at the centre of the wall to her right, below the thick and protruding chimney stack, were the remains of a bulky old oven. Freddie was at the hob of the modern oven he'd had installed as he made their lunch. The rain battered the thin strip of windows that ran along the top of the entire room.

'Do you think we'll hear anything soon?' she asked.

Freddie looked at her, then tilted his head and gave her the same sympathetic look he'd been giving her since the whole business had begun. 'Try not to worry, Lynn,' he said and sighed. 'I told you, I've already talked to my barrister friend, Jack, and he reckons they don't have a leg to stand on. It wasn't us who killed the poor girl and they've got no living witnesses to say we had anything to do with disposing of her body.'

'But what about the fact that we all sat in that cottage and spilt our guts about what happened?'

Wells stepped over to her and gently held her shoulders. 'Calm down, Lynn. I talked to him about that and he said we weren't under caution and that the confession was made under false circumstances. It wouldn't stand up in court.'

She sighed. 'You said there aren't any living witnesses, but there are, aren't there?'

He let go of her as he frowned. 'Who?'

'Us. If any of us start telling tales, then we're stuffed.'

'Well, it's me, you and that awful publican, but we're not about to talk, are we?'

'What about thingy? What's her name?'

Wells shook his head, blankly.

'You know, the woman with those awful dresses.'

'Oh, God, yes, I'd forgotten about her. We'll have to make sure… what is her name?'

'I don't know.'

'Well, whoever she is, we'll have a word with her and make sure she doesn't talk.'

The doorbell rang and they both froze, their eyes fixing on each other with wide stares.

'Who's that?' Bartlett asked.

'How should I know?'

'Are you expecting anyone?' She turned and looked along the narrow hallway and towards the front door.

'No, and I take it you aren't either?' Wells stepped around her and towards the hallway.

'Of course not. We need a weapon, just in case.'

Wells raised his eyebrows as he turned back to her. 'A weapon?'

Bartlett looked around the kitchen then spied a heavy wooden rolling pin, picked it up and handed it to Wells.

'Oh, thank you, I don't think.' Wells huffed then carried on down the hallway towards the front door, holding the rolling pin as if it was on fire. Bartlett followed him and as they got close to the porch, she thought she could see the silhouette of someone standing on the front steps through the stained-glass window that surrounded the front door. To her, it looked like a rather plump woman.

'It's a woman,' Bartlett said.

'Are you sure?'

'I can see them through the glass. Go on, see who it is.'

'It might be the murderer.'

'The murderer isn't a woman, is it?'

'How do you know?'

'The murderer cut someone's head off. Women killers don't do that.'

Wells let out a breath as he approached the door again, reaching out for the door handle. 'I hope you're right.'

He pulled it open and stared at whoever was standing there. Bartlett nudged him out of the way and looked past him and at the plump woman who was wrapped up in a waterproof coat spotted with rain, the hood drawn tight around her round, red, blotchy face.

'Hello?' Wells said. 'Can I help you?'

'It's her,' Bartlett whispered and elbowed him.

'Ouch. Who're you talking about?'

'Her. The one with those… dresses.'

Wells nodded and turned to smile at the woman who was still standing in the wind and rain, being pushed sideways.

'I'm sorry, I didn't recognise you,' Wells said. 'In your… coat. Come in, come in.'

The plump woman came into the house, smiling awkwardly as she unzipped her coat and took down the hood. Bartlett watched her as she looked around, seeming a little startled. All the time she examined the woman, she struggled to recall her name.

'So, nice to see you,' Wells said and held out his hand to her.

She took his hand after a little hesitation and then said, 'Sue.'

'Yes, of course, Sue,' Wells said and let go of her hand.

'Sue Bishopp. With two P's.' The woman smiled at them both in turn but Bartlett noticed she looked ill at ease and she guessed why.

'Is it true?' Bartlett asked. 'Did he really kidnap you?'

Sue nodded. 'He did. It was… awful.'

Bartlett grabbed Sue's damp coat and stripped it off her before hanging it up and guiding her to the front room. 'Make a cup of tea, Freddie,' Bartlett said as she sat the plump woman on the sofa, noting that she was wearing one of her frumpy dresses. 'How do you take your tea, Sue?'

'Milk, no sugar.'

Bartlett turned to Wells as he was standing in the doorway. 'Better put a couple of sugars in it, Freddie. I hear it helps with shock.'

Once Wells had vanished into the kitchen, Bartlett turned back to Sue and smiled at her, all the time her mind was drumming up questions. There was one particular question that kept rising to her mouth but she thought it best to keep it back. 'So, what happened?'

The woman looked down and took a breath. 'He must've been waiting outside my house. I always leave by the side entrance, where the alleyway is. He must've been waiting there…'

'Where did he take you?'

'To some old… shed…'

'You must have been terrified. You poor thing.'

'It was… it was very scary…'

'Here we go,' Wells said, bringing in a mug of tea. He handed it to the woman and stood by the sofa, smiling at her. 'Three sugars. Well, what an ordeal, Sandra.'

'Sue.' Bartlett glared at him.

'Sorry, yes, Sue.' Wells nodded. 'So, I wonder why he let you go? Why didn't he kill you like he did the others?'

Sue looked down at her mug of tea. 'I don't know. I just… I just begged him to let me go…'

'And he just let you go?' Wells asked, shaking his head. 'Why? I don't understand why…'

'What happened to him?' Bartlett asked. 'You got away, that much we heard, but what happened to the killer?'

Sue looked up. 'He's dead. He ran from the police… he must have got confused in all the fog and ran off the cliff.'

'Oh my God.' Bartlett put her hand over her mouth. 'So… so it's over? I wonder who it was.'

'James Headley.' Sue looked at them both, seeming to watch their reactions.

'Headley?' Wells said and let out an incredulous laugh. 'Jim? That's ridiculous. Jim wouldn't do anything like that…'

'He's dead,' Sue said and sipped her tea.

Wells looked at Bartlett and she stared back at him, both wearing the look of absolute confusion and doubt.

'But why?' Bartlett asked. 'I thought this was to do with that Polish girl? Did James know her?'

She had looked up at Freddie but he just looked at her blankly, lost in thought as he slightly shook his head. 'I don't think so. He never said anything…'

'But he wouldn't, would he?' Sue said. 'I mean, if he had moved here to get revenge for what… happened to her, then he wouldn't say anything, would he?'

They both looked at her, nodding in agreement. She was right, of course, Bartlett agreed. They had been fooled by him all this time while he waited to strike. She shivered a little at how close she had been to him all that time.

'I'm sorry,' Sue said as her cheeks grew red.

'But can I use your toilet?'

'Oh, right, yes,' Wells said, then turned towards the passageway. 'There's a set of stairs near the kitchen. It's at the top, you can't miss it.'

Bartlett watched the red-faced, plump woman get up awkwardly then waddle her way towards the passageway and disappear. She followed the sound of her heavy steps until she heard a door open and shut somewhere above.

'Why the hell did he let her live?' Bartlett said and jumped to her feet as she jabbed a finger at the low ceiling.

Wells put a finger to his lips. 'Quiet. She'll hear you, Lynn.'

Bartlett lowered her voice as she said, 'Why didn't he kill her? Why the others and not her? I'm sorry, but she's nothing special, is she?'

'Lynn!' Wells sighed and shook his head. 'Let's just be glad that it's over… although I still can't get my head around it being Headley. Jim Headley? Really?'

Lynn sat back down and let out a sigh. 'Let's not delve too deeply into a madman's mind. He's dead and that's an end to it.'

'We will go tandem as man and wife, Daisy, Daisy,' Morris could hear Dr Shaw singing somewhere in the autopsy room. *'Pedalling away down the road of life. I and Daisy Bell.'*

When they stepped into the long, lime-tiled room that had shining sinks and tables in each corner, she saw Dr Shaw, decked out in scrubs, leaning over a blue-ish body on the autopsy table. His eyes jumped to them and he grinned.

'I was just getting better acquainted with Mr Headley here,' Shaw said and straightened up.

'The conversation must be a bit one-sided,' Morris said and saw Radford step in and look down at the remains of their suspect.

'Au contraire,' Shaw said. 'Mr Headley still has plenty to say, don't you?'

'Is any of it relevant?' Radford asked, lifting his eyes from the body.

'It's all relevant,' the doctor said. 'For instance, Headley tells me that he did fall to his death. He's sustained subdural haemorrhages, skull fractures, and cerebral contusions. Not only that but there are also upper and lower limb fractures, pelvic and spine injuries all in line with a fall from a great height.'

'So he did run and fall from that cliff?' Morris asked.

'Yes and no,' Dr Shaw said and raised his eyebrows.

'What do you mean?' Radford asked. 'Did he fall or not?'

'He fell, but at least three days before he was found at the bottom of the cliff. And as far as I know, dead men don't run off cliffs.'

Radford looked at Morris, his eyes widening. 'Our killer is not dead, Morris.'

She shook her head. 'Then he must have run

up the steps and into the fog…He must have had the body there waiting.'

'Or he had already dropped it from the cliff.' Radford paced the room for a moment, then he turned and stared at Morris. 'Has Parsons already pulled the protection from Freddie Wells' house?'

'She has. There wasn't that much anyway, just the occasional…'

'We have to go,' Radford said, his voice tight as he made for the door. 'Thank you, Dr Shaw.'

Morris hurried after him, moving up a few gears to keep up with his long stride.

'The killer's still out there, isn't he?' she asked as they headed for the exit through a pair of double doors and then onto the lifts.

Radford reached the bank of lifts first and impatiently pressed the call button. 'Yes, I believe he is. Wells and Bartlett are in serious danger.'

'I'll call them and then try and get some uniforms over there.'

'Good.'

Morris let out a deep sigh. 'No signal. Shit.'

The lift pinged, then opened, and they both stepped in.

'He couldn't have known we would turn up like that,' Morris said as she watched the numbers above the doors.

'He was using Headley's boatshed. He must have known we would put two and two together eventually. He must have had Headley locked up for the past few days and then killed him before we got close and threw him off the cliff.'

'What about the photo of him and Anna Bajorek?'

Radford pinched the bridge of his nose. 'I'm not sure. Perhaps Headley did know her and the killer used that information to put us off the scent. Right now, we need to find Wells and Bartlett.'

Lynn Bartlett stared at Sue's mug of tea that was growing cold, then looked up towards the ceiling before she turned to face Wells who was staring at his phone. 'Where is she?'

Wells blinked up at her. 'I'm sorry, what?'

'Where is she? She went to the toilet ten minutes ago.'

'Sandra?'

'Sue. Jesus, Freddie.'

'Sorry. She looks like a Sandra.' He put his phone away and shrugged. 'She's probably having trouble up there.'

'Go and find out.'

Wells pointed a thumb at himself, his eyes widening. 'Me? I can't just go and ask. You go.'

'It's your house, Freddie. Go on, just go up the stairs and call her.'

Freddie shook his head and let out an unimpressed sigh before he went out into the hall. Bartlett heard him call out from the bottom of the stairs. At least he called out the right name this time, she thought. Then she heard the distant creak of the wooden steps as he went up, still calling out her name. After a while, she heard his footsteps return and Wells came back into the lounge looking perplexed.

'She's not up there,' he said.

'What?' Bartlett sat up. 'Where would she be? She must be up there.'

'I'm telling you, Lynn, she's not up there. Anyway, I better check the lunch.'

Lynn watched him head out of the lounge before she got up and tried to work out where the badly dressed, plump woman had gone. Then she thought of Sue's coat, hanging on the hook by the porch. She went to the porch and there it was, her coat where it had been hung up. She turned and faced the kitchen. 'Freddie!'

There was no answer.

'Freddie? Her coat's still here.' She listened out, but no reply came.

She headed to the kitchen and found the door open. She could hear the food bubbling away, but she couldn't see Freddie.

'Are you there?' she asked and went in and froze when her eyes fixed on Sue, holding a rolling pin. Then her eyes fell to Freddie who was lying still on the tiled kitchen floor.

'Freddie?' Anger and confusion burned through her as she looked up. 'What the hell've you done?'

'I'm...sorry.'

There was no time to move as Sue swung

the rolling pin.

The pain came in a sharp, blinding flash, and her skull rattled in her head.

Then the darkness came as she fell to her knees, close to Freddie.

CHAPTER EIGHTEEN

Two incident response cars turned up just after Morris drove her and Radford to Freddie Wells' house, which was tucked away at the end of a woody lane. It opened up to a small driveway with the old, unloved house behind it. It would have looked quite grand and picturesque at one time, but now the brickwork was crumbling and the paint was peeling from the window frames. A round sign to the right of the door read: Baker's Dozen. Beyond the house a thunderhead cloud hung heavy over the horizon, bringing a slight drizzle with the promise of another storm.

'Looks quiet here,' Morris said as they both climbed out and started towards the small cube-like porch that seemed tacked on as an afterthought.

The uniforms joined them, their radios

beeping and crackling. Morris pressed the doorbell but there was no sound or movement from inside.

'I have a bad feeling about this,' Radford said.

She stared at him. 'Are you quoting Star Wars?'

Radford stared back at her. 'No, don't be ridiculous. We need to get inside.'

'We need a warrant or reasonable suspicion.'

'Our killer, who we thought was dead, is very much alive, Morris, and seeing as he plans to murder the two people who are living in this house…'

Morris held up a hand. 'I get you. Franklyn, Mayhead, get the door open.'

Morris and Radford stepped out of the way as one of the uniforms brought a small, red battering ram towards the porch door and swung it at the lock. The door cracked open and hit the inner wall of the porch. The battering ram was used a second time and swung against the front door. It took two attempts before it sprang open and creaked into the hallway.

Morris went past the uniforms as she took out her Casco baton and flicked it to full length. She stepped inside, sensing Radford's bird-like shape following her.

'Freddie Wells?' she called out. 'Lynn Bartlett? It's Inspector Morris. Are you home?'

There came only silence and the creak of their steps as they went further along the hall. Morris saw the living area and went towards it, watching each corner for movement as her heart turned its beating up a few gears. The room was tidy with nothing on the coffee table.

'No one's home,' Morris said as Radford stood beside her.

'Upstairs?' he said, looking up.

Morris looked up above her and saw the bannisters crossing her vision, and the metal chandelier hanging high above her. 'Freddie Wells? Lynn Bartlett? It's the police.'

There came no reply, just the sounds of the two uniforms clattering around in the hallway and living room. Radford headed along the hall towards the back of the house. Morris followed him with her eyes and saw him push open a battered wooden door. As she followed him, she could see the pots and pans of a kitchen. It was a large room with a long table at one end and a proper wood-burning oven at the centre of the far wall. The whole place smelt of burning wood.

Morris stopped when she saw Radford had become frozen to the spot.

'Radford, what is it?' she asked.

He turned his head to look at her as he said, 'We need forensics here.'

Morris passed by him and stared at the floor where there were spatters of blood. A rolling pin lay on the ground, also stained with blood.

Morris came over to Radford with a takeaway tea that one of the constables had fetched along with some other drinks and snacks. She held it out to him, but he just stared at it as he rested against their car, a light rain hitting his face and suit.

'No, thank you,' he said, keeping his watch on the SOCOs.

'It's tea,' she said.

'I don't drink tea. Or coffee, for that matter.'

'It's hot.' She kept holding it out to him.

'So is molten magma, but I don't pour that down my throat either.'

'I know you're my boss now, but is it still OK to say you're very weird?'

He shrugged. 'It's fine. You are not the first. Anyway, I won't be your boss for long.'

'Really? Why?'

'Because after this investigation is concluded, I'll be moving on.'

'To where?'

He faced her. 'That I do not know.'

'It's nice here usually. The weather's usually better. There's lots of nice beaches, the people are lovely… when they're not murdering each other.'

'Do you work for the Lyme Regis tourist board?'

She laughed. 'Yes. Come to sunny Dorset.'

He looked away. 'There were no signs of forced entry, were there?'

'No. Not that I saw. I checked upstairs and

downstairs.'

'They let the person in. They knew whoever came knocking at the door out of the heavy rain we had an hour or so ago.' He looked at Morris.

'How do you know someone came to the door when it was raining heavily?'

'There was a puddle of water by the door, where the coat hooks are. But there is no damp coat, just an empty spot.'

'Clever. But we know the killer is one of the locals. But who? Headley's dead.'

'Yes, he is.' Radford took out the photograph they had retrieved from James Headley's apartment. 'We need to examine this photograph more carefully and take a look at his other home.'

'OK. What're we looking for?'

'The original of this.' Radford held up the photo. 'Do you notice that someone's been cut out of the photo?'

Morris took it and saw the arm of another person. 'I noticed that before but... do you think they're the killer?'

'I do not know. But we need to find the original and see who they are. Also, we need to find Jones, the landlord. He's in danger.'

'But no one knows where he is.' Then Morris had a thought. 'Hang on, we've been assuming that the killer is the boyfriend or family of Anna Bajorek, but what if it's one of the people who were there that night?'

'And their motive?'

Morris shrugged as she scratched around in her brain for an answer. 'I don't know... they hate the others for what they did... they feel guilt and want to punish them all, or something like that. Or maybe one of them knew her already and now they're taking revenge.'

'It's possible, but doubtful. But I think we should talk to Mrs Bishopp again, in case she knows something. I do get the feeling that she's holding something back. Let's go.'

Morris watched Radford climb in the passenger seat, so got in herself and started the engine. 'Parsons won't like us talking to Sue Bishopp.'

'No, she will not, that's why we're going to go and see her without informing her.'

Morris was about to put the car into first, then she looked at Radford and saw how calm and unaffected he was by everything that was happening. Even the mess left in his wake would do little to gain his attention, but she would suffer the consequences.

'I know you're thinking of leaving after this,' she said as she drove them away.

'I am leaving.'

'Well, remember that I'm staying and that I have to deal with the aftermath.'

Radford looked at her. 'I'll try and keep it in mind.'

'Thanks.'

There was a pounding coming from somewhere, a deep pulsing thud from inside the blackness. It ached to think, to try and open his eyes. Freddie Wells blinked into the light burning down at him. The harsh light made his head throb even more. He tried to move his hands and found they were secured behind his back. He looked around in a slow-building panic, his chest pounding out a wild beat as he tried to sit up. He was tied to a chair. He turned his head, even though it hurt to move.

His eyes widened to see Lynn tied to a chair next to him, her head flopped forward, her hair usually so neat and styled, now tangled and messy.

'Lynn,' he whispered. 'Lynn? Lynn? Are you all right?'

She didn't move, but he noticed that her chest rose and fell. She was alive. He let out a shaky breath as he took in the large, dusty room that had pieces of furniture scattered around. There was a bright spotlight positioned across the room and focused on them. His mind travelled back in time to the moment he found Sue Bishopp in the kitchen. She was going through the drawers as if she were searching for something. He asked her what she was looking for and she spun round as if she had been caught stealing. Then someone had hit him from behind. Sue had been there with someone else.

She must have let them in, he realised and turned to look at Lynn.

'Lynn?' he said, raising his voice a little. He could hear the wind whistling above in the rafters. Rain tapped at the windows. 'Lynn? It was Sue. She must have let him in. It's not Headley. I knew it couldn't be Headley. Lynn? Wake up, Lynn, please.'

He was about to call louder to her when he heard a sound from somewhere in the building. It was a creak, coming from above. He stared upwards and listened out for the noise. He swallowed as his heart thumped and the sound of it filled the blood that burned in his ears.

'Lynn?'

She was still out of it. He tried to pull his hands free again but they remained firmly tied together. Oh God, he thought, please don't let me die.

'I'm sorry,' he said out loud. 'I'm sorry we didn't call the police.'

Lynn moaned.

'Lynn?' He watched as her head moved. 'Lynn? Wake up. Please.'

But she stopped making any noise as her head fell forward again. He felt a desperate sob fill his chest, but he swallowed it down as he looked around the room for something that might help him get free.

His eyes shot up to the dark ceiling again as he thought he heard the noise once more.

The same creak. It sounded like a footstep above him. Someone was up there. His body trembled as a coldness swept over him. Whoever had attacked them and brought them to the house or whatever it was, was upstairs somewhere. There came another creak. Then another. Someone was walking above, moving around the building.

'Lynn?' he whispered, half looking towards her, and looking towards the door the rest of the time. 'Lynn? Please, wake up.'

Her head moved again and she let out a groan.

'Lynn? Lynn, for God's sake, wake up.'

Her head lifted and she blinked as she made a pained expression. Her make-up was smeared, her mascara smudged around her eyes.

'Lynn?'

She coughed and took in a harsh breath, her eyes closing again. 'My head. Oh God, my head hurts.'

'We're in trouble, Lynn. It was her, that woman. Sandra.'

Lynn lifted her head, taking in their surroundings. 'Sue. Her name's Sue.'

'I don't give a shit what her name is. She must have let him in.'

'Where are we?'

'I don't know. But there's someone upstairs. I've heard them moving around.'

Lynn turned her head, tears appearing in her eyes, looking around in desperation. 'He's going to kill us, isn't he? Like he killed all the others. I don't want to die…'

'You can't think like that, Lynn.' Wells pulled at the ropes that had his hands fastened behind him. 'We'll get out. We just need to find something…'

She turned to him, her eyes wet as her tangled hair fell over her face. 'What? What can we find? There's nothing here! It's no good. We're being punished…'

He watched as her head fell forward, and sobbing began.

'Lynn? Lynn? Look at me. We're going to find a way out of this. Listen to me…'

'We didn't do anything to help her.'

'No, Lynn, don't talk like that. Please.'

She looked up, her eyes red and swollen and lacking in fight. 'We should have called the police. We should have listened to her.'

'Who? Sandra?'

'Oh, my God!' Lynn let her head fall back, a strange strangled laugh pouring out of her. 'No wonder she did this. We never listened to her, never saw her. You can't even get her name right.'

Wells looked away from her and towards the door, as he realised she had already given up. The sound came again, the creaking footstep sound as it moved through the house. Lynn was sobbing harder, making it difficult for him to hear and follow the steps. They were getting louder.

'Shhh,' he said to her but it had no effect. 'Lynn, please be quiet. I can hear someone coming.'

At last, she sniffed and pulled back her tears as she stared towards the door. The room was quiet except for the creaking sounds that grew louder. Whoever was in the house, was coming towards them slowly. Wells followed the steps until he heard someone behind the door to the room.

'It's him,' Lynn said, visibly trembling. 'He's going to kill us.'

Wells shook his head, his heart had already started to throb in his chest and pump hot blood into his ears. He gave another few tugs of the ropes that held his hands tight together but there still wasn't any give. His head shot up when the door creaked. Lynn let out a gasp as the door started to open. The spotlight beaming down disallowed a clear image of whoever was standing in the doorway. All he could make out was a hazy shape that moved side to side a little.

'Please!' Lynn suddenly burst out. 'We didn't kill her. It wasn't us.'

'But you didn't help her, either,' a woman's shaky voice said.

The person moved across the room and came to rest between them. It was the woman who wore the awful flowery dresses. Sandra. No... Sue. *Get her name right.* That's what this was about, it must be, some kind of revenge for ignoring her all this time. He'd never meant to hurt her feelings, she was just so... forgettable. But now he could make her feel seen.

'Sue,' he said and smiled. 'Thank God it's you.'

She stared at him, her eyes quite blank. Then she stepped closer. 'You know my name?'

'Of course. Sue, can you untie us? Please?'

'Please, Sue?' Lynn said, her voice hoarse.

She looked between them, searching their faces. 'The thing is, you only know who I am because now you need me. You didn't even remember I was there that night. Did you?'

Wells swallowed and took a shaky breath. 'Of course, we remember... and we should have listened to you.'

'What did I say to you?' Sue stared at Wells as she brought her hand out from behind her back. The kitchen knife glinted as she clenched it tighter.

Wells tried to shuffle the chair backwards as she came towards him, her face flushed.

'What did I say that night?' she asked and he heard a sound deep in her voice that made his heart ripple into a wild beat. The knife came up close to his neck.

'Sue, please lower the knife,' he said.

'This is not you, Sue,' Lynn said, the tears now all gone from her voice. 'You're not a bad person...'

'No!' Sue's eyes widened as she lurched at

Lynn and pointed a thumb at herself. 'No! I'm not a bad person. I've always tried to do good, to be kind. But you lot, you're... you're... ugly inside. All you care about is how people see you. But now everyone knows what you are. Don't they?'

Wells tried to keep his voice steady as he said, 'Yes, they do, Sue. They know. And we'll have to live with that. We'll go to the police and make a confession...'

'They won't do anything! They never did anything back then. Why would they now? I can't live with that any more. I've been haunted by that night ever since. I've never had a proper night's sleep. But you lot probably forgot all about her, put her out of your mind, the way you put me out of your minds.'

'Listen, Sue,' Wells started to say, but Sue grasped her own face with one hand as if she meant to tear it off. 'Shut up! Shut up! Shut up!'

Then she took a few breaths and glared at them. 'This is the only way to put things right. He's going to come back and when he does, he'll... he'll deliver justice. Justice for Anna Bajorek. Justice for Anna Bajorek. Justice for Anna Bajorek!'

Wells looked at Lynn and she returned his look of horror, the tears returning to her eyes.

Radford had the photograph in his hand as they reached James Headley's other home, which was a white three-bedroom Victorian house in

Charmouth, on the west side of the village. It had a white-painted iron fence running along the tiny front garden.

Morris got out of the car but Radford stayed where he was, observing the building, as if by merely staring at it, some clue might magically appear and help him solve the case. He sighed, wondering where the killer would have taken Bartlett and Wells as he climbed out and stretched. The truth of the matter was that they didn't have long to find them.

The grey front door was already open, and Radford could hear the sound of the police officers going up and down the stairs and across to the different rooms. He still held the photo of Anna Bajorek cuddled up next to James Headley, both of them smiling. Half of someone was missing. Was it the killer? He moved into the house and straight toward the kitchen, which had shiny white units and dark woodwork surfaces. He looked down at the photo again, then closed his eyes as he tried to run it through his brain and make sense of it all.

He heard heavy footsteps coming down the stairs and turned to see Morris carrying a box in her gloved hands. Her eyebrows were raised as she put the heavy box on the work surface.

'Photos,' she said. 'Lots of photos.'

Radford put down the photo he had been carrying around, then looked into the box as he pulled on some gloves. 'Then let us begin.'

'It might not even be here,' Morris said as she started taking out some thick albums, and then some pouches of photos.

'But it might.'

'Who prints out photos these days? Mine are all on my laptop or my phone.'

Radford looked up at her. 'I do. I have mine all in order too. I organise them by date…'

'Of course you do… boss.' She rolled her eyes, he noticed but he continued to examine the many photographs contained in the box.

'This is going to take a while,' Morris said as she started flipping through pictures.

'Call the uniforms down and get them to help.'

'Good idea.' Morris put down the photos she had been looking through and headed for the stairs.

Radford sighed, looking at all the photos still in the box. He pushed aside the ones on the counter to make room as he heard Morris upstairs talking to the uniforms.

Then hurried steps came down the stairs before Morris appeared, a photo frame in her gloved hands and her eyes wide. 'You're not going to believe this!'

Morris turned the frame around and showed him that it was almost the same photograph, only larger and containing more people. There was a crowd of people tucked into the corner of what looked like a pub. Anna

Bajorek was cuddled up to James Headley and on the other side of her was the missing man. Radford didn't recognise him.

'Who is the man next to Anna Bajorek?' Radford asked.

'I don't know. The killer?'

'But it has to be a local.'

She shrugged. 'Does it? Maybe we've had this all wrong. We thought it was a local, but maybe we were wrong.'

Radford shook his head, then took the photo frame from her hands and opened it up. He took out the photo and examined the back. There was writing on the back, the careful neat print of someone who had written, "The gang, London, 2018".

Morris looked over his shoulder. 'Well, then Anna Bajorek worked with Headley in London and they had a relationship…'

'And what? Headley is dead. Someone threw him off that cliff because he knew the truth about the photograph.'

'But what is the truth?'

Radford examined the photo, running his eyes over the crowd of people on the right side of the picture that had been cut off in the other version. Some were further back, the image quite grainy. Radford looked up at Morris. 'I think the killer is here somewhere. It's the right side that was cut off in the image we have. Perhaps the killer planted the other photo we found at

Headley's flat so we would think he was the killer.'

'You could be right. Do you recognise any of them?' Morris took the photograph from him. 'It's hard to see them.'

'Get the uniforms down here. Let's see if there's any more photos of that night. Because I'm certain our killer was there.'

CHAPTER NINETEEN

'Sue?' Wells called out, causing Lynn's head to jerk up and her eyes open. She had fallen asleep and he had felt a little jealous that she could sleep through the hellish situation they were in. At some point, Sue had walked out, leaving them alone. A door had shut somewhere and he was convinced they were alone. There were no more sounds, no creaking floorboards above them. One thing he was sure of after talking to Sue was that her anger hid her fear. She was so terrified that the killer might come for her that she decided to join him.

'What's it called when a hostage starts to identify with their captor?' Wells asked and looked at Lynn.

Her eyes had closed again. She opened them but didn't look his way. All the pain and fear was dug deep into her face. 'Stockholm Syndrome.'

He nodded. 'That's what she's got. Stockholm Syndrome.'

'She's a crazy bitch.' Lynn turned and stared back into his eyes. There were no tears now, only determination and anger. 'We need to get one of us free, and when she comes, that person jumps on her.'

'What if *he* comes?'

'He? What if there is no he? What if it's been her all along? She's angry and crazy because we never noticed her. She's just using this as an excuse to get back at us...'

They both looked towards the door when there came a noise that rippled through the house. Then there were footsteps, the creak of the floorboards. Wells swallowed hard, his whole body tensing. The door handle rattled, followed by a slow, eerie creak as it opened.

He took in a harsh breath when he saw that it was not the frumpy, pear shape of Sue standing in the doorway, but the taller, broader shape of a man. He stepped closer and that's when Wells saw the white mask he was wearing and the hood that framed it. He said nothing, just stood looking at them through the blank eyeholes.

Lynn started to sob.

'We know why you're doing this,' Wells said. 'We're so sorry. We're sorry about what happened to Anna...'

Wells nearly toppled backwards as the killer

tore at him and grasped his face in his gloved hand. His fingers dug into his jaw as the killer's mask came closer.

'Don't you ever dare to say her name!' the killer said in a growl.

Wells shook his head. The killer let go and stood back, his head turning back and forth between them.

'Look at you,' he said. 'Pathetic. Weak. You've spent your lives thinking only about yourselves. Me, me, me. All you had to do was protect a young, defenceless girl…'

'We didn't know…' Wells started to say, then stopped when the masked man put a finger to his lips.

'You have to be quiet and let me think,' the killer said. 'I need to decide which one.'

Wells looked at Lynn and saw her eyes fill with tears as she trembled. 'Which one?'

'Which one dies next.' The killer turned, taking them both in. 'It's not like I can flip a coin, leave it up to fate. No, wait. That's what you did, didn't you? You left fate to decide what happened to Anna. My poor Anna. Well, let's let fate decide, shall we?'

'Please, listen…' Wells said but the killer was already moving his finger back and forth as he sang, 'Eeny meeny miny mo, catch a tiger by the toe, if he squeals let him go, eeny meeny miny…'

The killer pointed to Wells. '…mo.'

Wells struggled again, pushing his chair

back as the killer pulled out a clear plastic bag and stretched it wide, moving quickly towards him.

In the end, Radford decided it would be best to bring all the photographs to the station. They would be laid out on a table in the incident room for some of the uniforms to go through.

He stood at the head of the table, staring at the small team as they went to work. Morris and DS Scott were there too, both hurriedly going through the packs of photos. Occasionally he saw Morris looking up at him.

'Is there a problem, Morris?' he asked.

'Well, you know you could join in, don't you?' she said, raising her eyebrows at him.

'My father used to say, why have a dog and bark yourself.'

Every one of the uniforms, and DS Scott, popped their heads up and stared at Radford, none of them looking very pleased.

'You're not comparing us to dogs, are you?' Morris' eyes blazed at him.

He looked over all their faces, sensing that the comparison to dogs was going to be an issue. His mind scrambled about for the appropriate answer. 'The drinks will be on me later. Fifty pounds for the person who finds the photograph first.'

He breathed a sigh of relief when the scowls became smiles and they went back to work.

'I hope you're not bribing my people, Radford.'

He turned to see Parsons standing a little way behind him, her eyebrows raised.

'I wouldn't dream of it,' he said. 'Just trying to motivate them.'

Parsons stood next to him, her narrowed eyes taking in all the photos before she looked at him and said, 'Why have you got them going through someone's holiday snaps?'

'We are trying to find the killer,' Radford said. 'Before he executes Lynn Bartlett and Freddie Wells.'

'What? But I thought the killer was dead. Wasn't it James Headley?'

'No, ma'am,' Morris said, looking up from her stack of photos. 'The pathologist said he'd been dead at least three days before we found him.'

'So who fell off the cliff?' Parsons looked between them.

'It was an illusion,' Radford said. 'Morris saw the killer run into the mist ahead of her. Then a shape disappeared off the edge. All the killer had to do was throw something off into the sea. Headley's body was already there, caught on the rocks. The body was meant to put us off momentarily while he snatched Wells and Bartlett.'

Parsons rubbed her eyes as she sighed. 'So, he's managed to get hold of two more potential victims. We're not doing very well, are we?'

'We need to find another photo like the one we found at James Headley's house. If there's more than one photo taken in the pub in London…'

'Pub? What pub? You know what? Never mind. Just do what you're doing and catch the killer. Let me know when you do.'

As she was about to walk away, Radford said, 'I have another request.'

'Go on.'

'We need to bring in Sue Bishopp.'

He watched as her eyes closed and another heavy sigh escaped her lips. 'Can't you leave the poor woman alone, Radford? Hasn't she been through enough?'

'Why did he let her go? He ruthlessly kills the rest, but lets her go. A man with revenge at his heart would not just let her go.'

'You think she's in danger?'

'I'm not sure. But I think we should bring her here.'

Parsons puffed out her cheeks. 'Fine. Bring her here, but no interrogations. Got it?'

He nodded, then watched her walk off.

'No interrogations?' Morris repeated. 'What's the point of bringing her in?'

'She said no interrogations. She did not say no friendly chats.'

'Crafty. Well, still no photo.'

'Keep looking. He must know he's running

out of time so we need…'

'Radford!' Parson's voice rang out and he heard some urgency within it. He turned and saw her short frame and pinched face coming at him. Something bad had happened.

'We've got another body,' she said to him. 'It was found in Anthony Jones' pub of all places.'

Morris stood up. 'Jones is dead?'

Parsons shook her head. 'No. Apparently, it's Freddie Wells. You two had better go and take a look.'

The uniforms had already set up a cordon around the Lyme Inn which sat at the top of the hill, overlooking the gardens and the rest of the town. It was a large, white-washed block building with black timber framing it. Now the place was swarming with uniforms and SOCOs that had finally arrived from Bournemouth. Radford drank from a bottle of water as he was huddled in his coat, the wind tugging at his hair. The storm cloud was hanging low over the whole of Lyme Regis, seeming to push down and smother it. He thought he heard a rumble of thunder in the distance as he ran through everything that had happened. He was missing something and he sensed it was all in the missing photograph, if there even was one.

'Are you coming in?' Morris said as she snuck up on him.

'Is he still in there?'

'He is,' she said and started up the pavement and towards the door of the pub where one of the uniforms held the crime scene log. Morris put on some gloves and overshoes after she signed in, then disappeared inside. Radford followed her lead and went in after her. The large bar area was glaringly bright with spotlights beaming in from the corners. One of the SOCOs was already taking photos of the body, which Radford hadn't concentrated on yet.

'Poor Freddie Wells,' Morris said as she knelt by the body.

Radford looked down and saw the clear bag and the blue face beneath it that was staring up at him. Even from there, he could see the petechiae in his eyes. There was a ligature as well, a cable tied around his neck. Radford straightened up and looked around the pub, noting the usual dark wood bar at the back and the toilets to its right. Then he noticed something as he turned. There were two framed photographs on the wall opposite the body. He stepped closer, eyeing them all the time as they came into focus. He let out a harsh breath when he saw a framed photo taken from the same bunch they had been examining. It was the night in the London pub, with Anna Bajorek, James Headley and various other people he didn't recognise. 'Morris, he's been watching us.'

'What?' Morris walked over as Radford pointed to the two framed photographs.

'Look at the photo. Taken in the same London pub. These have been hung recently. He knew we must have been looking for this. He knew we would see the photos in Headley's house and put two and two together. He's here somewhere.'

'Look at the other photo,' Morris said, shaking her head.

Radford stared at it. It was a shot of all of them, all the Isles of Scilly cast, taken on the harbour, most smiling, oblivious to what was coming for them. The killer had drawn a red cross through each of their faces. Only Anthony Jones and Lynn Bartlett remained.

'He's taunting us,' Radford said. 'Drawing us in. He knows that he'll be caught but he's trying to finish his mission before we catch him. Three left.'

'Two left, isn't there?'

'I don't think he'll let Sue Bishopp live. He sees her as guilty as the others. He only let her go to confuse us, put us off the scent and use her.'

Morris scrutinised him. 'Use her for what?'

'For luring in Wells and Bartlett. I think it was her who came to Wells' house. They let her in and she let in the killer.'

'Sue? No, not Sue.'

'She's terrified and she'll do anything to live and she hates them all. Now we must go and find her and Anthony Jones.'

'Why did he leave Wells in Jones' pub?'

'Because he believes once Jones finds out what happened here, then he might put his head over the parapet. He's probably right. Ask the SOCOs to print and check these photos, although I doubt he's left anything for us.'

Radford was about to walk away when he saw one of the men in the photograph who was looking straight at the camera. He was a man in his late twenties, maybe early thirties. He had dark medium-length hair and a neat beard. There was something familiar about him, although he was too far back to get a good look at his face. 'Who is this?'

Morris took a look. 'I don't know. Could be anybody.'

'No, not anybody. He's the only one looking at the camera. He picked this photograph because he's looking directly at the camera. Not only the camera.'

'What do you mean?'

Radford stared at her. 'He's looking at us. Chances are, he's watching us now.'

Morris turned and raced out of the pub and Radford followed. Over on the other side of the road, all done up in warm coats, people had come to stare at the scene. Some of them had their phones out, pointing them at the pub.

'Check all those people, especially the ones with their phones out,' Radford said. 'He will be watching.'

'OK.' Morris went and started ordering

uniforms to interview some of the bystanders, while Radford looked down the town. There was another rumble of thunder as Radford wondered where the killer had Lynn Bartlett held captive. She was running out of time.

As he lit another fag and relaxed on the sofa, Anthony Jones tried not to hear the crackle of pop music his niece was playing in the kitchen. The TV was on, but he kept looking at the French windows beyond it where the sky had come down to wage war on the earth. He saw a flash and a little while later a rumble travelled up the sofa.

'Really getting bad out there, Rio!' he called out.

Rio, his frizzy blonde niece who was in her early forties, came tottering in and stood at the end of the sofa, frowning. 'You still lying there?'

'What else am I supposed to bloody do?'

She shrugged. 'I don't know. Just don't mess up my poor sofa. Anyway, when are you going back home?'

'Not any time soon, not when there's a nutter out there trying to knock me off.' He sat up and took a drag of his cigarette.

Rio sighed, then tutted. 'Well, Mike will be back from working away soon, and I don't want this place looking messy.'

'Isn't he on the rigs for another couple of weeks?'

'Yeah, well, that's pretty soon. Look, I just don't want him coming back to find your stinky socks all over the place.' Rio was about to speak but the musical jingle of her mobile sounded from the kitchen. She pointed a warning finger at him, then wandered off. He got up and stretched as the rain started hammering at the windows. Now there was a proper storm wrapping itself around the house. The thunder was now right overhead. He turned as he heard Rio's voice rising and falling with excitement. She was coming his way, the phone clenched to her ear as she chatted.

'Oh my God!' Rio said, engaging his eyes as her own widened. 'That's terrible… but exciting. Yeah, he's right here. I'll tell him.'

'Tell me what?'

'OK, Linda, yeah, talk later.' Rio hung up and let out a harsh breath. 'Well, what a turn-up.'

'What?'

'There's police all round your pub.'

'What? What's happened?'

'Well, Linda wasn't sure, but looks like maybe they found a dead body in there.'

'What?' Jones took the fag from his mouth with a trembling hand, scared to ask his next question. 'Whose body?'

'How would I know?' She tutted, rolling her eyes.

'Didn't the daft mare say?'

'Don't call my friend a daft mare. And no,

she didn't say, but she did say that Freddie Wells and Lynn Bartlett have gone missing.'

He could only stare at her for a moment while it all sunk in. Then he took another shaky drag of his cigarette as he thought about it all, knowing there was some sick bastard out there wanting his blood. He'd had enough. He went over to the ashtray, stubbed out his cigarette and then barged past Rio and went into the kitchen and started pulling out the drawers. If he was going back home, he'd go armed.

'What're you doing, you nutter?' Rio came in and stood staring at him.

He turned to her after he pulled the large kitchen knife out of the drawer. She shuffled backwards, horrified.

'What are you going to do with that?'

'Where's your tool bag?'

'My tool bag? Tony, what the hell're you thinking of?'

He ignored her and went straight to the cupboard under the stairs, where he knew he'd seen the tool bag. He went out into the hall and opened the first of the three doors. There it was on the back shelf. He dug his hand in and brought out a claw hammer. When he turned around, there was Rio, her eyes on him, obviously thinking he'd gone mad.

'I'm not being terrorised any more,' he said and looked for a bag to put them in. He dropped the items into a carrier bag and then grabbed his coat before he headed for the front door.

'Tony!' Rio called, but he didn't want to stay and hear it. His blood was up, his body shaking with anger as he went to his car and put the weapons in the boot. He climbed in and started his car, staring round at the street for a moment before he put the car into first and headed for Lyme Regis.

CHAPTER TWENTY

Radford's head sprung up when he saw Morris waving at him from across the road, beyond the police tape. The onlookers were dispersing as the storm picked up, with rain blowing up the street. Morris was standing with a woman wrapped up in a thick and bright pink parka, blonde hair poking out and being toyed with by the wind.

He crossed the road and slipped under the tape so he could stand close to Morris and the woman.

'What's occurred, Inspector?' Radford asked, noting the woman didn't look too happy.

'This is Linda Rickard,' Morris said. 'I happen to know that Linda is friends with Tony Jones and frequents this pub quite often. In fact, she used to work there, sometimes.'

'That's not a crime, is it?' the woman

groaned.

Radford pointed down the street. 'Why don't we get out of the wind and rain and go along to the cafe and I'll buy you a coffee or tea?'

The woman looked round, then shrugged. 'I suppose I've got time. If you throw in a pasty.'

Morris put Linda Rickard's latte in front of her and then sat down and sipped her cappuccino. Radford had declined a drink and was now sitting upright, his keen and watchful eyes on Linda as they all sat in the far corner of the busy cafe. With her big damp pink coat on the back of her chair, their potential witness now brushed strands of her bleach-blonde hair out of her face. She was mid-thirties, quite attractive and large-chested, which was the reason why Jones had put her to work in the pub, Morris remembered being told.

'Why's he staring at me like that?' Linda asked, leaning towards Morris.

'He's right there, Linda, you can ask him yourself.'

She stared at Radford. 'I know what he's doing. He's sizing me up, trying to work out what sort of person I am. He's staring at me and trying to unsettle me. It won't work.'

Radford leaned forward. 'No. I noticed that you have lipstick on your teeth and I was wondering whether I should tell you.'

'Have I?' Linda gritted her teeth, pulling her

red lips back as she turned to Morris.

She did. A red tooth. Trust Radford. 'You do. Here…'

Linda wiped at her tooth with the serviette Morris gave to her, then looked between them. 'Go on then, start your interrogation. Don't be shy.'

'Do you know where we might find Anthony Jones?' Radford asked.

Linda looked down as she sipped her coffee. 'No, no idea.'

Morris watched as Radford leaned back. 'Did you murder the man we just found in the public house across the street?'

Linda's head shot up as her coffee rattled against her saucer. Her eyes bulged. 'What? No, I had nothing to do with it. Why would I? I am a… a good person…'

Radford held up a hand. 'Please calm yourself, Mrs Rickard. That was simply a test.'

'A test?' Her eyes bulged again.

'A demonstration. You can tell a lot from the way a person answers a question. For example, when I asked if you know the whereabouts of Anthony Jones, you said, and I quote, "No, no idea". Not I have no idea or even no, I don't know. When I asked if you murdered the man in the pub, you said, "What? No, I had nothing to do with it. Why would I? I am a good person".'

'So?' Linda rolled her eyes at Morris, who hoped Radford was going somewhere.

'When they lie, people tend to forego the word I. For some reason, that letter falls out of their brains. It wasn't me. It had nothing to do with me. No, no idea. Do you understand what I'm saying?'

Linda huffed. 'Where's my pasty?'

Morris stood up and went up to the till and found the pasty waiting. She put it in front of Linda Rickard and sat down again.

Linda broke off a piece of the pasty, allowing a billow of steam to emerge from inside it. 'He's insinuating that I'm a liar.'

'No. I'm saying you lied just now. You know where Anthony Jones is.'

'Tony,' she said as she ate some of her pasty. 'Anthony makes him sound like he's posh or something. He's not. He's Tony, a right slob. But yeah, I know where he is.'

'Where?' Morris said. 'He's in danger. Whoever killed the man in that pub, wants to murder Tony. We need to know where he is so we can keep him safe.'

'He is safe,' she said and laughed. 'He's not here. End of story.'

Then the large pink coat started to ring, so Linda scrabbled around in the pockets until she pulled out a smartphone. 'Excuse me. Hi, Ri. Are you all right? What? Oh no, what a bleeding fool. Can't you get hold of him? Hang on, he took what?'

Morris noticed Linda's eyes jump to Radford

as she said, 'OK, better go. It's all right, I'll call you back.'

Linda put the phone away then sipped her coffee and smiled.

'Anthony is on his way here, isn't he, Linda?' Radford asked.

'No, course not. He'd have to be stupid to come back here.'

'But Anthony is stupid, is he not? Plus, he's probably upset and angry that someone was murdered in his pub.' Radford turned to Morris. 'We had better put a couple of cars on the major routes in here and try to intercept him.'

'You're going to protect him, aren't you?' Linda said as Radford stood up.

'Of course.'

Morris smiled apologetically to Linda then hurried out after him and caught up with him as he was standing on the street, glancing up and down.

'So, we intercept him and take him to the station or some safe house?' Morris asked.

Radford looked at her as if she had flashed her boobs at him. 'No. We're going to use him as bait. If he's stupid enough to return, then we might as well use it to our advantage.'

Morris hurried after him as he stormed on, taking his usual long strides as he moved towards the seafront and the wind and rain attacked them both. 'So that's our plan? Use Jones as bait? He could end up…'

Radford stopped and faced her, his usual calm eyes filled with what could be seen as anger or perhaps frustration.

'Have you got any better suggestions?' he asked, a definite edge to his usual calm voice.

She shook her head.

He nodded and started to move again, as he said, 'Then call in and make sure officers are waiting on all the routes into Lyme Regis.'

She took out her mobile. 'Where are you going now?'

'I have hardly slept in the last two days, and when I don't sleep, I cannot think straight.'

'You're going to sleep?' Morris tried to keep up as they turned along the promenade of Front Beach as the wind pushed around the sand that already covered the ground.

'I'm going to meditate.' He quickened his pace.

'Have you got any idea who the killer might be?'

He stopped dead again, so she stopped. He faced her, his skin now tight to his bones, his eyes dead again. 'Quite frankly, no. James Headley seemed a likely suspect but now we have none. Perhaps I was wrong and the killer has only been watching them from a distance. I'm not sure any more. Anyway, go to the station and organise the uniforms to catch Anthony Jones. Let me know when you do.'

Radford went to move on again, then

stopped and started to rifle through his pocket. He took out the photo they had found with the bearded man and held it out to her. 'Get someone in IT to see if they can enlarge this. Get them to try and identify the man with the beard. Now, Morris, I need to sleep.'

Morris was about to speak but he had already turned on the spot and stormed on. She was left alone on the promenade, the sand and rain battering her, wondering exactly what they were going to do next. Then her phone rang in her pocket, so she headed back to her car as she answered the call. 'Inspector Morris.'

'Hey, it's DS Scott,' the detective said. 'Thought I'd let you know that we've got Sue Bishopp here to be questioned again. Radford wanted to interview her again, didn't he?'

She turned and looked towards where the shack was, wondering if she should disturb him or not. He needed his sleep, he had said. 'He did. But he's indisposed. You and I can talk to her.'

'OK. Oh, and Nigel Oldroyd has turned up wanting to talk to someone. Think he's got some information but he only wants to talk to Radford.'

'He'll have to talk to me as well then. I'll be there soon. Oh, I nearly forgot, we need cars on the routes into Lyme Regis. Tell them to look out for Tony Jones and take him into custody.'

'Is he the killer?'

'No, but we need to get hold of him. Bye.' She

hung up, a panic rushing over her as she sped up her pace. She had no idea what to do next and she was starting to feel that Radford didn't either. They were lost and Jones seemed like the only bait they had.

Morris kept on moving, the wind now battering her, and the dark storm clouds even more ominous looking as they raced overhead. As she looked up and blinked into the rain, she saw a figure wrapped up in a dark raincoat. They were making a beeline for her, and it was only when the person was feet from her that she recognised Nathan Sharpe, the journalist.

'Inspector Morris,' he said, holding down his hood. 'Where's your partner in crime? I was hoping to catch him.'

'He's busy,' she said and started storming on. 'So am I.'

As Sharpe followed her along, he pulled out his phone and held it out to her. 'Can I get a quote on how the case is going?'

'No.' She hurried on, thinking, the photo burning a hole in her pocket as she kept imagining Jones on his way back to Lyme Regis. Her mind jumped back to the photo again as her eyes took in the nosey journalist still following her. She stopped dead and took it out. 'Look at this photo we found in Headley's house. You said you'd seen the other photo before that we found in his flat. Have you seen this one before?'

Sharpe looked quizzical as he took hold of

the photo and wiped off the drops of rain. He stared at it and nodded. 'I have. That's when he and some of his colleagues had a night out in a pub. Same as that other photo you found. Why? Is this important?'

The journalist pushed his phone in Morris' face again, so she lowered his hand. 'Like Radford said last time, when this case is over, then you get the exclusive. Now, take a good look at this photo, and see if you recognise anyone else.'

Sharpe gave her a suspicious look and then examined the photo again. 'I don't think so. Who am I looking for exactly?'

'What about the bearded guy near the back?'

Sharpe held the photo closer as the wind tried to rip it from his grasp. 'Sort of... familiar, I think. Are you thinking this is your killer?'

Morris snatched the photo back. 'I can't discuss that. And don't you go printing any of this.'

Sharpe sighed. 'Well, at least give me a quote or something. Anything.'

'We are pursuing lines of enquiry,' she said and then hurried on as she stuffed the photo back into her coat.

'That's it?'

'You'll get your exclusive!' she called out, her mindset now on interviewing Bishopp and Oldroyd. With or without Radford she was going to do her best to find out what they knew.

Radford shut the door to the shack, blocking out the rain and wind that fought to follow him inside. He then went to the windows and looked down Monmouth Beach where the sea charged and roared dangerously close to the mobile homes set almost within its grasp. He shook his head and turned to see the dark snake-like shape of the Cobb against the grey and wild waters. As he stared at the wall, a great fist of water punched into it, a plume of foam exploding high into the air. He shuddered. There were no figures on the Cobb, no one was mad enough to chance it that day.

'Where are you?' he said to himself. 'Where are you, Carr? I need you.'

'No, you don't.'

He turned and there she was, sitting on the sofa, radiant and pristine as ever. Her smile was as enigmatic as the Mona Lisa, he decided. 'I'm losing.'

'You never lose.'

He stepped closer. 'I might this time. I simply cannot figure out who the killer is.'

'Because your mind is clouded.'

'Is it? By what?'

She looked towards the windows. 'Look where you are. In the middle of a storm, close to the sea. Lyme Regis is a beautiful place, even when a storm is pounding at it, but is it the place for you? I used to visit here when I was a little girl.'

'Did you?'

She laughed. 'I'm in your head, Radford. I'm not real. Maybe I did. Or maybe Carr did, I should say. Maybe this is the problem. You're too wrapped up in what happened and you feel guilty over my death.'

He looked down, a wave of pain filling his chest.

She stood up and came towards him. 'You need to let me go. I'm not here. I'm ashes somewhere or six feet beneath the earth. I'm gone. But you're still here. You can do this. Just shut out the storm and concentrate. Lay down on the sofa and close your eyes.'

Radford did as she said, and closed his eyes, the rattle and patter of the rain in his ears. The shack sounded as if a giant hand was trying to pull off the roof. He closed down the sounds as he took deep calming breaths. In and out, slowly.

At some point, he fell deeply asleep.

DS Scott met Morris outside interview room one, a cup of hot tea in his hand, and a smile on his lips.

'Is that for me or Mrs Bishopp?' Morris asked.

Scott suddenly looked guilty. 'Oh, sorry, I didn't think...'

'It's OK,' she said. 'Let's just go and talk to Sue.'

'I thought you'd better do this one by yourself,' Scott said.

'Why?'

He shrugged. 'You know, woman to woman. She might open up to you.'

Morris stared at him. 'I'm sure there's probably something sexist in there or something, but I can't be bothered to care at the moment. Come on, just get in there and we'll ask her a few quick questions.'

Scott looked a bit awkward but nodded and opened the door for her. Morris went in and saw that Sue Bishopp was sitting back with her arms folded over her chest. Her face was red around the cheeks, her mouth tight shut.

Morris pulled out a chair for Scott before sitting down herself. 'Thank you for coming in, Mrs Bishopp. Can I call you Sue?'

'Is Chief Superintendent Parsons here?' Sue asked, her voice strained.

'No.'

Scott pushed her tea towards her, but she only stared at it briefly as she fidgeted and said, 'When will she be here?'

'Sue.' Morris leaned forward. 'I've got some bad news. Freddie Wells is dead.'

She nodded. 'I know.'

'You know?' Morris exchanged surprised glances with Scott. 'How do you know?'

She looked up briefly with a shrug. 'Heard someone say. You know what gossip's like.'

'When was the last time you saw Freddie Wells?'

Bishopp kept staring down at the desk. 'Can't remember. Not for a long while.'

'You must have seen him since the trip to the Isles of Scilly,' Morris said, trying to engage her eyes.

'I suppose.'

Morris took out Headley's pub photo and pushed it across the desk towards her. 'Have you seen this photo before, Sue?'

She raised her eyes and looked at it. 'No, I haven't. But that's… that's James Headley.'

'Do you recognise the girl?'

Sue nodded as tears filled her eyes. 'That's her, isn't it? That poor girl?'

'It is. Do you recognise anyone else in the photo? Could anyone there be living in Lyme Regis, Sue? Take a close look.'

Sue's red and teary eyes took in the photo. 'I don't think so.'

'No one there that was on the holiday with you all?'

Sue looked up, her eyes jumping to Scott. 'Why don't you ask him?'

Morris stared at DS Scott and saw his face had become a little red. 'What does she mean?'

Scott shrugged. 'I don't know.'

'He was there,' Sue said, nodding.

'You were in the Isles of Scilly?' Morris let out a harsh breath.

Scott looked at her. 'For one day. I went over on the morning ferry a couple of days after they went and came back in the afternoon. That's it.'

'Why didn't you mention this?'

Scott looked down. 'I wasn't there when this all happened, I never met the girl and no one else seemed to even remember I was there. Except Sue here.'

'No one sees you, do they?' Sue was staring at him intently, her eyes wide, making Scott lean back a bit.

Morris' head was spinning, not knowing what to do. What the hell would Radford do? 'How can I trust you now?'

Scott spun his head around to her. 'You can trust me. It's me, good old DS Scott. How long have we known each other?'

'A fair while, but what if you knew her?'

'Who?'

'The dead girl. Anna Bajorek. James Headley knew her. Why not you?'

Scott just stared at her, then shook his head. 'I didn't. I've never met her. I swear. I was there for one day and I wish I'd never gone. They were all miserable, hardly talking. Now I know why. Please, Morris, you've got to believe me. I'm not a murderer.'

Morris sighed, half believing him. She had known him long enough to get a good sense of him. He wasn't a killer. But then again, one of the people in the town was a cold-blooded killer walking around smiling and pretending to be just an average local. She looked away and faced Sue Bishopp again and saw her fidgeting with her dress. Then her head jumped up, her face red. She smiled. Why was she smiling?

Then something caught Morris' eye, something on the brightly coloured flowery dress she was wearing. She stared at what looked like a stain.

'What's that stain on your dress, Sue?' Morris asked, her tone sharpening.

'Just some ketchup or something,' she said quickly without even looking down.

Morris felt her temperature lower until it was icy. 'Is that blood?'

Bishopp laughed loudly but her eyes didn't join in. 'Oh, no, of course not. Blood? No, that's… ketchup or something.'

'Sue.' Morris leaned towards her. 'Were you there when Freddie Wells and Lynn Bartlett were taken?' She recalled Radford saying someone had arrived during the heavy rainfall.

Sue shook her head, but then the tears came as her body shuddered. She started mumbling through her tears, her voice rising until Morris could hear she was saying, 'I'm sorry, I'm sorry, I'm sorry…'

'Did you help kidnap them, Sue?'

She nodded. 'I'm sorry, I'm very sorry. He made me do it. He said I had to or he'll find me and kill me. He said he'd always be close by. What could I do?'

Morris sat back, her trembling breath escaping her open lips. 'Sue Bishopp, I'm arresting you on the suspicion of aiding and abetting in the kidnap and murder of Freddie Wells...'

'I'm sorry, I'm sorry!' Bishopp collapsed face-first onto the desk, burying her head in her arms.

Scott looked at Morris, and she stared back at him, both open-mouthed.

Scott whispered, 'What the hell's going on?'

CHAPTER TWENTY-ONE

To bide the time while they sourced a solicitor for Sue Bishopp, Morris hurried to the IT department, which was made up of two people; one was a frumpy, blonde-haired woman called Fran, the other was a young, long-haired man who spent his days in a Metallica T-shirt and wearing jogging bottoms. He called himself Tonto. The two of them didn't get along at all, and usually kept themselves at a distance on either side of the narrow room on the third floor. Morris knocked and then waved at the two figures sitting at their desks.

Fran raised her head without much expression, just her usual sour half-smile, while Tonto took off his headphones and leaned back in his chair.

'Well, well, here she is,' Tonto said, his eyes

travelling up and down Morris. 'The love of my life.'

Fran snorted. 'Listen to him. You'll have a sexual harassment case on you, you will, my lad.'

'Oh, keep your cakehole shut,' Tonto said, then grinned again at Morris as he stood up and stretched. The acrid smell of body odour drifted her way as he moved closer.

'And what can I do for you, gorgeous?' Tonto said as he gave her a wiggle of his eyebrows.

She sighed and shook her head as she took out the photo they had found at James Headley's house. 'Can you examine this photograph for me?'

He snatched the photo from her fingers with a wink, then dramatically raised it to his eyes. 'Hmmm… a group of ugly people in a pub. Important, is it? Crucial evidence, is it?'

'It is. See the fellow with the beard? Can you enlarge and try and remove the beard?'

Tonto smiled. 'Of course. Anything for you, my darling Morris.'

'Leave her alone!' Fran said. 'Do you want me to put in a complaint, Inspector?'

She laughed. 'No, it's quite all right, Fran. Look, Tonto, identify the bearded guy and I'll buy you a drink.'

The IT guy's eyes widened. 'Really? You're not pulling my leg, are you?'

'Would I? Just get to work and call me when you've cracked it.'

As she turned to hurry out, Tonto shouted, 'I'll have it sorted in no time, darling. You and me will soon be sipping cocktails!'

She laughed then headed back along the corridor and found DS Scott waiting for her, his hands dug in his pockets and looking worn out.

'Are you all right, Scott?' she asked, part of her brain thinking about the fact that he had lied about the holiday to the Isles of Scilly.

'Yeah, just here to remind you that Nigel Oldroyd is still waiting to talk to someone,' he said, nodding to the interview room door.

'Oh bugger, I forgot what with Sue Bishopp,' she said. 'Let's go in.'

Scott was about to open the door then stopped and looked at her. 'You don't think I'm the murderer, do you?'

She put on a smile that she hoped hid her doubts. If he was the killer, she didn't want him to know that she suspected him. 'No, of course not. Come on.'

Morris followed Scott into the room and found a sour-faced Oldroyd on his feet, looking as if he was about to leave.

'Oh, there you buggers are,' he said, with a grunt. 'I was just about to sling my hook.'

'I'm very sorry, Mr Oldroyd,' she said and sat down. 'We've been rather busy.'

Oldroyd looked Scott up and down with disdain. 'You're busy? I'm the busy one. Where's the other one, the big streak of piss?'

'He's not here.'

There came a knock on the door before it opened and Radford stepped in.

'Oh, here he is,' Oldroyd said as he sat down. 'The bird man of Lyme Regis.'

'Get Mr Oldroyd a cup of tea, Scott,' Radford said as he took a seat. Morris watched as Scott's face reddened and he threw his hands up before sloping out.

'I like you, Radford,' Oldroyd said. 'You have a certain something, a je ne sais quoi, as the French say.'

'I'll take that as a compliment, Mr Oldroyd. Now what is it you wanted to tell us? Is it about your failing business and your bankruptcy?'

Oldroyd lost his smile, a flicker of anger appearing along with plenty of confusion. 'Who told you that pack of lies?'

'Your suit,' Radford said.

Oldroyd looked down at it. 'This is Armani.'

'It's fake. I used to have a colleague in the fraud department and he taught me how to spot the fake from the genuine. You, for example, are a fake.'

The businessman's face grew redder, which made Morris want to hug Radford.

Then Oldroyd seemed to calm down as he wagged his finger at Radford. 'You nearly had me going there for a minute. Come on, who told you?'

'Your suit and your Rolex,' he said. 'Both

fake. The young lady staying with you. Some kind of escort?'

The businessman stared at him, then slapped the desk as he laughed and shook his head. 'Jesus, you're good, Radford. You could go on TV.'

'What did you want to tell us?'

Oldroyd sat back. 'Actually, my friend with the photographic memory...'

'The good memory.'

'Whatever. She remembered something that happened a while back. It was the night that I had a few of the lads round...'

'Who are the lads?' Morris asked.

Oldroyd looked at her. 'James Headley, Nathan Sharpe, Ben Gardener, Peter Mayfield, and Freddie Wells.'

'Hang on,' Morris said. 'Since when do they all hang around together?'

'Since I started having a poker night at my place.' He grinned.

Radford folded his arms. 'About the time you found yourself needing a large amount of cash, by any chance?'

Oldroyd nodded. 'You're a very clever bastard, aren't you, Radford?'

'Only compared to some,' Radford said, staring at the businessman. Morris found herself wanting to hug him again.

Oldroyd leaned forward, still staring at Radford. 'As I was saying, we had a poker night. I did pretty well, although Mr Money Bags, Parsons, didn't turn up until late. The sod started going on about one of his investment opportunities, the chance to make a lot of money by putting a little in.'

'Meaning a lot?' Morris asked.

Oldroyd looked at her. 'Twenty grand each, he wanted. Like I had that kind of money in my back pocket. I couldn't tell him that, though. So there he is, saying how they'd all make a fortune if we all put in. Gardener had had a few too many by then, so he started having a go at Parsons, saying ridiculous things like he should be investing in the people and doing something about the cliffs. Ridiculous stuff. Anyway, it nearly came to blows and the night came to an abrupt end.'

'And that was it?' Morris asked. 'Was that all you had to tell us?'

Oldroyd huffed. 'No, it wasn't just that. Parsons was the last one to leave, and I saw him off. He must have been heading to his car. Well, my friend with the photographic memory heard something outside, so looked out the window and saw someone come out of the dark and grab hold of Parsons. She said that whoever assaulted him was shouting at him, really having a go at him. She thought they were going to hit him, or worse.'

'But your so-called friends didn't see who the person was?' Radford asked with a sigh.

'No, it was dark. But it was a man, she reckons.'

'And why is your friend not here telling us all this?' Radford raised his eyebrows.

'Because she's had to go to London to see her family. I said I'd tell you.' He smiled briefly, as he sat back. 'Make of it what you will.'

Radford folded his arms. 'We will have to talk to your… friend, to get an official statement.'

'Very well. She'll be back in a couple of days.'

'What's her name again?'

'Amber,' he said as he folded his arms.

Radford made a note. 'Surname?'

'Marsh.'

Radford nodded. 'Amber Marsh. I remember now. Thank you, Mr Oldroyd. We'll be in touch unless you have any other information?'

'No, that's it.' The businessman stood up and adjusted his suit and tie. 'Nice seeing you again, Radford. Inspector Morris.'

'So, what do you make of that?' Morris said after Oldroyd had left the interview room.

Radford pinched the bridge of his nose and closed his eyes. 'Well,' he said, 'If it's true, I think that might have been the moment our killer reached his breaking point. Imagine you're witnessing one of the men who allowed your sister or daughter or friend, to die and helped dispose of her body, discussing money in front of you, going about his careless, money-oriented life. How would you feel?'

'Like killing him,' Morris said. 'So he decides he's waited long enough?'

Radford nodded. 'Possibly. But why not kill Parsons first? Why Ben Gardener?'

'Because it would be easier to get to Gardener? Chances are he'd never killed anyone before... all he had to do was wait until Gardener was drunk and follow him.'

Radford nodded and looked at her. 'Yes, I think you're right, Morris. Well done. He kills Gardener first because it's easier. He was working his way up. I mean, the way he dispatched Adrian Parsons was particularly conspicuous and brazen. I think you've got it.'

Morris found herself smiling but then turned it off as she thought on. 'But it doesn't get us any closer to solving it, does it? Oh, I just realised. We've arrested Sue Bishopp!'

Radford stared at her and nodded. 'For aiding and abetting the killer?'

'How did you know?'

'The killer let her go. Why? We already know he has no compunction, so why take pity on her unless her release would help him in some way? Plus, Wells and Bartlett let in the person who abducted them. At a time when they were fearing for their lives, for them to have let someone in, it would have to be someone they felt posed no threat.'

Morris let out a deep sigh. 'Wow. OK. Well,

she says she did it because he threatened her life. He promised her that he would always be close, close enough to kill her at any moment.'

'And she cannot identify him?'

'No, because he wore a mask. Other than he's white and probably average height, we don't have much else to go on.'

'Wonderful.' Radford sat back, staring into space.

'He's going to kill Bartlett, isn't he?' she asked.

'Not if we stop him in time. Has there been any sign of Anthony Jones?'

She shook her head. 'No, no sign yet. But if he's coming, they'll spot him.'

'I hope so.' Radford turned to her again. 'And the photograph?'

'With the IT people. They're trying to work their magic.' She laughed.

'What's so humorous?'

She shrugged. 'Sorry. It's just that I promised I'd buy the IT guy a drink if he manages to get something from the photo…'

'Meaning you'll take him to the pub?'

'Yeah, but what I'm going to do is buy him a bottle of water or a beer.' She laughed again, but Radford just let out another sigh as he stood up and said, 'You are a genius, Morris. I hope they do work their magic. I have this feeling that all the answers are in that photo, we're just not seeing what they are.'

'What now, then?'

'We wait for Anthony Jones to be taken into custody and for the photograph to be examined. We must be patient.'

Her eyes fluttered open again as her head throbbed. Darkness surrounded her. Bartlett felt strange, her arms and legs heavy, while a deep sickness filled her stomach. The last thing she remembered was drinking from

the bottle of water being held to her lips. Oh God, she thought and felt like vomiting. She hadn't seen him open it. He must have put something in the drink before he gave it to her. She'd been drugged.

She tried to see beyond the wall of darkness that surrounded her. She wasn't on a chair but was propped up against a cold wall. There was tape over her mouth. Her heart started to throb in time with her head. She tried to move her hands, but they were tied together somehow. Oh God, please. No. Please help me. An image flashed into her head. The bag was pulled over Freddie's face, his eyes bulging with panic and horror. She closed her mouth and tried to swallow the sob that threatened to escape. She was trembling all over.

She looked up, trying to hear beyond the pounding of her pulse in her ears. She heard a door shut. Then footsteps. The steps were getting louder, and closer. And then a door was opening nearby. She prayed to whoever was listening that it was someone coming to rescue her.

A door was pulled open and light flooded in, burning her eyes. She blinked and focused on the shape standing looking in at her. She let out a muffled sob as she shook her head. No. No. Please.

The killer stepped inside and looked down at her, a mask covering most of his face, sunglasses hiding his eyes. He put his gloved hand into his pocket and took out a phone. He held it up and aimed it at her, just the way he had with Freddie before he'd killed him. And after, he had taken photos. This was it, she thought and trembled violently as he put the phone away. She tried to plead into the gag while he stared at her. Then he reached out his gloved hand to her and ripped the tape from her mouth.

'Please, please, don't do this,' she begged, unable to hold back her tears.

'Don't do what?' He straightened up.

'Don't kill me. Please. I beg you. I'm sorry.'

He laughed. 'You saw what I did to poor, dear Freddie, didn't you? You know what I did to the others, right?'

She nodded weakly, her body trembling.

He crouched down until she could see herself reflected and distorted in his sunglasses. 'Then what hope do you have, really?'

She let out the tears as she knew he was

right. She would die in that room, that bare, unloved room. She didn't even know where she was. There was a bed, unmade, worn slippers on the floor.

'This is Tony Jones' place,' the killer said, as if he had looked into her thoughts. 'It's disgusting, like him. It stinks, like him. Ugly, like you all are. Now, we wait.'

She stared up at him, wanting to ask what they were waiting for.

He laughed. 'Now, you're wondering what we're waiting for. Well, we're waiting for someone to arrive. Your friend and mine, Tony Jones. Then when he's here, you can watch him die.'

He reached down for her, but she started to scream and kick. He grabbed her jaw, stuck the tape back over her mouth and then took hold of her ankles and dragged her across the carpet.

Jones had stopped at a service station on the way and stuffed himself with a fry-up. He'd felt a little better with some food and a cup of tea inside him. At least he'd felt a little calmer as he continued to drive towards Lyme Regis on the A35. He was on the Bridport Road when his phone started ringing. He looked over at it as it flashed and vibrated across the passenger seat. He saw it was Rio calling and groaned. He decided to ignore her call, but then his mind whirred for a moment, and he wondered if she might have news for him.

He looked for the next turning and saw a signpost for a garden centre. He slowed, signalled and pulled into the large car park. Rio had stopped calling, so he rang her back.

'What do you want, Rio?'

'Oh God, Tony, where are you?'

'Australia. Does it matter?'

'Listen, Tony, the police are looking for you!'

'Why? What's happened now? You didn't tell them what I was going to do?'

'No, I didn't... it was Linda. But listen, the police are camped out, waiting to catch you on the way into town. You've got to turn around!'

'No! No bloody way. I've had enough, Rio. This bastard's got it coming. He desecrated my pub!'

'Listen to me, Tony. If they stop you, you've got a knife in your car. They'll bang you up. You know what the law's like.'

He lowered the phone from his ear and let out a shout. She was right, there was no way he was going to be able to get into town without the filth picking him up. Shit. He took a breath, trying to think straight. Then he thought of something and raised the phone back to his ear.

'Rio, listen to me,' he said, trying to make himself heard. 'You're going to get in your car and come and meet me...'

'Oh no, Tony, no way...'

'Yes, you are. Come here and I'll climb in

your boot.'

'Tony, you're nuts. I can't do that. It's crazy.'

He took a deep breath, knowing he had no choice but to lay it on the line. 'Rio, remember I know what you and your fella get up to on the side when he's not on the rigs. Also remember what I turned a blind eye to in my pub. Do you remember?'

'You threatening to go to the police?'

'I won't have to. I just need you to do this for me. All I have to do is get in your bloody boot and you drive into town and drop me off at my flat! That's all!'

There was the sound of her breathing on the other end for a while before she said, 'You're a tosser, Tony. You'll get yourself nicked.'

'Let me worry about that. Just get your arse down here. I'll send you my location. Hurry up.'

'For fu... OK,' she sighed, 'send me the bloody location.'

She hung up and he fired off his location as he looked around the mostly empty car park. It would be fine. All he had to do was squeeze in her boot and then get to his place. From there he could come up with a plan to get the better of the psycho.

CHAPTER TWENTY-TWO

Radford was busy at the far end of the large open-plan incident room posting the victims' photographs on the whiteboard and making notes under them, when Inspector Morris came in and stood by him.

'I'm pretty sure we didn't have a whiteboard,' she said, staring at all the photos.

'You did not, which is why I sent a couple of uniforms to fetch one.'

She sighed. 'We have murder books these days.'

'I'm quite aware, I just find this way helps.' He taped up the next photograph, which was one of Amber Marsh, their newest witness.

'Amber Marsh? Oldroyd's special friend? Why is she there?'

'Everyone in the chain of events is here, or

will be.' He wrote her name on the board. Then he raised his eyes to the photo he had placed at the top. Anna Bajorek. He stepped back and tried to take it all in, to somehow find the pattern in it all.

'Still no sign of Jones,' Morris said.

'He'll turn up.'

'What if he's on a train?'

'Anthony Jones? No, he doesn't seem the train type to me, does he you?'

She shook her head. 'Well, I hope he does turn up, because he might be our only way to find our killer.'

'No, I'm sure there's something else we're not seeing. Has the IT department come up with anything yet?'

'No, but I'll give them a call.' Morris took out her phone and walked off, leaving Radford in a kind of peace although at the other end of the massive room were the cubicles and desks of the other team members. Phones were ringing, fingers were tapping on keyboards. He sighed and pinched his nose as he looked over the photos and notes he had made.

'DCI Radford,' Parsons said from behind.

He turned and faced her, unable to keep his disdain from his face. 'Yes?'

She folded her arms. 'Yes, ma'am, you mean? I am your boss.'

'Did you want something?'

'I wanted to know if you're any closer to

finding Lynn Barlett or Anthony Jones, or our killer for that matter?'

'I would be if I didn't keep getting disturbed.'

Parsons' face reddened. 'You're rude, Radford, do you know that?'

'People keep telling me.' Radford faced the board. 'It's here. Somewhere in all this mess is the answer. Who is our killer? He's white and average height.'

'That's half of Dorset.'

Morris came back over and stood next to Parsons. 'Ma'am. Radford, Tonto is coming down.'

Radford stared at her, his eyebrows raised high. 'Tonto?'

'The IT guy,' Parsons said. 'God knows why.'

'Did someone say God?' a man's voice called out behind them, and they all turned to see a long-haired young man in a Metallica T-shirt. He was grinning but lost his big smile when he realised Chief Super Parsons was standing close by.

'Boss,' Tonto said and nodded to her. 'Sorry, I was just coming to update you on the photo.'

'Have you learned anything from it?' Radford asked.

'Not much. I'm still working on it, running it through a few programs. Trust me, I'll come up trumps. Oh, are these all the crime scene photos? Cool.'

'People died!' Morris said, elbowing him in the ribs.

'All right, I get it. Just don't often get to see all this. Is that her?' Tonto reached up and tapped the photo of Anna Bajorek.

'Yes, that's her,' Morris said, 'and we might be able to stop our killer if you get back to work.'

'All right,' he said and stepped back, still staring at the board. 'That's funny.'

'Oh, yeah, it's hilarious,' Morris said and tutted.

'No, I mean that.' He pointed to the board.

Radford looked at him. 'What do you mean?'

'Nothing really. Just Anna Bajorek and Amber Marsh, that's all.' He shrugged.

Radford stepped up to him. 'What are you getting at, exactly?'

Tonto walked up to the board. 'Anna Bajorek. Amber Marsh? Does no one see it?'

'No, obviously not, Tonto,' Morris moaned. 'Please just spell it out.'

'I'm guessing no one here speaks Polish?'

'Do you?' Morris asked with a laugh.

He made a face. 'Yes, I'm part Polish. My surname is Toncheva. Bajorek means Marsh or Marsh dweller. I just thought it was a funny coincidence.'

Radford stared at Morris as she looked back. 'Amber Marsh. She pointed us towards Sue Bishopp. She's been right there in front of us...'

'Laughing at us.' Morris let out a deep sigh.

'Hang on,' Parsons said, turning all eyes on her. 'I thought you said the killer was a man?'

Radford pinched his nose. 'I think the killer is a man. In fact, I'm certain of it. But what if she's his accomplice? Think about it, it would take more than one person to pull off the stunt at the cliffs the other day.'

Parsons approached the whiteboard, looking it all over. Trying to look as if she had a clue what was going on, he decided. Then she looked at him, putting on her most authoritative expression. 'Well, Radford, you'd best bring her in for questioning.'

He nodded and looked at Morris. 'We had better go.'

As they started to hurry through the incident room, Tonto called out, 'Does that mean I solved your case?! Does that mean you'll definitely go for a drink with me?'

'No!' Morris shouted back.

'You don't look very comfortable,' Rio said as she looked down at Tony, all curled up, his teeth gritted and his face red.

He widened his eyes. 'I'm not bloody comfortable, you dozy cow. Couldn't you have got a bigger car with a bigger boot?'

'Talk about ungrateful. Why can't we use yours?'

'Jesus, you are stupid. Because the filth has

probably got eyes out for my car, haven't they?'

'All right. Leave it out. Just hold on, I'll be as quick as I can.'

'You'd better!' he said, but she shut the boot, half tempted just to leave him there for a while. She tutted, then, with her heart starting to race a little, got in the car and started the engine. She turned around and headed out of the car park and towards Lyme Regis. The drive seemed to take ages and she could hear Tony moving around in the boot, and muffled, pain-filled grunts. She almost laughed, but then she caught sight of a police car pulled up by the side of the B-road she was on. She tried not to look, but she found her eyes jumping to the lone police officer sitting in the car. He looked right at her. She carried on driving, watching in the rearview mirror. Her heart pounded when she saw the police car pull out and start to follow. Shit. Bugger.

The police car flashed its light and briefly sounded its siren. It was over, and Tony would be caught. He'd never forgive her, but she had no choice but to pull over and sit there.

The car pulled in right behind, and the police officer remained behind the wheel for a moment, before he climbed out and slowly approached the driver's side. She lowered her window as she tried to raise a smile.

'Afternoon,' the constable said, glancing around inside her car. 'Where are you off to today?'

'Lyme Regis,' she said. Her heart was rattling in her chest.

He nodded, then took out his mobile phone and held it up. Her eyes almost popped out of her head when she saw Tony's driving licence photo staring back at her. He looked like a right criminal in it.

'Have you seen this man?' the policeman asked.

'No. Sorry. Has he done something?'

'We just need to talk to him. If you do see him, call the police, OK?' The policeman smiled, then walked back to his car.

She let out a trembling breath as she watched him in the rearview mirror. He got back in his car, turned it around and headed back to his previous position.

She started the engine and drove off again. Her hands were trembling on the steering wheel and she kept looking in the rearview mirror for the police car as she got closer to Lyme Regis. Soon she was heading down Broad Street, then up Church Street as the rain started pelting her car. She put her wipers on and listened to the screech of them as her eyes jumped to the view of the grey sea that smashed against the town's stone defences.

It wasn't long before she was parking up on the side street, a hundred yards from where Tony's flat was. She jumped out and opened the boot to see a pained Tony staring up at her, tears in his eyes.

'You all right?' she asked, trying to help him out.

'Do I look all right?' he groaned as he managed to sit up. He let out a sudden cry of pain. 'Oh, my back! Oh, Jesus. I'm crippled.'

But he managed to move and somehow get out of the boot. He was standing hunched over for a while, groaning as he rubbed his back.

'You'd better go,' he said, looking at her. 'I'll be all right from here.'

'What're you going to do?'

'I don't know yet. Probably take a hot bath first with some Radox and think about it. Go on, get lost.'

She huffed, shook her head and went to get back in her car.

'Rio,' he said.

She looked at him. 'What?'

'Thanks,' he said but turned and walked awkwardly away.

Nigel Oldroyd opened his front door and let out and tired-sounding sigh when he saw Morris and Radford standing there.

'What now?' he asked, leaning on the doorframe. 'I do have a business to run, you do know that, don't you?'

'Where is Amber Marsh?' Radford asked, stepping forward and looking over Oldroyd's head.

'She's not here. Why? Is this because of what I said? I'll tell her to come and see you when she gets back.'

'You said she's in London, didn't you?' Morris asked.

'Yes. Why?'

'We need to question her,' Radford said. 'We believe she's been helping our killer. She might even be related to Anna Bajorek.'

'What?' Oldroyd looked between them. 'What are you talking about? This is ridiculous.'

'What do you know about her, Mr Oldroyd?' Radford asked.

The businessman stared up at him. 'Enough.'

'Where did you meet her?' Morris asked.

'In a pub,' Oldroyd said. 'Does it matter?'

'Did she just wander up to you one day and start chatting away?' Radford asked.

Oldroyd stared at him, his eyes showing the annoyance and embarrassment building. 'So, she came up and talked to me…'

'She is using you. She wanted to live here because you knew the victims pretty well. Did she ask you all about them? All the people who have died recently?'

Oldroyd lost his annoyance as Morris could see the coin was beginning to drop in his mind. 'She asked me about them, I think, but that was ages ago. She can't be…'

'Do you have a phone number for her?' Morris asked.

'Yes,' he said. 'But this is all a mistake.'

'Her phone number.' Radford glared at him.

Oldroyd took out his phone, brought up her number and held it up. 'What are you going to do?'

'Find her,' Radford said, glancing at Morris. 'We need to track this phone.'

Tony Jones watched Rio drive off, then unlocked the front door and went into the hallway, and up the red-carpeted stairs to his flat. The fast beat of crappy music was coming from the flat below as usual. He sighed, lacking even the strength to knock on the door and complain. He let himself in, took out the large kitchen knife, and placed it on the small phone table by the door. There were several letters on the floor, mostly junk mail with a few local newspapers thrown in. He picked them up and put them on the kitchen bar that separated it from the small front room. He looked around the place, making sure everything was as he had left it. He nodded, his mind jumping to what the hell he was going to do next to find the bastard who wanted to kill him. He swore under his breath as he hobbled to his bedroom, his back moaning with the pain.

He stopped dead, his heart rumbling to life.

The door was open a little. He'd definitely shut it, he thought. He went and grabbed the knife, then approached the door again and slowly nudged it open. He rushed into the room, swiping the air with the blade. Nothing. No one was there. He looked around and even looked in the wardrobe. Nothing. He shook his head as he let out a sigh of relief. The thud of music was still pounding up from downstairs, louder than ever. He stamped a couple of times on the floor, but it only hurt his back more.

Surprisingly, the music became quieter. That's a first, he thought as he looked towards the tiny bathroom. He went in and put the knife down on the windowsill before he had a well-earned piss while staring at the bath. He still had some Radox left, and it was a muscle relaxer kind. He shrugged, thinking the killer could wait for now. He put the plug in and turned the taps on with a deep grunt of pain. Men his size were not meant to be squeezed into the boots of toy cars. He tried to stretch, but his muscles spasmed in protest. A nice relaxing bath would set things right, and perhaps he could have a little nap on the sofa afterwards. He nodded to himself, found a cigarette and lit it. As he smoked, he checked the temperature of the water, and it was a little too hot. He put more cold in and poured in plenty of Radox. Then he stood there, thinking as took a few more hungry puffs and then rested the fag on the side of the bath as he undressed. With a great deal of pain, he managed to climb into the lovely warm water and then lower himself down.

'Ah, that's the stuff,' he said, picked up his cigarette and took a puff. Then as he lay there, he thought to himself, if he kept his door locked and the knife by his side, the killer wouldn't be able to get him. He was in no state of health to go chasing after some psycho anyway.

The beat of music from downstairs got louder again. Bastards, he thought.

'Can't even enjoy a relaxing bath in peace.'

The bathroom door creaked open a little. He spun his head towards it.

'Hello?' His heart fired up. 'Who's that?'

No answer. Must have been a breeze, he decided and took another puff. He looked for the knife, then he saw it was up above him, out of reach. Shit.

The door smashed open, a dark blur racing at him. Then hands pushed down on his body, submerging him in the water. The thud of muffled music filled his ears as he looked up and saw the man wearing the mask, the crazed eyes looking down at him as he flailed his arms, trying to get a grip of the bath. No, no, no. The hands were strong, keeping him under. He needed to take a breath, his lungs burning.

The eyes kept staring down at him. He knew those eyes. He fought and struggled but he kept sliding around as his chest ached and his heart pounded. He needed a breath. His mouth opened.

The darkness seemed to colour the water,

taking away the light.

It was Morris who drove them down through the town and along Church Street. The phone was on, and it was somewhere in the backstreets. They had a small area to search, but they had a car with two uniforms following them. Radford was gripping the dashboard as she took a left turn down a narrower street and then a right until they were on a road filled with a few craft shops, a chippy and a garden restaurant. The rain was coming down a little harder as Morris parked up. The response car with the uniforms in swung in behind them. Radford got out first and Morris watched as Radford took out his phone. He was ringing the number and listening out for the ring. She got out and went over while the uniforms waited in their car. It was quiet, only the sound of the wind and rain keeping it from being silent. They listened out. Radford ended the call, then rang it again.

'Hello, who's this?' a voice suddenly said on the other end. Radford and Morris stared at each other. She grabbed his phone and put it to her ear. 'Hello, is Kelly there?' she said, shrugging at Radford.

'No, this isn't Kelly's phone. You've dialled the wrong number.' It was Amber Marsh's voice.

'Oh, sorry.'

'How did you get this number?'

'I don't know. Must've pressed the wrong

number.'

'Kelly your friend, is she? Your best friend? Don't you have her number already saved?'

'She's just got a new number…'

'Who is this?'

Radford snatched the phone back. 'Amber Marsh?'

There was only breathing on the other end.

'Or is it Amber Bajorek? You are her sister or a very close friend? Is that correct?'

There was a laugh, a strange kind of empty laugh. 'Cousin, actually. But we were like sisters. She didn't deserve to die like that.'

'No, but neither did those other people you had killed.'

She laughed, but there was a sharp edge to the sound. 'Didn't they? They could have helped her. Or they could have called the police after… so we could have… those weak, cowardly, horrid people.'

'Tell us where you are, and we'll leave the station and pick you up.'

'Trust the police? You lot didn't help. You won't deliver justice. You're to blame too.'

Then the line went dead.

'Now what?' Morris asked.

'We wait.' Radford looked around the street, up and down as the rain blew in. The dark, thunderhead clouds had started to blot out the sky. A rumble of thunder sounded but it was far off.

A door opened behind them. They spun round and saw a woman in a dark red waterproof coat, the hood up, shutting the door behind her. She turned and saw them. Amber Marsh stared at them, the anger flickering in her eyes. Before they could react, she had the door open and was disappearing inside.

'Kick the door in,' Radford ordered the uniforms, who rushed over and did as ordered. It took a few goes before the door swung in and hit the wall. They all went rushing through the small cottage, searching for Marsh. There she was, standing in a tiny, cramped kitchen at the back of the house, the windows behind her were being pelted mercilessly by the rain. Morris followed Radford as he moved closer. Marsh raised her right hand, revealing a knife clenched in her fist. She was scowling at them, her teeth bared like an animal about to bite.

'Amber,' Radford said.

'Lena,' she said, her voice trembling and breaking up. 'Lena Bajorek. I should have stopped her from ever going there. She wanted me to go with her, but I had a boyfriend… I chose him over her. I hate myself for it.'

'Put down the knife,' Morris said. 'It's over now.'

Lena's eyes snapped to her. 'Over? That's funny. It's not over. There's two left.'

'Three,' Radford said. 'Anthony Jones, Lynn Bartlett and Sue Bishopp.'

'Anthony Jones will be dead by now. Go check his flat, if you don't believe me. Lynn Bartlett will die soon and there's nothing you can do. But you're used to that, aren't you, you police people? Doing nothing?'

'We have Sue Bishopp,' Morris said. 'You won't be able to kill her.'

She laughed. 'But it's not me. I didn't kill them. That was my friend. He's out there, ready and waiting. He'll get her eventually, and you have no idea who he is. Do you?'

Lena Bajorek lifted the knife, smiling, then dropped it to the floor. The uniform rushed at her, turning her around and restraining her.

Morris looked at Radford. 'She's right though. We don't know who he is.'

'We had better go to Anthony Jones' flat.'

CHAPTER TWENTY-THREE

Two uniforms went in first, using the key they had taken from Lena Bajorek to gain entry. Radford pulled his gloves on as they followed them into a small, dusty hallway. Morris was behind him as they went up the worn carpeted stairs and reached the magnolia-painted door. Radford held his hand out for the key and opened the door when it was placed in his palm.

He sniffed the air when he went in, his nostrils filled with only damp and the acrid smell of stale cigarette smoke. He looked round at the untidy living room as he heard everyone entering after him.

'Touch nothing,' he said as his eyes jumped to the bathroom. The door was open a little, but he could only make out the tap end of the bath. He went slowly to the door and nudged it open.

Radford stepped in and looked down at the pale, misty sight of Anthony Jones looking up at him through the bubbling water.

'Jesus,' Morris said as she appeared and looked over his shoulder. 'We're too late.'

Radford nodded, then pinched the bridge of his nose. 'Your observational skills are excellent.'

'Thanks very much.' Morris sighed. 'Now what?'

But Radford was reaching out a gloved hand to the windowsill. He took hold of a large kitchen knife and showed it to Morris as he said, 'So near, yet so far.'

'Us or Jones?'

'Bag this and get the SOCOs over here. His killer might have left us something, but I doubt it. Next, we interview Lena Bajorek.'

The young woman's formerly deep tan seemed to have deserted her as she was sitting in the interview room, dressed in an oversized sweatshirt and jogging bottoms that had come from lost property. Lena Bajorek looked up when they took their seats opposite her. Radford watched her, observed her eyes that had little of the sting they'd had earlier. He supposed she'd had time to mull it all over as she sat in her cell after being booked in and medically examined. She had almost completed her mission of revenge and he wondered how it felt to her now. To him, she looked empty.

Morris started the interview process, reading out the names of those who were present and the time and date. As she had nearly finished, there came a knock on the door. It was the duty solicitor, a man in his forties, hay-coloured hair that was greying. He wore glasses. He sat down and introduced himself as Adam Linnell. Morris added his presence to the tape and sat back.

'Now you have had time to think,' Radford said, sitting forward. 'Would you care to tell us where your accomplice is?'

She lifted her dark eyes to him. 'You want me to make it easy for you? Do you think my cousin had it easy?'

'No, I know she didn't. But from what I hear, she did not suffer…'

Lena slapped both hands down on the desk, her eyes burning out to Radford. 'Didn't suffer? She's dead. Gone. I feel like my heart has been ripped out.'

Radford watched as Lena clawed at her own chest. The solicitor stared at her, open-mouthed.

'She's gone,' Lena said, quietly. 'I'm gone.'

'No, you're still here, Lena,' Morris said, her voice gentle.

The suspect looked at her and gave a hollow laugh. 'I'm going to prison, you stupid bitch. I might as well be dead.'

'If you help us now,' Radford said, 'and tell us where he is, then it may help your case.'

Her face changed, some of the anger seeming to dissipate. 'Would it?'

'I could put in a good word.'

'And that might help reduce my sentence?' Lena asked, leaning towards him.

'Radford,' Morris said, but he ignored her.

'It would, I'm sure,' he said.

'You want to know who he is and where he is?'

He nodded. 'It would help.'

Lena Bajorek leaned even closer. 'He's... a ghost... and you'll never find him, you stupid policeman bastard.'

Radford sighed and sat back. He stared at their suspect, the way she grinned victoriously. She knew she had won. 'Morris, let's pause it there.'

Radford decided to go for a walk outside the station for a while, to be alone with his thoughts. He would have enjoyed the view, but there was only the car park and the road to look at. The wind was blowing, the big thick thundercloud rumbling overhead. The storm was getting worse and mirrored what was going on in his head.

He had failed. Just as he had failed his colleagues and Carr all that time ago.

'You didn't fail me.'

He turned and saw Michelle Carr standing behind him, wrapped up in her coat and smiling at him.

'I led you down into that tunnel, he said. 'I should have gone by myself.'

She stepped closer. 'You didn't know what was down there, you idiot. How could you?'

He sighed. 'I'm sorry.'

'Don't be. Just find her accomplice and save Lynn Bartlett.'

'But where is he?'

'It's all in the photograph, you said. It's all there.'

'Is it, Carr? What's there? I cannot see it.'

'Just go and see about the photograph. Go on, hurry up.'

Radford stared at her until she faded from his mind, then hurried inside and up the stairs until he managed to find the small room where the IT people were working. He stood in the open doorway and coughed. Both the woman and the scruffy young man looked round at him.

'Can we help you?' the woman said, but she sounded fed up.

Tonto stood up, smiling. 'DCI Radford, welcome to our part of the world. Do you want a tour?'

'I want to know about the photograph. Have you examined it?'

Tonto smiled. 'I certainly have, boss. It's bogus.'

'I'm sorry? Bogus?'

Tonto went over and brought back the photograph and pointed to it. 'See this fella next to the girl?'

'James Headley?'

Tonto shrugged. 'Well, whatever he's called, that head doesn't belong on that body. It's Photoshop. Brilliantly done, I might add, but didn't fool me.'

Radford stared at it, his mind trying to grasp wildly at what it all meant. 'And what about the girl?'

'Oh, she's not been touched.'

Radford pointed to the other man in the photograph, the one in the crowd. 'What about him?'

'Bogus. If you ask me, someone's been yanking your chain.'

Radford took the photograph and stared at it. It was all fake, and the killer had been toying with them all along. He had lost. He looked at Tonto as his heart sank. 'Is there anything about the photograph you can tell me?'

'Well, it was made recently,' Tonto said, looking at the back of the photo. 'Three days ago.'

'What?' Radford turned it round.

'Whoever photoshopped this wanted you to think it was real, so they must've had it printed in a photo-finish shop. Problem is, those places always print the date on the back. You can't really see it very well, but someone's tried to erase it, but under a microscope, you can just make out the remains of a date on the back. It was taken three days ago. Someone's been messing with you.'

Radford turned and started moving out of the room, blindly walking towards the stairs as his mind grasped for some kind of sense. He ran back over the last few days. Then he stopped at the top of the stairs, recalling talking to one of the locals about the photograph and what he said about it. He started running down the stairs, passing by uniforms coming the opposite way.

He saw Parsons hurrying off to somewhere when he reached the floor where the incident room was.

'Chief Superintendent!' he called out. 'I'm about to arrest the killer.'

Before she could say anything, Radford was jogging into the incident room and found Morris standing chatting to DS Scott.

'Morris!' he called out. 'Get armed response here. I know who murdered them all.'

She hurried towards him, her face stamped with shock. 'Who?'

'Nathan Sharpe.' Radford went down the next flight of stairs with Morris trying to keep up.

'The journalist? What? Why?'

As he pushed out through the side door and into the car park, he said, 'The photograph is fake. It was meant to confuse us. But it was only made a few days ago. Get armed response to meet us at the newspaper office.'

'OK.' Morris unlocked their car and got in as she made a call to request armed response to meet them there.

After Radford had climbed in and put on his seatbelt, he said, 'Nathan Sharpe said he'd been shown the photograph ages ago by Headley. Well, he couldn't have, could he?'

'He said something similar to me. But he could be mistaken.'

'No, he's not. He's seen the photograph before because he made it. Let's head for the newspaper office.'

Morris drove them off at speed, heading back into town as the rain pelted the car. Radford hated the car being jerked sideways by the horrendous wind and clasped hold of the sides of his seat. It was only minutes later that Morris swung the car into a space close to the newspaper office.

'We'd better wait for armed response,' she said.

Radford was watching the building, his mind racing. Time was running out for Lynn Bartlett.

He climbed out and Morris followed.

'What're you doing?'

He looked at her. 'Confronting him.'

'Wait.'

Radford heard a car engine revving near

them, then the beep of a car horn. Both he and Morris looked round to see two people sitting in the car. There was Lynn Barlett in the passenger seat, gagged, her eyes wide with terror. Behind the wheel was Nathan Sharpe. He had a strange smile on his lips.

'Ah, there you are, Radford!' he called out through his open window. 'Took you long enough. Is it time for my exclusive?'

'We have Lena,' Radford said. 'Give yourself up.'

'But I haven't disposed of Lynn here. What do you think? Throw her off the cobb and into the stormy, treacherous waters? Race you there!'

Then the car roared as it raced off down Broad Street, swung sharply, and vanished.

Radford started running as hard as he could towards Front Beach, heading along the promenade, his heart pounding with the effort. The rain lashed in, the sky darkening. He saw the abandoned car near the beach, the doors open. His eyes jumped to the cobb, where the sea was raging, a giant wave clawing at the wall. He swallowed but moved on, taking quick steps as his eyes found the silhouettes of Sharpe and Lynn. He was pushing her up the steps and then along the cobb. The waves kept crashing over. When one wave went down, he saw Sharpe shove Bartlett along. Radford jogged towards them, his body starting to shake. A cold sweat broke all over him as his heart pounded at the sight of the sea exploding against the sea wall.

He hardly noticed the car driving beside him.

'Radford!' Morris called out. 'Wait for armed response!'

'I haven't got time!' He rushed on, diagonally across the beach, his feet sinking into the wet sand. He reached the stone steps and froze. He tried to take another step, to lift his leg, but nothing happened. He looked up and saw the shape of Sharpe and Bartlett at the far end. In between, the waves pounded the wall, clawing with its grey hand as great clouds of foam exploded into the air.

'Come on, Radford!' he heard Sharpe shouting.

He couldn't move.

'I'll go!'

Radford saw Morris standing a little behind him, her hair soaked from the rain.

'You can do this,' Carr said. She was standing close by, nodding. 'You can save her, Radford. You really can.'

He took a step and started to climb. He wobbled a little as he reached the top of the wall. There was a roar as the latest wave came exploding against the cobb. He moved closer, feeling the rain hammer at his face. His teeth chattered and a terrible sense of dread huddled his stomach as he saw the wild sea below.

'That's it, Radford!' Sharpe called out. 'Come

and get her.'

A wave came crashing down. When it retreated, he made a bolt for it and ran towards the two figures.

Nathan Sharpe had his arm around the bound and gagged Bartlett, a knife in his hand.

'I wasn't sure you'd make it,' Sharpe said. 'Well done. You've conquered your fear. I planned on this, right from when I learned how scared you were of the water. That's why I put the box with the dress in here, to test you. You failed, of course. But I knew you wouldn't let me down today.'

'What was Anna Bajorek to you?' Radford asked, as his eyes took in the angry sea all around, and then the knife close to Bartlett's throat. The sea raged behind him, slapping at the Cobb.

'Anna? I didn't know her that well. But I love Lena. I would do anything for her, and here I am. Have you ever loved anyone so much, Radford, that you would kill for them?'

'No,' Radford said. 'But I suspect that you liked the killing really. I mean, you murdered James Headley for no reason but to frame him.'

'No. He saw us one night. Lena and I together, talking outside Oldroyd's house. We thought no one was around, but suddenly there he was. He had to go. But like I said, I would have killed anyone for Lena. Anyone she asked me to.'

'People don't just kill because somebody

they love tells them to.'

Sharpe stared at him. 'Then you don't understand love. I don't think you're capable of it. You're a broken man.'

'Then so are you. Let her go.'

Sharpe looked at Lynn, then grinned as he started to push her towards Radford. Her eyes grew large, full of panic as she got closer.

'You want her?' Sharpe asked.

'Let her go. We can talk.' Radford's heart raced, his body trembling.

'I asked if you wanted her.' Sharpe pushed her closer.

'Be careful, Sharpe.'

'Here!' Sharpe shoved Lynn out of the way and threw himself at Radford. He felt the force of his body knocking him sideways. Then they were falling. His body hit the water, its icy burn grasping him, pulling him under. It was dark as he panicked, his arms flailing, his legs kicking to get him to the surface.

His head broke the surface and he gasped for air before a wave came crashing down and sank him back down into the cold and dark. Something grasped hold of him, and he swivelled in the water to the wild eyes of Sharpe staring at him as he fought to get hold of Radford. He tried to get away, kicking at him while the terrible cold enclosed his body. Sharpe came again, his hands grasping at Radford's coat, tearing at it like a wild creature. He kicked again and started pulling himself away until he broke the surface again and tried to grasp the wall. His hands slipped against the wet rock, the waves pounding against him.

Sharpe's head broke the surface, his eyes just as crazed. 'Radford!' Then another huge wave came smashing down and Radford dived below it, spinning in the dark. He swam up to the surface and grasped the wall in desperation.

'Radford!'

He looked up and saw her leaning over towards him, her hand reaching out to him. Carr. But she wasn't real.

'Take my hand!' Carr shouted.

He threw his hand out and felt her grasp him. She pulled and he got a foothold and scrambled up. The next thing he knew, he was rolling onto the cobb and lying there, staring up at the dark sky. Seagulls screeched and passed over.

A silhouette appeared over him.

'Carr?' he asked.

'It's me, Morris. Are you OK?'

Then he realised as he sat up. 'Thank you.'

'For what?'

'Pulling me out of there.'

Morris helped him up. 'I didn't. I had to stop Bartlett from falling in. I don't know how you managed to get out. I thought you were a goner.'

Radford looked around, still trembling, confused. He shook his head. It didn't make sense.

'Where's Sharpe?'

Radford looked round at the sea that was battling against itself and smashing angrily at the cobb. 'In there. Drowned by now.'

'Good,' Morris said. 'Let's go.'

Radford paused as they reached the end of the cobb and looked back over the sea. 'I used to be scared of the sea.'

'Oh really? I never would have guessed.'

CHAPTER TWENTY-FOUR

When the phone call came that Nathan Sharpe's body had been found by the divers after the storm had passed, Radford put on his coat and left the shack. As he walked, he thought about the last few days and what had happened. He no longer feared the water, well, not quite as much as he did before. He still had a healthy respect for its duplicitous nature.

His mind rewound to the moment he thought he was lost below the waves, destined to drown. He saw her, Carr reaching out and rescuing him. But that wasn't possible, as she was only in his mind. She was haunting him, in a way. No, that wasn't correct. He was haunting her. Perhaps it was time to let her go. But he didn't want to.

He arrived at the beach in time to see a body bag being lifted by some of the diving team. Morris was there, still sporting a warm coat even though the clouds had parted and the sun glistened on the calmer water.

He stood near her and stared out to sea. It was a beautiful part of the world.

'Oh, there you are,' Morris said and joined him. 'That's Sharpe taken care of. Lena goes before a magistrate in the morning. I still feel sorry for her and Anna and her family.'

'So do I.' He looked at her.

'So, there is a heart in there?'

'Of course.'

She nodded. 'Bartlett got away with it.'

'Did she really? I think she's had her punishment.' He looked at her again, a question rising. 'Did you really not help me out of the water?'

'I told you already. No. You must have found the strength to climb out.'

'You didn't see anyone else there?'

'No. Did you?' Morris stared at him strangely.

'No.'

'Hmm. So, where are you off to now?'

'I'm not sure.' He turned and looked along the coast.

'You know, Parsons told me she hoped you'd stick around.'

'Really? Parsons?'

'It surprised me too. So, what do you think?'

He smiled. 'I'm wondering if the shack is for sale.'

She smiled and patted his shoulder. 'Good. I'll find out.'

He looked at her.

'What?' she asked.

'Go on, then. Leave me alone.'

Morris sighed, shook her head and trudged off up the beach.

Radford faced the sea again, wondering about it all, thinking of the past. He was out of the tunnel, no longer buried in the earth.

He breathed deeply. He would like living here, he decided.

GET TWO FREE AND EXCLUSIVE CRIME
THRILLERS

I think building a relationship with the readers of my books is something very important, and makes the writing process even more fulfilling. Sign up to my mailing list and you'll receive two exclusive crime thrillers for FREE! Get SOMETHING DEAD- an Edmonton Police Station novella, and BITER- a standalone serial killer thriller.

Just visit markyarwood.co.uk

or you can find me here:

https://www.bookbub.com/authors/mark-yarwood

facebook.com/MarkYarwoodcrimewriter/

@MarkYarwood72

THEY WILL DIE

DID YOU ENJOY THIS BOOK?
YOU COULD MAKE A DIFFERENCE.

Because reviews are critical to the success of an author's career, if you have enjoyed reading this novel, please do me a massive favour by leaving one on Amazon.

Please leave a review on AMAZON

———————

Reviews increase visibility. Your help in leaving one would make a massive difference to this author. Thank you for taking the time to read my work.

Printed in Dunstable, United Kingdom